RESERVATION 1

The Makanza Series
Book Two

KRISTA STREET

FREE E-BOOK!

Join Krista Street's Newsletter and receive a FREE copy of
Siteron.

A YA Sci-Fi Short Story

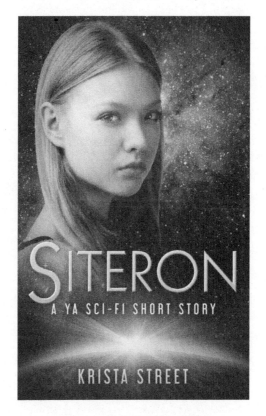

1 – VACCINE

"We'll never get out of here," Sage muttered. He sat on a couch in the Kazzie's locked and airtight entertainment room, sipping a soda. The Canadian occasionally flicked his fingers, emitting tiny sparks into the air.

The entertainment room held a movie screen, stadium seating with comfortable couches, and a kitchen and billiards area at the top. It put any entertainment venues in Sioux Falls to shame.

Sage flicked sparks into the air again. "This could be our home forever. Eh, Meghan?"

The other Kazzies mumbled similar comments.

Shifting on a chair beside them, I shook my head in my large biohazard suit. "No, that's not going to happen. There's a lot happening in Washington D.C. right now. The MRI is working to release you all back into the public. It's the politicians causing problems. Some of them are fear mongering, but that won't stop the Summit from happening next week. I'll be there along with numerous other Makanza Research Institute employees. We'll once again educate our senators and congressmen on the efficacy of the vaccine. After the Summit, the representatives will vote."

I leaned forward in my chair. On the horseshoe-shaped couches, sat all seven people within Compound 26 that were infected with *Makanza*, or Kazzies, as the general public called them. The Kazzies sitting closest to me regarded me warily. I knew they didn't believe they'd ever be free.

Clasping my hands, I took a deep breath. "Please don't lose hope. I'm going to do everything I can to set you free, and remember, a huge percentage of the public doesn't think you should be imprisoned here. Even though a lot of them are afraid, they still want you free."

"Even if that means they could become infected with a mutated strain of *Makanza*?" Victor sat on the opposite couch from Sage, his forearms resting on his thighs. His bright, red skin was very noticeable in his t-shirt and shorts. "Isn't that what they fear? That the virus will mutate, creating a new strain and it'll be set free to wreak havoc, creating a Third Wave?"

"Which means we'll *never* get out of here." Sara sighed.

I shook my head again. "That won't happen. No scientific evidence supports that will *ever* occur."

Sara didn't look convinced. She sat on Victor's right side, her blue skin appearing strangely normal beside his, like primary colors lined up next to one another. Although Sara's skin shimmered when she spoke telepathically to her twin sister, Sophie, whereas Victor's red skin was simply a protection against heat.

Even though I'd been working with the Kazzies for over nine months, I was still amazed at how their various *Makanza* strains had Changed them.

"So most likely we're stuck here for the foreseeable future," Sage concluded.

Davin nodded at Sage. "Most likely."

Davin sat beside me, as he usually did when I visited with Compound 26's entire group of infected survivors. With broad shoulders, dark hair, striking blue eyes, and chiseled features, he always got my heart fluttering.

"So, are we ever going to watch the movie?" Sophie squirmed in her seat. Whenever our discussions turned to the political turmoil regarding the rare survivors of the *Makanza* virus, Sophie became visibly nervous.

Sara, her twin, squeezed her hand.

I could easily tell the twins apart now, without looking at the tattooed markings on their wrists, but it had taken me a few months to get there.

"We can wait, if Meghan has more to tell us," Dorothy replied. The oldest Kazzie in the group lounged on a recliner. Her plump cheeks and round shape gave her a matronly look.

"I should go anyway." I checked my watch. "I still have work to do."

I stood awkwardly from the hard, stiff desk chair. All seven Kazzies lounged on the deep sinking, comfortable furniture. Not me, though. In my bulky biohazard suit, trying to push up from a plush sofa was rather embarrassing. So I always opted for the desk chair Davin had carried in for me months ago.

I sighed. The suit was incredibly annoying. Even though I'd received the vaccine, protecting me from all forty-one strains of *Makanza* two months ago, Dr. Sadowsky still insisted I wear my biohazard suit when I was with the survivors, *just in case* something happened.

I tried to tell Dr. Sadowsky, the Director of Compound 26, that requiring all MRI researchers to still be suited up around our Kazzies did not instill much confidence in the vaccine—

the vaccine the entire public had now been inoculated with. However, he said we were too valuable to lose. He wasn't taking any chances in case *Makanza* mutated.

His caution frustrated me to no end. I had yet to talk to or touch any of the infected people that I considered my friends without wearing one of these monstrous things. It was annoying.

Davin joined me. "I'll walk you out, but let me get the elevator first."

In his blurred Kazzie speed, he raced to the elevator, pushed the button, and was back at my side before I could blink. I was used to his speed by now, but sometimes, his sheer power and blindingly fast moves took my breath away.

Back at my side, he took my hand. Even with my gloves on, I felt his heat. It did funny things to my heart. For months now, I'd been in love with Davin, but I'd never told him that.

At times, I was convinced he was in love with me too, but we'd never talked about it. Not once.

Every day it was the same. I visited with him, sometimes briefly if I had a lot of work to do, other times for hours, if it was a slow day. Regardless, neither of us had ever brought up our feelings for one another. The reason I never had was simple: I was too afraid to make the first move.

As for why *he'd* never said anything, I could only speculate. But I did know he felt a relationship with anyone in the Compound was impossible. He'd commented a few times about lack of privacy and the constant surveillance.

However, his grabbing my hand was nothing new. The biohazard suits were bulky and awkward. Walking could be difficult, but Davin's hand always steadied me. I'd never looked in a mirror, but I knew I resembled a glutinous marshmallow. In other words, super attractive.

When we reached the elevator, we descended to the main floor and stepped into the back hallway that connected the Kazzies' living areas to their cells. The hallway was wide, probably ten feet and curved, following the circular pattern of the Inner Sanctum. Gray concrete floor and walls surrounded us. The lighting was dim, not like the harsh fluorescents in the hallways outside of the Inner Sanctum and entertainment facilities.

Davin's cell was number six. Each door leading into a Kazzie's cell was numbered. We were currently at three, Dorothy's cell.

"When are you flying to D.C.?" Davin asked.

I shrugged, or tried to in the bulky suit. "I'm not sure. I haven't received the flight schedule yet from Dr. Hutchinson, but the Summit's on Wednesday, less than a week away, so I have to be there by then."

Davin grinned devilishly. "Of course, we couldn't have a government hearing without the poster child for the vaccine."

I grimaced at which he chuckled.

The attention I received seven months ago, when I helped unlock the secrets to extracting a stable version of the virus for a vaccine, didn't go unnoticed. I'd been interviewed by several magazines and newspapers. America News Network, or ANN, our only national broadcasting network, interviewed me for their morning show a few months back.

During each interview, I'd vomited before and after. My anxiety had been through the roof. And Dr. Cate Hutchinson, my idol, who also happened to be the Director of Compounds 10 and 11 in Washington, had taken me under her wing since my discovery.

I could be wrong, but I had the feeling she was grooming me to take her position one day. I wasn't sure how I felt about that. In the past ten years, South Dakota had become my home. My parents lived here, and even though we weren't close, it was nice having them nearby. All of the Kazzies I knew were here too, although that could change once they were released.

Most importantly, though, Davin was here.

He'd never leave South Dakota. I was sure of that. As the last remaining Sioux Indian, he had a tie to this land. That and his mother lived in Rapid City and had done so for the past thirty years. I was positive she had no intention of moving.

Just the thought of leaving either of them made my heart ache. But for all I knew, once Davin was out, he would find someone else to spend his life with. After all, despite our close bond unlocking the secrets to the vaccine, he'd never professed his undying love and devotion to me.

Not like he had years ago to someone else.

I bit my lip as I often did when I thought about that. Davin had been in love once, before the First Wave. The only reason I knew about it was because Sharon had told me last year. However, whoever that girl was had moved away. Sharon presumed she died in the First Wave.

I tried to picture Davin with another woman. My stomach dropped at just the thought.

Perhaps moving wouldn't be so bad if that happens.

"You're kind of quiet." Davin glanced down at me. We just passed door five, and I hadn't said a word in the past few minutes.

"Just thinking."

"About what?"

"Nothing really, just about the vaccine and all the interest Dr. Hutchinson's giving me. She's hinted a few times at me moving out to Washington to work directly with her."

Davin's hand tightened over mine for the briefest second. "She must see a lot of potential in you."

"She seems to."

"She'd be a fool not too. You've done more in your short time here than most researchers have done in the last ten years."

Davin constantly lavished praise on me. He made it no secret, to anyone, how impressed he was with my accomplishments. It was yet another reason I loved him so much. He didn't have an ego. My success only made him proud.

Regardless, I still rolled my eyes as my cheeks flushed, even though I *had* played a huge roll in the vaccine's discovery.

Despite the Compounds opening two years after *Makanza* struck, it wasn't until last year, ten years after the First Wave started that any advancement had been made on creating a vaccine. It was Dr. Hutchinson's discovery regarding mind-body genomics that had begun the progress. And it had been *my* discovery that love stabilized the virus that ultimately led to the vaccine.

I peeked up at Davin as best I could in the suit's viewing shield. "If I did take Dr. Hutchinson's offer, I'd have to move to Washington state."

He was quiet for a few steps. "Is that what you want?"

"Um . . . not right now. There's still too much to do. And I believe I made someone a promise last year that if it was the last thing I did, I'd get him out of here."

Davin chuckled. "I wonder who that was."

"Just this Kazzie I know. He's pretty good at poker."

"Pretty good? Didn't I beat you in every hand last time we played?"

"That was only because Sara was distracting me. I'm

7

positive she was cheating. Didn't you see her skin shimmering during most of the game? She was obviously talking telepathically."

"She was doing that to distract everyone, not just you. I'm sure she wasn't actually talking to anybody other than Sophie, who wasn't even playing. Sara doesn't have a poker face. She has poker *skin*."

I laughed. Door six came into view a few steps later.

"I'll be fine from here. I'm sure I can manage to walk across your cell without falling." We often joked that if I ever did fall, I'd be like an upside down beetle on the sidewalk. Legs flailing about with no help of ever getting upright. "Ugh, these suits are getting beyond annoying."

"It's still better than risking your exposure to *Makanza*," Davin replied.

I sighed. Davin on the other hand, had a mindset similar to Dr. Sadowsky. It was better to be safe than sorry. At least, for me. Davin didn't care if any of the other researchers wore their suits or not.

"So what's supposed to happen when you get out of here?" I put a hand on my hip. "Am I never allowed to visit you since I won't have a suit? Will we just be pen pals?"

He chuckled at my syrupy tone and batting eyelashes. "We'll talk about that when the time comes."

As always, a stone settled in my stomach when we broached that topic. Davin wanted to get out of the Compound, just like every other Kazzie here, but he also wanted to make sure I was safe. I had a sickening sense of dread that pen pals may, in reality, be all he was okay with.

"All right, I'll see you tomorrow." I typed in my code to the keypad beside Davin's door. With a hiss, it opened.

"Are you going to let me know when you find out about

D.C.?" Davin lounged against the door frame and crossed his arms.

"Yes, I'll let you know."

"My mom said she expects a postcard this time."

I laughed. They didn't even make postcards anymore. Not since all of the borders were closed between states as a way to prevent the virus from spreading. "I'm guessing she was joking."

"You know her well."

I waved goodbye and walked into his cell. Davin waited in the hall. I felt his gaze follow me until the door closed behind me.

SERGEANT ROSE GLANCED up when I entered Davin's cell. He was in the watch room, on the opposite wall by the windowed hallway, where he always was. He was Davin's daytime guard Monday through Friday.

"Davin got a call while you were gone." Sergeant Rose leaned over the control panel, pushing the microphone button so I could hear him in my earbud.

"From who?" I asked as I walked to the containment room.

"His mom."

"I'm sure he'll call her when he returns. It wasn't important, was it?"

"I don't think so."

"They're going to watch a movie now." I stepped into the small containment room. The door closed behind me as the dials turned and switches glowed.

"Can you give him the message when he returns?" A fine mist that decontaminated my suit and everything it touched descended like a fog around me.

"Yeah, I just know he doesn't like missing her." Sergeant Rose's voice still sounded in my earbud despite the fact that I couldn't see him.

It had only been in the past month that the Kazzies were given personal phones in their cells. Before then, they weren't allowed contact with the outside world under Dr. Roberts' rule. Ever.

That was one thing Amy and I had worked hard to change. It hadn't been possible while Dr. Roberts worked here. However, once my old boss left, Amy and I wasted no time.

Dr. Hutchinson's support had helped tremendously in that department. She'd helped convince Dr. Sadowsky to install them. But when the Kazzies weren't in their cells and their phones rang, the guards answered. Sergeant Rose joked that he was now a glorified message service. Davin and his mom spoke daily, sometimes several times a day, and Davin often wasn't in his cell.

The mist around me evaporated, and the light above flashed green. All clear. Any particles of *Makanza* that were potentially on my suit or in the room had disintegrated.

The door to the watch room opened as Sergeant Rose entered. He hustled to help me out of my suit. "Dr. Sadowsky also called while you were in the entertainment rooms. He wants to see you before he leaves and said it was important."

Those words made me pause. Compound 26's Director was a very level-headed man not prone to dramatics. If he said it was important, that could only mean one thing.

It was related to the Summit.

2 - WASHINGTON D.C.

I hurried to Dr. Sadowsky's office as soon as I left the Inner Sanctum. The Director's office was on the top floor, level four. I took the rail system. Otherwise, it would have been a fifteen minute walk.

I murmured hello to Dr. Sadowsky's secretary, Emma Lehmann. She typed at her desk, outside of his office. Emma and I had a good working relationship now, but it hadn't started that way.

After Dr. Roberts had fired me from the Compound last year for breaking policy, I'd called Dr. Sadowsky hourly in hopes of talking to him. Of course, the Director never answered his incoming calls, Emma did.

Needless to say, Emma had not been impressed with my persistent phone calls. However, we got along just fine now.

"Is he in?" I asked Emma.

"Yes, he's expecting you. Go ahead."

I knocked before entering but didn't wait for a response. Plush carpet softened my steps when I entered the large room.

The Director's office was huge, easily five hundred square

feet. I was greeted with the scent of eucalyptus. Emma had a thing for the dried plant. She'd placed it everywhere throughout upper management. Compared to the stale air in most of the Compound, it smelled fresh and light.

Dr. Sadowsky sat in a chair by the bookshelf. His image, as always, was striking. At over six feet with graying hair and sharp blue eyes, he embodied the rich, older gentleman look to a tee. He also dressed immaculately. I'd never seen him in anything but a perfectly fitting suit and expertly knotted tie. Before *Makanza* emerged, he had been a distinguished scientist who worked for a large medical company. When the Compounds were built, almost nine years ago, he quickly rose in the ranks. He'd been the Director of Compound 26 for the past seven years.

He stood when I entered, putting down whatever he was reading. "Meghan, I'm glad you made it."

"I just got your message. You said you wanted to see me before you left for the day?"

"Yes, please have a seat."

He waved toward the deep seated armchairs by the floor to ceiling windows that covered half of his office. On the top floor, we had to be at least eighty feet above ground.

The smooth windows faced south. Rolling fields extended as far as the eye could see. Since it was June, the South Dakota field was alive with color. Asters, clovers, geraniums, balsamroots, and ragworts were just a few of the wildflowers dominating the landscape. They rolled in waves as the wind whipped through them, a beautiful rainbow sea.

He settled in his chair. "Has Dr. Hutchinson been in touch with you about D.C.?"

"Not recently. She called a few days ago to talk about the Summit, but I haven't heard from her since."

Dr. Sadowsky crossed his legs. "You'll be hearing from her shortly as you'll be flying out Saturday. Since you essentially discovered how to stabilize the virus enough to create a vaccine, we'd like you attending all of the meetings, even when you're not presenting. People associate your face with the vaccine. You represent hope. We believe that may help sway them."

I balked but didn't say anything. Just the thought of going to the Summit meeting next week, in which every state leader and the president herself would be there, was intimidating enough. But to also attend every meeting? With all of those people?

Already my heart rate increased. I balled my hands into fists. They were ice. My usual anxiety-provoked response was nothing new. It was something I'd lived with most of my life.

"How many, ah . . ." I cleared my throat. "How many times will I speak?"

"Just once. We'd like you to talk about those infected with *Makanza* that survived. You work so closely with them and know them so well. We need you to assure our representatives that they're people just like you and me but with extra abilities. The public still doesn't know enough to not be afraid. We're hoping you can change that."

I took a deep breath. *Public speaking. An evil necessity.* It wasn't the first time I'd done it in the past few months, but I'd never spoken at a government meeting as crucial as the Summit. Somehow, I would have to get through it.

Davin's face flashed through my mind. His midnight hair, deep-set striking blue eyes, bronze skin, and chiseled features. My heart rate slowed. *I'll do it for him.*

"Can you be ready to go Saturday morning? Dr. Hutchinson is landing in Sioux Falls around ten if the weather cooperates, and the MRI only wants to run one flight so everyone's traveling together."

"I'll be ready."

It wouldn't be the first time I'd flown in the Makanza Research Institute's plane, but those trips had been rare. Oil production was almost non-existent and only two refineries in the country made jet fuel.

Another scent of eucalyptus wafted toward me as I nervously pushed my long brown hair behind my shoulder. "What should I prepare for the meeting?"

"The usual speech you give, about how the Kazzies have been imprisoned since contracting *Makanza*. How they've done their duty by helping us formulate a vaccine. How it's only fair that we now set them free."

For someone who still didn't want his employees exposed to *Makanza* despite our vaccinations, he made an impassioned argument. It was the trait I admired most about him. He still had compassion. It was something a lot of the researchers in the MRI had lost, or buried away, as inhumane treatments were done on the Kazzies under Dr. Roberts' rule.

A chill raced down my spine at the thought of my old boss.

I tucked my icy hands under my thighs. "Do you have the schedule yet?"

"No, but Dr. Hutchinson does. She can give you the details."

We spoke for a few more minutes before I said goodbye. It was almost five o'clock. Normally, I didn't leave until seven in the evening or later, but what I'd originally planned to do this weekend would no longer be possible if I flew to D.C. on Saturday.

I returned to my wing in the Compound to grab my things,

and then I sailed through security and out the door. It would take almost an hour to drive there from the Compound, and curfew was approaching.

THE CEMETERY WHERE my brother lay buried was in Vermillion. That was where we'd been living when he died on June 8, almost seven years ago. At the time of his death, he was only sixteen.

Today was June 6. The anniversary of my brother's death was in two days, the day I'd be flying to Washington D.C.

Curfew didn't begin until nine at night in the summer, so I had a few minutes to cut a bouquet of wildflowers from the vast fields surrounding the Compound. For over ten years, curfew had remained in place. It had been a regulation for so long, that it almost felt normal, like the state border closings.

After *Makanza* hit, as a way to control public movement, the MRRA had shut state borders and imposed curfew. Their argument was that tracking movement across state lines was harder at night. Therefore, nobody was allowed out of their homes during dark hours. It was another way they were trying to control human movement should a Third Wave ensue.

My hands ripped flowers from the ground as I tried to keep myself occupied with thoughts. There was so much that I needed to get done before I flew out Saturday. Not to mention, my speech was coming up, and I needed to practice it more. But once I was driving toward Vermillion, it was harder and harder to keep myself distracted.

The inevitable tears came when I pulled into the cemetery's parking lot. Every year, it became a tiny bit easier, but it still created an aching void in my chest. The pain at times was still overwhelming.

I put my car into park. The electric motor died, leaving me

in nothing but silence. Acres of tombstones stared back at me as the descending sun blazed on the horizon.

One of those tombstones belonged to my brother.

A tear rolled down my cheek. My brother had meant more to me than anybody in my life. He'd been with me for as long as I could remember. He was my childhood playmate, the one I went to when I needed a shoulder to cry on, the one who always brought a smile to my face. For many years, he'd been my best friend.

My only friend.

Throughout our childhood, it was him and me. We moved around a lot as kids, so usually, it was only the two of us. We often didn't stay anywhere long enough to make other friends. Our entire lives we'd been inseparable. It had always been like that, even when we were teenagers. Naturally, I thought we'd walk side by side through the journey of life.

Only . . . we hadn't.

My heart had shattered on the day of his death. During the weeks following, I'd fallen into a bottomless chasm of despair. I'd managed to claw my way out, my fingertips bloody and shredded from the ordeal, using a singular purpose to reach the top: to obtain a job with the MRI and to find a vaccine.

To stop *Makanza*.

My heart still hurt when I thought of my brother. I doubted that would ever fully stop, but with Davin's unyielding support and never-ending understanding, I was better than I'd been a year ago. I no longer pretended that my brother was alive.

Before Davin, I would pretend Jeremy was at my apartment when I really needed to talk to him. I'd make up conversations between us, as if he were actually alive and there, living and breathing.

The day I admitted that to Davin, I'd expected him to look at me like I was crazy. After all, what kind of sane person conversed with her dead sibling? But when I finally got the courage to meet Davin's sapphire gaze, I'd been amazed at what I'd seen.

Mirrored understanding.

He'd also lost his youngest sibling in the Second Wave. He had been as close to her as I was to Jer. Meeting someone who experienced the exact same loss, and knew just how deep my grief went, helped me heal. I wasn't there yet, but each day it became a little easier.

Taking a deep breath, I grabbed the wildflowers off the passenger seat and stepped out of my car. I clutched the flowers to my chest, their fragrant scent tickling my nose as I walked across the emerald graveyard.

The evening wind whipped my long, coffee colored locks around my face. Stone markings jutted up from the grass. The oldest part of the cemetery had graves from over two hundred years ago. The newest part, the section built solely for the victims of *Makanza*, stretched for acres.

No actual bodies were buried in the new section. Federal law deemed anybody who died from *Makanza* be cremated as a way to prevent the spread of infection. However, people still wanted a grave to visit. Therefore, victims of *Makanza* had headstones even though only their ashes lay buried underground.

Jeremy's grave was toward the center, close to a single maple tree. I'd sometimes sit against the tree, staring at the headstone that was the only remainder of my brother's existence.

When I reached his grave, I knelt beside it and pushed the excess grass clippings away from the headstone. I stared at the inscription.

Jeremy William Forester
Beloved son and brother
Taken from us too soon, but never forgotten

Another tear streaked down my cheek. My vision grew blurry. I blinked and wiped my eyes before setting the flowers against his headstone.

"I miss you," I whispered, staring at the headstone. "Every day, I miss you."

I leaned to my side and curled my legs beneath me. Soft grass tickled my ankles. "You'd be so proud of everything we've done to stop the virus. I wish I could tell you about it. We finally developed a successful vaccine two months ago. Since we only discovered how to stabilize the virus seven months ago, it took every single Compound in the country working together to pull off that feat. And in the past two months, the entire country has been inoculated. Sooner or later, the whole world will have the vaccine. Life might go back to normal one day, Jer, just like it used to be. People will be able to get in their cars and drive until the sun goes down, borders forgotten. Children will be able to play at nighttime, curfews extinct. Someday, we may restart world trade."

I rubbed my hand along the rough headstone, the rock like sandpaper. "I might even be able to visit a different country someday. It could all happen again, the rebirth of our world."

I sat by his grave, murmuring all of the things I wanted to tell him, wishing I was speaking to him and not a rock.

When the sun finally bathed the sky in red, I knew I needed to go. It was a forty-five minute drive back to my apartment. Curfew was curfew. I stood and wiped the grass clippings from my pants. I was sure my face was a blotchy mess. My head ached from all the tears, and fatigue slowed my movements. Someday, this trip would be easier, but I doubted it would be anytime soon.

I pressed my fingers against my lips and touched them to his gravestone.

"Bye, Jer. I'll see you next year."

ON THE DRIVE back to Sioux Falls, I felt the scratchy feeling in my head that indicated Sara was trying to reach me. I opened the door to the telepathic connection we shared.

Hi, I said.

Hey. Davin wants to talk to you, but he hasn't been able to reach you.

I grabbed my bag and fished around for my cell phone. I'd left it in the car when I'd visited Jer. When I found it, I pushed the power button. The screen lit up. Three missed calls. All from the Compound's central line. In other words, Davin.

Right, I see that now. Tell him I didn't have my phone on me, and I'll call him when I get home.

Will do. She paused. I could tell she knew something was up with me. *You okay?*

Yeah, I'm fine. It's just been a big night.

Hmm. I could tell she wanted to ask more. *You sure you're okay?*

I'll be fine.

Okay, talk to you later.

We both shut down the telepathic link. Sara and Sophie had *Makanza* strain 30. It was one of the rarer strains. It created telepathic links between twins or siblings, but if a person contracted strain 30 and all of their siblings were dead, they only had blue skin and didn't share a telepathic link with anyone.

Sara, however, had an extra ability. She was the only person to have it in the United States, as far as I knew. She not only had telepathy with her twin, but she could also form telepathic links with anyone she chose, as long as they were open to it.

She and I made that connection last year, when I was doing everything I could to help her and the six others imprisoned within Compound 26. In the time since, she'd become like a sister to me.

The sky grew darker as Sioux Falls neared. It was quarter to nine when I pulled into the parking lot outside of my apartment building. My stomach grumbled. I hadn't eaten dinner.

I hurried to park and ran upstairs. Once in my apartment, I called Davin's private number as I opened the fridge.

He picked up on the second ring. "Hi, Meghan."

The only people who usually called him were me or his mother. Hence, his readied greeting.

"Hey, Sara said you called?"

"Yeah, nothing important. I just wanted to say hi."

My heart skipped. Despite being exhausted from visiting Jer, Davin still got my pulse racing. "Oh . . . hi."

He chuckled. "What have you been up to tonight?"

I bit my lip and stopped rummaging through the cupboards. The fridge had been empty. "I went to see Jer."

"Oh." He was silent for a moment. "I thought you were going on Saturday?"

"I was but now I'm flying to D.C. Saturday morning. If I didn't go tonight, I would have had to wait until I got back. Tomorrow's going to be too busy."

He was quiet for a moment. "Are you doing okay?"

"You mean have I had a nervous breakdown? No."

"I know it's been hard for you."

I chuffed. "You mean since it's been months since I've pretended Jer's in my living room?"

"Yeah." His tone stayed serious despite my flippant replies. "How'd it go?"

My facetious façade crumbled under his gentle probing. He knew me so well. I bit my lip harder, but tears still blurred my vision. "It was hard. I'm exhausted."

"Yeah, I imagine you would be. Can I do anything?"

"No. Just talking about it helps." I closed my eyes and took a deep breath. I loved that I could hear the soft sound of his breathing.

"Did your parents go with you?"

My eyes snapped open. "No. I didn't tell them I was going."

"You don't visit the cemetery together on the anniversary of his death?"

"No. We never have." I could just picture that awkward encounter. My mother's distant manner, my father's anxious smiles. "It's best that I go alone. Trust me."

"When was the last time you talked to your mom?"

"Last month maybe. Or the month before that."

"Hmm." Davin tried to understand the dynamic I shared with my parents, but he couldn't. He and his mother had the exact opposite relationship of me and my mother.

Where Sharon was kind, personable, and warm—my mother was standoffish, critical, and cold. I honestly couldn't remember her ever hugging me, let alone sitting me down for a long, girl-to-girl chat. The second time I'd met Sharon, she'd done both.

"How is your mom by the way?" I shut the cupboard door

and turned to the next.

"She's good. I talked to her earlier. I guess she's started a new hobby. Knitting or crocheting? I can never remember the difference between the two."

Sharon was a homebody. It seemed like the perfect activity for her.

"She said to tell you hi and that she misses you," Davin added.

"Yeah, I need to drive out and see her again." It had been three weeks since our last visit.

"She was actually hoping to come to Sioux Falls this time. She doesn't think it's fair that you're always driving to see her."

My searching movements paused in the cupboard. The farthest Sharon ever traveled was to her Food Distribution Center. "Really?"

"Yeah, you should talk to her about that."

I smiled. "I will."

"Are you gonna have time to stop by tomorrow?"

"Of course. When have I ever missed a day?"

Davin chuckled. I loved the deep, rich sound. "The other Kazzies and I are meeting in the gym to play soccer at four. Can you come before that?"

"You mean I'm not invited to play while wearing my biohazard suit?"

He laughed. "That would be rather entertaining. Maybe you *should* join us."

"I can only imagine what Sage and Sara would say."

"No kidding." Both Sage and Sara had competitive streaks. The Kazzie group sports could get serious, and low blows were not unheard of when trying to distract an opponent.

"So are you ready for D.C.?" Davin asked.

My stomach twisted. I closed the cupboards, all yearnings

for a meal gone. "I guess. I'm only speaking once, so that's good, but I don't know the schedule. Dr. Sadowsky said I'd be hearing from Dr. Hutchinson soon."

"You'll be fine. Just do your deep breathing beforehand. And if your anxiety gets too bad, call me."

I sank to the floor and wrapped my arms around my legs. Love for Davin coursed through me. The feelings were so strong, they threatened to crush me. The words he just uttered were one of the many reasons why. He accepted me. All of me. Not just the smart, hardworking, determined side of me. But the vulnerable, anxious, unconfident side too. He knew all of my weaknesses. All of my less than perfect traits. I never had to pretend with him.

He was the only person I felt that way with.

"Thank you," I whispered.

"For what?"

I shrugged, even though I knew he couldn't see it. "For being you."

"You know I'm always here for you."

I know, but I want more. As much as I'm trying to have your friendship be enough, it's not.

"I'm always here for you too." I swallowed thickly and not for the first time wished I had the courage to say the words I thought, but I didn't.

"I should let you get to bed," he said.

"Yeah, right." I pushed myself to a stand. "I need to eat something anyway."

A disapproving sound came from his end. "Did you not eat supper again?"

"I got too busy."

He sighed. "Meg. Eat something."

"I will, promise."

We hung up, and I placed my cell on the counter. Even though I'd lost my appetite, I returned to the cupboard. It was a bad habit I had. Anytime my anxiety got out of control, I lost my appetite. Consequently, I was a little thinner than someone my height should be. And getting too thin in today's world was never a good idea.

3 - SUMMIT

The MRI's jet landed ten minutes late on Saturday morning. I waited on the tarmac, bag in hand. Even though the Summit wasn't until Wednesday, all of us were flying there now since the Director and research managers were needed earlier. Jet fuel was precious, hence why we all flew at once.

Since I had a few days before I presented, I had ninety-eight hours, nineteen minutes and a few seconds to stress about it.

Not that I was nervous.

Good thing I went for a run this morning. With how I was feeling, I'd probably be running daily in D.C. before the Summit started.

The jet glided to a stop after taxiing from the runway. Warm, summer air shimmered off the concrete in the distance.

I waited for the door to open and the stairs to descend. Dr. Hutchinson's head poked out. She waved and smiled, her dark, solid rimmed glasses firmly in place.

Like Dr. Sadowsky, Cate was striking despite her age. She was tall, thin, with shoulder-length blond hair, and smooth skin. Both Directors carried an aura of authority. I had no idea why Dr. Hutchinson would be grooming me for her position. I cringed anytime I drew attention. *Hardly the trait one needs in a Director.*

"How are you, Meghan?" she asked as I climbed aboard.

"I'm good, Dr. Hutchinson. How are you?"

She gave me a disapproving look. "You know you can call me Cate. We're not as formal in Seattle."

I glanced down sheepishly. "Right. Sorry. How are you, *Cate?*"

"Very well. I'm so pleased you could make this trip with us."

I bent over once in the airplane. The private jet could hold twelve passengers, but it wasn't tall enough for anyone over five feet to stand fully upright.

I knew a few of the other researchers on board. There were the heads of research at Compounds 10 and 11, Dr. Martin and Dr. Zheng. And then there were the MSRG researchers, like me. Paul Kelly had a position similar to mine. He worked closely with Compound 10's Kazzies. Fiona Garrison sat behind him. She also had a similar position to Paul and me, but she was at Compound 11.

Both were in their thirties, in other words, at least a decade older than me. Half a dozen other MRI employees were also onboard. I didn't recognize them. Thankfully, Dr. Hutchinson just stated who I was and that was it for introductions. All of them just nodded hello or waved.

My heart still hammered, and my fingers were ice when I strapped my seatbelt in place. I took a deep breath, counted to ten, and released it. *Just breathe, Meghan.*

Dr. Hutchinson sat across from me. The pilot revved the engines, and we moved slowly forward. Flying was still a novelty to me even though I'd been to D.C. three times now. I leaned back in my seat and looked out the window. Whirring from the engines increased and with a release of the brakes, we took off.

Once we reached cruising altitude, Dr. Hutchinson glanced at her watch. "We have three hours until we land. Would you like a drink?"

"Sure. What's onboard?"

"The usual. Water, carbonated flavored water, soda, coffee, and tea."

"Coffee sounds good." I unclicked my belt to get up, but she waved me down.

"I'll get it." She sailed to the back before I could refuse.

I used the time to stare out the window and continue my deep breathing. It was getting easier, since everybody was ignoring me, but it didn't help that the cabin interior was so crowded. I was within arm's reach of Dr. Hutchinson and the researchers sitting in front and behind me.

"Here you go."

I snapped my gaze away from the window. Dr. Hutchinson stood over me. I took the steaming cup of coffee she held. It smelled delicious.

"I added a little cream. Just the way you like it."

"Thank you." Learning how I took my coffee was one of the ways she seemed intent on wooing me to the west coast.

"Now tell me, how are the people infected with *Makanza* in 26 doing?" She sat down and sipped her coffee.

I took a sip and held the mug between my hands. It warmed my cool fingers. "They're all doing okay but anxious to get out."

"Has Davin caused any more problems?" Davin's reputation spread well beyond Compound 26.

"No, none since Dr. Roberts left."

She made a disgusted sound. "I'm surprised he was never fired."

I shrugged helplessly, a tight frown on my face. "He did a good job of brainwashing his researchers. He had everyone convinced the way our Kazzies were treated was the standard. And since he quit before he had the chance to be fired, his record remains clean." It was one thing that bothered me. That Dr. Roberts never suffered any consequences for his actions.

Dr. Hutchinson glowered. "Regardless, I'm surprised Dr. Sadowsky didn't know what was going on right under his nose."

I'd felt the same way, when I'd found out a few months ago that Dr. Sadowsky was truly ignorant to the sinister sides of Compound 26, but I didn't judge him. He'd done a lot to correct things recently, as if trying to make up for his lapse in attention. I also gave him the benefit of the doubt. He had a lot on his plate, more than I could really know. Micromanaging his direct subordinates simply wasn't feasible. Still . . . What happened in our Compound should have never occurred.

I took another sip of coffee. "At least, Dr. Roberts is no longer in control of the Inner Sanctum."

"But how much damage did he do while he *was* in charge?"

I nodded. She had a point.

When I'd started at the Compound a year ago, Dr. Roberts was three months into his new position as Director of all research within Compound 26. Before that, he'd only been in charge of the MSRG, Makanza Survivors Research Group.

During his reign of terror, when he was Director of the *entire* research department, none of the Kazzies were allowed to interact. They were all in isolation, except for the twins, and truly barbaric research practices had been done on them.

Things changed after I was fired and rehired. Dr. Sadowsky became very involved, so Dr. Roberts was no longer allowed to do as he pleased. Still, I was never entirely comfortable with Dr. Roberts continued control of the Inner Sanctum.

Luckily, I didn't have to worry about that long. Dr. Roberts left the Compound for a job with the MRRA in D.C. a few months ago.

Our parting hadn't gone well. The last conversation we'd had, he'd alluded to believing that *I* was responsible for his downfall at Compound 26 which was absurd.

I shuddered. With any luck, I'd never see him again.

"Is Dr. Sadowsky still not letting you into the cells without your suit?" Cate leaned back in her seat with her mug between her hands.

"No, he's still not."

"All of my researchers move freely with their survivors, now that they've been vaccinated."

"And no one's been sick." I gripped my cup tighter when the plane jostled.

"No. Neither dead nor Changed. A few of our researchers have had stronger immune responses than others. Most of them felt unwell for a day or two as their bodies created antibodies to fight off the live vaccine, and one moved into the second stage of symptoms, but all of them recovered successfully." Dr. Hutchinson cocked her head, looking thoughtful. "It's been the same nationwide in all of our drug trials. Nobody's been around a Kazzie and died or Changed. It's very promising."

My stomach churned as a thought cropped into my mind. "I hope that's all they'll want to talk about in D.C."

"What do you mean?" She tucked a short strand of blond

hair behind her ear.

I shrugged. "It's just that . . . well, how am I supposed to convince our representatives that the vaccine is safe when my own Director won't let me be around the Kazzies without my suit on? Your researchers have all been exposed and they're fine, and the researchers in other Compounds have been fine, but I personally haven't been exposed. It seems rather misleading for me to preach things I haven't done."

Dr. Hutchinson took a deep breath and straightened her suit jacket. "We're not going to tell them that if we can avoid it."

"Don't you think they'll ask?"

"It's possible, but I'm hoping we can steer the conversation away from that if it arises."

"I hope you're right."

The plane dipped a little, and this time coffee sloshed onto my hand. I wiped it off with my napkin and took another large drink, just to get the level down in case there was more turbulence.

"Have you heard that Canada's vaccination program is coming along nicely?" Cate asked. "So is Mexico's."

I tightened my seatbelt as we hit another patch of turbulence. "What about Europe and Asia?"

Dr. Hutchinson leaned forward as she launched into details about the global efforts to stop *Makanza*. We'd shared our research with every functioning country. Vaccine production was now occurring worldwide. Sooner or later, the entire world would be inoculated. The progress she revealed had me grinning ear-to-ear.

WE LANDED AT Dulles International Airport not long later. The name was deceiving. It had been ten years since any international flights had departed or landed here.

The large airport was eerily quiet when we disembarked. The only sounds were a few birds flying overhead and the infrequent, distant sounds of traffic on the highways and interstates. The air was heavy and humid, the smell of jet fuel present.

An abandoned air traffic control tower had all of its windows broken. I could only imagine how many rocks had been thrown by local teenagers to achieve that. The building's windows had to be at least forty feet from the ground.

A large van waited for us, the driver leaning against its hood. He pushed away from it and held his hand out to Dr. Hutchinson. "I'm Harry. I'll be your driver today."

Dr. Hutchinson shook his hand. "Thank you, Harry. It's nice to meet you."

Since we all only had one carryon, there wasn't much to pack.

"I've been instructed to take you to your hotel right away. Is that all right?" Harry opened the sliding door on the large van.

"Perfectly fine." Dr. Hutchinson climbed inside. "It's been a long trip."

The ride to our hotel was fast. The streets in D.C. were numerous, but there wasn't much traffic or people. A lot of the buildings had been neglected. Some had broken windows, others had been reclaimed by nature. Weeds grew several feet tall in sidewalks that were rarely or never used.

After *Makanza* hit, there had been talk of moving our government headquarters away from the east coast. The coasts had been harshly affected by the virus. It had been sheer willpower on the president's part at that time, preventing the move.

Most of D.C. was now a ghost town, but the major government buildings and a few neighborhoods were still occupied and well cared for. It was like crossing a border between two countries, going from an abandoned neighborhood to an occupied one in some parts of the city.

Since Washington D.C. was now exclusively government, the universities, shopping centers, and tourism areas were long gone. The only people that lived here were federal employees and they all tended to congregate in the same area.

The drive took a little over twenty minutes, and the hotel came into view once we turned down the street. It was the same hotel we stayed at each time we traveled to D.C. Most of the meetings we had were held inside. During one trip, I'd never gone farther than a block from my room.

The brick building with its impressive array of windows felt familiar. Flags flew above the parking garage, the colors vivid and welcoming in the summer breeze. The trees lining the boulevard were trimmed and groomed, the sidewalk without cracks or weeds.

It was an unusual sight.

"Here we are." Harry pulled up to the front doors.

We all stepped out, each of us carrying our bags before entering the building. Inside, the lobby was impressive. Grays, whites, and neutrals dominated the color palette. Several large chandeliers hung from the coffered ceiling. Wingback chairs lined the walls.

The government helped fund the hotel now since it was an official meeting site for out-of-state business. Practical, really. Your guests could stay here, eat here, and conduct business here. No transportation was needed, other than to and from the airport, and the amenities were luxurious.

It was so different from my life in Sioux Falls.

THE NEXT FEW days passed agonizingly slowly. Since the Summit was held in the hotel we stayed at, we never had to leave the building. The only time I left was to run. It became my daily routine as I waited for Wednesday: run every morning, sit in meetings all day, and call Davin each evening.

At each meeting, I sat in the back and listened. I made sure my presence was noted, since that's what Cate and Dr. Sadowsky wanted, but it was still difficult when representatives wanted to speak to me.

Not surprisingly, when Wednesday morning finally rolled around, I was an anxious mess. I'd barely slept the night before, tossing and turning as I thought about all of the things that could go wrong. As much as I tried to prepare, as much as I rehearsed my presentation, and as much as Davin tried to calm me, I still threw up two times before leaving my hotel room.

It was my usual response to public speaking. If the day ever came where I only threw up once, I'd count it as a victory.

Fiona and Paul—the MSRG researchers from Compounds 10 and 11 in Washington state—had agreed to meet me in the lobby before going to the conference room.

"How are you?" Fiona asked when she saw me. Her white-blond spiky hair look freshly styled.

"Fine," I managed.

"You're looking a little green." Paul frowned and pushed his glasses up his nose.

"I am?" My voice took on a high pitched, panicked tone.

"No, you're not. You look fine." Fiona elbowed Paul to the side before fingering the multiple piercings in her ear. "In fact, you look great. That suit fits you well, and you look very professional. And I like your hair up like that. You look at least five years older."

Her teasing tone made my shoulders relax. The whole country knew how young I was.

She winked. "Now, come on. We don't want to be late."

I followed them to the room where the Summit had been taking place for the past few days. Today, the tables and chairs were lined up in a circular pattern. At the front stood a podium. *That's where I have to stand.*

To me, it looked like a crucifix. I swallowed the sudden lump in my throat.

Dr. Hutchinson approached as soon as we entered the room. "Meghan, how are you?"

There was an edge to her tone. She'd seen first-hand what my anxiety could do. At one presentation, I'd run out of the room just before I was due on stage. It was either that, or I'd have thrown up all over my shoes, or on the shoes of the person sitting beside me.

"I'm fine. Really, I am." I straightened my suit jacket.

The anxious lines around her mouth lessened. "Good. Now, you'll be presenting right after I do. I'll probably take twenty minutes to go through my material. Just sit tight until then."

"Right. Okay."

My cheeks flushed since everyone coddled me. *Why can't I be as tough as Davin?*

Nothing seemed to faze him. I'd bet he'd walk into this room, his expression unflinching, while he told each and every one of the senators and congressmen exactly what he thought of the Compounds. Whereas I, the person with two PhD's, years of experience in virology, and the founder of the vaccine, was ready to throw up *again*.

It was sadly, laughably ironic.

"I think I'll wait in the hallway until I present." I fingered the notecards in my pocket. *Maybe practicing one more time will help.*

Dr. Hutchinson nodded. "Good idea." She gave my shoulder a quick, reassuring squeeze before she turned.

My cheeks blazed when I returned to the hall. *Get a grip, Meghan. Seriously!*

I pulled out my cell phone as I brushed shoulders with two men walking into the room. I recognized them. One was a senator from Minnesota. The other from Virginia. Behind them trailed Senator Douglas from Arkansas. His shrewd gaze met mine. He was one of the loudest opponents of freeing the Kazzies.

Somehow, I managed to hold my head high as he passed. Once he entered the room, I slumped against the wall.

I tapped in Davin's number into my phone. My fingers were icy cold and shaking.

He picked up before the first ring even finished. "You'll be fine. Just breathe."

The sound of his voice calmed my racing heart. "How is it that you always know what to say?"

"I do? Well, that's a relief."

I laughed, feeling some of my tension ease. "I'm speaking after Dr. Hutchinson."

"I know. I've been watching the clock all morning. Most of the others are in the pool right now. Dorothy found a water aerobics DVD in the library, so they brought in a portable TV and DVD player so she could try it in the swimming pool. For kicks, the twins, Sage, and Victor joined her."

I smiled despite myself. Dorothy was convinced she could lose weight if she just tried hard enough. Her researchers had explained to her, numerous times, that wasn't possible because of the *Makanza* strain she carried. Strain 8 had caused her to grow pounds of brown fat. That, along with changes in her kidneys, allowed her to go weeks without eating or drinking.

I leaned against the wall in the hallway. "So you're just hanging out in your cell, waiting for my frantic phone calls? Instead of doing water aerobics?"

"Yeah, I think it was Jane Fonda or someone like that. Not really my thing."

I laughed again.

A squeak sounded in the background, like Davin just laid down on his bed. "So it was either water aerobics or I joined Garrett for a painting session. He's working on a portrait right now, but since I struggle to paint stick figures, that wasn't a good option either."

I could picture it. Davin sitting beside Garrett, the large-eyed Kazzie who worked as an artist before catching *Makanza*. Garrett was the quietest of the group. He was often drawing, painting, or sculpting. He had a gentle soul. Of all the men with *Makanza* in Compound 26, he had the least intimidating presence. Not like Sage's large build or Victor's hot temper.

Leaning against the wall more, I turned and quieted my voice when a woman in a business suit walked by. "I'm sorry that you've turned into my personal therapist."

I felt his shrug. "At least I'm employed. Got to earn my keep somehow."

"You don't mind? Seriously?"

All joking left his tone. "Not at all. I'm glad I'm able to help."

I felt a little better after he said that, but I still felt guilty. Sooner or later, I knew I'd have to learn how to deal with my anxiety completely on my own, but right now, it was too hard.

"What if I throw up on stage?"

"You won't, because if you start panicking, I want you to

picture me sitting in the audience listening. Just picture it and stare at me. Pretend I'm the only one there. Just you and me."

I took a deep breath, counted to ten and let it out. "Okay."

"Do you want to go through your presentation one more time?"

"Yes."

BY THE TIME I returned to the conference room, I felt less shaky. I also didn't feel the urge to throw up. *Baby steps, right?*

Dr. Hutchinson announced me when it was my turn. I walked with my head high and didn't look at anyone. *Just breathe Meghan. Just breathe.*

When I reached the podium, I set my notecards down, my fingers shaking as I rearranged them. The room was eerily quiet, the rustling from my papers amplified in the speakers. I could almost feel Dr. Hutchinson's nerves. She stood off to the side, shifting from foot to foot.

Am I that bad? Does she really think I could lose it any second?

I looked up and took another deep breath. *You can do this, Meghan!*

A sea of faces stared back at me. My stomach flipped, so I shifted my gaze higher until I was looking at the blank wall in the back. *Just pretend they're not here.*

I pictured Davin, sitting by the back wall, his midnight hair curling around his ears. Those intense, bright blue eyes shining with encouragement. My heart rate slowed, and in that moment, I felt anchored to why I was here.

The Kazzies deserved to be free. My speech could help make that happen.

It was imperative I didn't fail. *This one's for you, Davin.*

"Good morning," I began. "As Dr. Hutchinson stated, my

name is Dr. Meghan Forester. I'm a researcher at Compound 26 in South Dakota. I helped develop the vaccine, and I work closely with the survivors infected with *Makanza* in our facility. I'm here today in hopes of convincing you that it's safe to release them back into the public, and to help you see the science behind why that is so."

I continued on, telling the congressmen, congresswomen, and all of the state senators, about the efficacy of the vaccine, breaking down the physiology behind it, and explaining how the immune response worked. In detail, I described how researchers worked with their survivors, unsuited, and how nobody had contracted the virus since the vaccine.

I went on to emphasize the mundane, imprisoned life the Kazzies led. How they deserved more than to be locked away simply because they survived the virus. My voice became impassioned, all nerves leaving me as I pictured Davin being free, of all the infected survivors being able to have a normal life.

"I hope you strongly consider everything we've told you today. The infected survivors have done their part. They've given us a vaccine so that *Makanza* can no longer ravage the earth. Please set them free. They're people who've never committed any crime. They simply survived."

When I finished, the room was quiet. Dr. Hutchinson was the first to applaud. A grin spread across her face. Everyone else followed suit. Clapping echoed in the room.

"I'd like to open the floor to questions," I said, when the applause died down. I took a deep, uneasy breath.

This was the part I dreaded most.

A senator from Utah, Al Rosting, was the first to chime in. Similar to Senator Douglas, he'd been adamantly against releasing the Kazzies since day one. I tensed, waiting for his question.

"You say the vaccine is one hundred percent effective, yet we can't guarantee that, can we? After all, we'd have to expose every single person in the U.S. to *Makanza* to know that for a fact. Right?"

"In every drug trial, it's been one hundred percent effective. We have no reason to believe that will change."

"But you can't guarantee that, can you?" he persisted.

Dr. Hutchinson had helped prep me for these kinds of attacks. I knew what I needed to say. "All evidence supports its effectiveness, one hundred percent."

"But what if that's not true? What if someone in the public comes into contact with a Kazzie and dies because of it?"

"There's no evidence supporting that will ever happen. We can't base a decision on what-if's. We have to base decisions on science." I kept my voice cool and even. I knew part of this was an attempt to rile me into saying something to support his claim.

"What if your mother died? What if your father died? What if your brother died?" he persisted. "From being exposed to a Kazzie?"

I flinched. "My brother *did* die, in the Second Wave. If we'd developed this vaccine before then, I'm one hundred percent certain he'd be alive today."

He had the decency to look contrite after I said that. Senator Rosting obviously hadn't done his homework on me.

"What about the immuno-suppressed people, or people who might not respond to the vaccine as well as others?" a congresswoman asked. I glanced her way. She represented Maine.

"As you know, very few immune suppressed people are still alive," I replied. "Those that are, have all received the vaccine. We haven't seen any negative symptoms from them. They have tolerated the vaccine acceptably."

"But what about fear in the public?" another asked. "What if releasing the survivors causes riots or violence?"

"Since when are civil rights not upheld for fear of violence?" I challenged.

"But some of them are so different," Mary Goldberg, a representative from New York said. "I want them to be free, but I'm afraid for *them*. You've explained how different the strains are in your previous talks, and how some strains have turned the survivors into people that don't even look like humans anymore. Aren't they afraid of the public's reaction to them?"

I bristled as a fierce protectiveness rose in me. "Let me ask you a question, Senator Goldberg. Do you know anyone with Down's Syndrome?" I knew she did. I'd thoroughly researched every state's representatives.

She sat up a little straighter, her tone defensive. "Yes, my niece has Down's."

"In a way, your niece is no different than the Kazzies. She was born with an extra chromosome. Her genetic makeup is different than yours or mine. So does that mean we should lock her away? Keep her away from the public? For fear of how others may react to her?"

"Of course not," she said hotly.

"Then why should it be any different for those that survived *Makanza*? They may look different, but they're still humans. They're still like you and me."

She grew quiet after I said that, a penchant look on her face.

"And what about you, Dr. Forester? Have you been exposed to *Makanza*?"

I dreaded turning toward that voice. When I finally did, Senator Douglas' dark beady eyes bore holes into me. He sat three rows from the front, his arms crossed over his paunch belly. He raised an eyebrow as he waited for my answer.

Swallowing sharply, sweat erupted across my brow. I avoided the urge to seek out Cate's supportive presence. I was on my own. "No, I haven't been exposed."

His look turned smug. "I didn't think so. It's a bit hypocritical to be lecturing all of us on the safety of the vaccine, if you don't have the guts to expose yourself, now is it?"

A murmur erupted around the room.

"That's not it," I said through gritted teeth. "I'm not afraid of being exposed. My boss . . ."

I stopped myself. I was about to say that Dr. Sadowsky wouldn't allow his researchers to be exposed, but it was too late. I'd played right into Senator Douglas' hands.

"Oh, I heard," the senator continued. "Your own boss won't allow his scientists to mingle with their Kazzies. Hardly something a renowned Director would do unless there's cause for concern. If the vaccine truly is as safe as you claim it to be, why won't he allow it?"

I opened my mouth to respond, but the voices in the room rose as the leaders of our nation began discussing the topic Senator Douglas presented.

"Please!" I called when my efforts to control the rising energy in the room failed. "Please, listen! *Every* researcher and scientist in other Compounds in the U.S. that have been exposed have all survived and remain healthy."

"So why the concern from your Director?" a voice shouted from the back.

Avoiding the urge to pinch the bridge of my nose, I

replied, "I cannot speak for someone else, but as Dr. Hutchinson can confirm, every scientist in her Compound has remained healthy and unharmed."

My gaze swept the room as my heart plummeted. It didn't matter that everyone exposed had been okay. Already, I could see fear and skepticism on faces that only minutes ago had seemed open and hopeful.

Senator Douglas smirked.

It took all of my self-control to not glower at him.

I was exhausted by the time the session came to a close. Cate waited for me when I stepped off the stage.

"What a bastard." She seethed quietly.

My shoulders fell as she guided me out of the room. "I'm sorry. I should have been more prepared for that."

"It's not your fault." She tapped her foot after crossing her arms. "He knew what your weakness was and exploited it. Never mind that you would be fine if exposed. He pounced on your boss' irrational decision to keep you separated from Compound 26's Kazzies."

"And it was going so well."

She nodded. "It's a pity it had to end on that note."

It wasn't until I returned to my hotel suite that my nerves finally gave out. I threw up one last time before collapsing on the bathroom floor. With shaking fingers, I brought a glass of water to my mouth and rinsed it out. My stomach felt hollow and empty. I was surprised there'd been anything left to vomit.

Pale, clammy skin stared back at me when I finally stood and looked in the mirror. After retreating to the living room, I called Davin.

He picked up immediately. "Go okay?"

"For the most part." I summed up how well it had gone until Senator Douglas piped in.

Davin's tone turned grim. "So there's no guarantee we're getting out."

"No." I sank to the living room floor and drew my knees up. "No guarantee but let's hope for the best."

4 - BACK TO THE COMPOUND

We flew back the next day. Everyone was quiet during the flight. Tension hung in the cabin, like a thick oppressive fog. My thoughts kept returning to Senator Douglas and the fear he stoked. It was very possible he'd thwart any progress for the Kazzies.

When I disembarked in Sioux Falls, warm summer air swirled around me as I walked to my car. It was early evening by the time I arrived at my apartment, too late to drive into the Compound, even though I really wanted to see Davin.

I was toweling off from a shower, still biting my lips over thoughts of Senator Douglas, when my cell phone rang. One look at the screen, and I smiled. Amy.

"Hey," I said.

"Hey, yourself. Are you back in town?"

"Yeah, I got back an hour ago."

"How'd it go? Mitch, Charlie, and I are currently in a bet on what's gonna happen."

Since Mitch, Charlie, Amy, and I were Davin's researchers we all worked closely together. Over the past year, my anxiety around them had mostly disappeared.

I sighed and leaned against the bathroom counter. Water dripped down my back from my wet hair.

"As much as I'd like to say I'm certain of a positive outcome, I'm not." I explained how my speech went well and the question and answer session seemed fine until Senator Douglas spouted in.

"What a douche," Amy grumbled. "So I'm probably out twenty bucks then? I bet they'd all be free within a month. Charlie said it would be over a year."

"And Mitch?"

"He said they'll never be free."

My stomach dropped. "I really hope he's wrong."

"Me too." She paused. "They said on the news tonight the president will be addressing the nation on Monday."

"That's the plan. The state representatives are supposed to come to a decision by tomorrow. If they don't, they'll be working through the weekend."

"As long as they make a decision."

"Exactly."

I ARRIVED AT the Compound at my usual six o'clock the next morning. The huge, four-story building stretched a quarter mile. Its exterior walls were gray concrete and dotted with windows. A few lights were on, but most of the building was dark.

Most employees didn't arrive until seven or eight, but I'd been working longer days than most for so long, I didn't think twice about it.

Since I was impatient to see Davin, I took the rail system to the Inner Sanctum. Most of the Kazzies were asleep when I entered. Garrett, the Sisters, and Victor's cells were all dark.

However, Dorothy and Sage were awake.

Dorothy sat at her desk, eating breakfast. Gray streaked through her dark hair. Her ample bosom pushed into the desk. I could practically hear her adding up the calories. She'd recently asked the kitchen to reduce each meal to four hundred calories. I think she'd actually gained weight instead of lost, but she was still trying. She was stubborn. I'd give her that.

Sage waved when I entered his hallway and motioned me toward his watch room. I stepped inside as the Kazzie approached the window.

As usual, there was a swagger in his step. He was an attractive looking guy, and he knew it. The only overt difference to his appearance was the subtle change to his skin. If I stood close enough, I could see it. His skin looked almost reptilian. Small looking scales covered his entire body. They were constructed of myelin and metal. The combination was highly conductive and was how he generated electricity.

The rest of him looked like any other guy. He had dark hair, brown eyes, and angular features. He was big, too. He stood around six-three with broad shoulders and muscular legs. I felt fairly confident that he'd been a ladies man before the First Wave.

He made a motion to the guard. The guard reached for a switch on his control panel and pushed something.

"Meghan, can you hear me?" Sage asked.

I smiled. "Yes."

"Sweet. You look good by the way. That color's nice on you."

I just rolled my eyes. I wore a brown blouse and tan slacks, hardly earth-shattering in its attractiveness. "Is that all you wanted to tell me?"

He chuckled. "No, I want to show you something. It's

something I've been working on lately."

He stepped back and raised his hand and then glanced at me again. "Ready?"

I shrugged. "Sure."

He flashed a smile before his face tightened in concentration. A second ticked by and nothing happened.

Then, a few sparks shot from his fingers. Actually *shot* from his fingers, not like the usual small sparks he achieved from mundanely flicking them.

I crossed my arms and leaned forward.

Sage's eyebrows drew together as a few beads of sweat popped up on his brow. He brought his arm back, like he was going to throw something, and shot his hand forward. A flash of light flew three feet in front of him.

"What the . . ." I mumbled, my arms falling to my sides.

Sage brought his arm back again before throwing another bolt of electricity from his hand. This time, it shot all the way across the room, hitting the concrete wall as a loud *boom* echoed around us.

"Sage, you're gonna have to stop that!" his guard said disapprovingly. "He's been getting it farther and farther all week." He glanced over his shoulder at me.

Sage turned to the window, grinning. Sweat dripped from his face. "Did you see that?"

I just stared at him, my mouth gaping. Sage had *Makanza* strain 27, which meant he could generate electricity along his skin, rather like an electric eel. However, I'd never heard of a Kazzie with that strain being able to *shoot* lightning bolts.

"Are you okay?" I finally managed.

He just laughed. "Of course, why wouldn't I be?"

I glanced at the small hole in the wall and wondered what the state representatives would think knowing a Kazzie could do something like *that.*

I switched off the microphone. "Keep this between you and me, okay?" I said to the guard.

"His researchers already know."

Crap. "In that case, don't tell anyone else."

"What are you two talking about?" Sage asked.

The guard pushed the microphone button again and pointed at Sage's wall. "Just that Liam's not going to be happy about that."

Liam Nichols and Tom Madison were two of the technicians that serviced the Kazzie's cells. They'd no doubt be the ones repairing Sage's handiwork.

Sage had the decency to look sheepish, although I could tell he'd throw another bolt in a heartbeat. "Think you could convince the higher powers to give me a room to practice this stuff in?"

I sighed. "I'm not sure that's a good idea. You could get hurt."

Or you could hurt someone. Senator Douglas would have a hay day with this . . .

Sage laughed. "Meg, seriously, even if I was put in the electric chair, I wouldn't die. I can't get hurt from electricity."

"You don't think millions of volts from a bolt of actual lightning would kill you?" I retorted.

He shrugged. "You wanna let me outside during a thunderstorm and we'll try it out?"

I smiled. "Nice try." Like all of the Kazzies, Sage was always coming up with some reason to be allowed outside. "But hopefully, with any luck, you soon won't need an excuse."

"So your trip was a success?" His voice rose in hope.

"We'll see."

I said goodbye a few minutes later, after Sage promised to not damage his cell further. With his new skill, his researchers would probably be making a few adaptations to it. I had a feeling there'd be a large shipment of rubber coming within the next week.

I hurried into the next cell. Victor was still asleep. The last access door waited. In a few steps, I'd be in Davin's hallway.

Just the thought got my heart racing, my breath coming a little shallower. How could it be that I'd known Davin almost a year, yet this reaction never changed. If anything, it grew.

"Seriously Meghan," I whispered to myself. "Get a grip!"

He was awake when I entered his hall. I knew he would be. Davin had always been an early riser. When our eyes connected, he grinned.

That look stopped me in my tracks. Davin's midnight hair, blazing blue eyes, and broad shoulders would make any woman look twice, but when he smiled like that, my stomach flipped, and I felt lightheaded. I was thankful for the four inches of bullet proof glass that separated us. I was pretty sure he would have heard my thudding heart otherwise.

Sergeant Rose was sitting on his stool in the watch room when I stepped inside.

"Morning, Dr. Forester." He took a sip of coffee. "How was D.C?"

"Still there."

He chuckled. "Going in today?"

"Yes. Will you help me suit up?"

We entered the containment room, attached to Davin's cell, and proceeded to do all of the biohazard suit's safety checks. I grumbled at how unnecessary it was. If Davin and I lived in Washington state, and this was Compound 10 or 11, I'd have been visiting with him for months without a suit.

I sighed audibly.

"Everything okay?" Sergeant Rose raised his eyebrows.

"Oh, yes. Sorry, I'm just tired of this suit. That's all."

"Hopefully you won't need it much longer. I hear the president's addressing the nation on Monday."

"She's supposed to. With any luck, it will be good news."

We finished the safety checks, and Sergeant Rose exited to the watch room.

Davin's face appeared in the door's window as the dials began to turn, depressurizing the room. We both smiled at one another, and my heartbeat answered in reply.

Calm down Meghan, it's not like you've never seen him before.

When the door finally opened, Davin did his usual. He took my hand and guided me to his chair. It had become such a ritual, it was like neither of us thought twice about it.

I could feel his heat through my gloves. He rubbed my thumb absentmindedly. He probably didn't know he was doing it.

Shivers traveled up my arm. I took another deep breath when I sat on his desk chair.

"It's good to see you." He perched on the edge of his bed and clasped his large hands. He wore his usual jeans and tee, with his bare feet planted on the floor. It always amazed me that he never minded the cold concrete on his soles.

"You too. How was your week?" I asked.

"The usual." He shrugged. "Read a few books, hung out with the gang. Do you really want me to go into the details?"

I laughed. "No, I'm sure I can guess."

"So, do you want to come down here on Monday and watch the president's speech with all of us?"

"Yeah, of course. You know I'll be here."

Monday couldn't come fast enough.

5 – STATE OF THE UNION

Monday finally rolled around, and its effects on everyone were obvious. Researchers were more quiet than usual. No music played in any labs. The cafeteria was like a ghost town. The jittery snacking apparently keeping workers full.

Everyone seemed on edge.

Tonight was the night. We'd finally know the outcome for the Kazzies: freedom or continued imprisonment.

"I never thought I'd be so nervous." Amy sat beside me at our bench, pipetting solution by hand. We'd decided the only way to make time pass faster was to work. "I mean, after tonight, everyone's lives could change. If the Kazzies are free, what becomes of the MRI? What becomes of our jobs?"

I frowned. "I've never thought of that."

Her eyebrows rose. "You haven't? How could you not? In a few years, we could be unemployed. I feel it's safe to say we'll have a job until then. We still have a lot to learn about *Makanza*, but after we figure everything out, then what? Will the MRI still exist? And what the hell are they going to do with all of the Compounds?"

I thought of the fourteen empty cells in our Compound alone. They'd been sitting vacant ever since I started. *Is that what will become of the Compounds? Will everything in them be sealed up and locked down? Like it had never been?* Funny how that thought made me smile.

"That seems like progress." I snapped on a new pair of gloves. "We never had Compounds before *Makanza*. Isn't that a good thing?"

"Yeah, I guess so." She didn't sound convinced.

"Don't worry, I'm sure you'll get a job *somewhere*."

She chuckled. "I am pretty marketable." She held up her gloved hands. "I come with mad skills."

I laughed. "Are you going to stay tonight and watch the president's speech with the Kazzies?"

"Yeah, I think a lot of the researchers are."

I tried to picture dozens of my colleagues in biohazard suits in the Kazzies' entertainment area. I couldn't. Usually, it was just me and the Kazzies. They didn't have an affinity to anyone quite like they did to me.

It probably didn't hurt that Davin and I had been behind the vaccine breakthrough—all of the Kazzies knew that. It also didn't hurt that I had a telepathic connection with Sara.

"Come on girls!" a booming voice called.

We turned to see Mitch and Charlie standing at the lab's entrance door.

"Let's grab something to eat before the party starts." Mitch's lab coat draped open. A typical comedic shirt appeared. *Sometimes I wonder, "Why is that Frisbee getting bigger?" Then it hits me.*

I chuckled and nudged Amy. "I take it they're staying too?"

"Yep." Amy glanced at her watch. "Wow, it's already half

past five. The address starts soon!"

We joined Mitch and Charlie and hurried to the rail system. When we reached the cafeteria, a hum of voices, and scents of freshly cooked food, filtered into the hall from the cafeteria's open doors. It was jam-packed.

Great. People everywhere. "Looks like everyone's appetite is back." I shrank closer to the wall when someone brushed against me.

"And it looks like everyone's sticking around for the big announcement." Charlie crossed his thin arms over his chest, surveying the room for an open table. He had a small Asian build and only stood a few inches taller than me.

Mitch towered over all of us. A thousand years ago, Mitch would have been a Viking. I was sure of it. His Nordic ancestry was apparent in every line of his body. Sandy blond hair, pale blue eyes, and a brawny build that towered to at least six-four made him one of the most physically intimidating men I'd ever met.

However, Charlie had one of the sharpest minds I'd ever encountered. If it came down to a game of wits, Charlie would be the more worthy opponent.

"There's an open table over there." Amy pointed. "I just saw a group stand up."

"Ready, set, go!" Mitch joked. He took off, striding towards the table before anyone else could swoop in and take it. When the rest of us caught up, we draped our lab coats over the chairs before getting into line for food.

"Be quick about it." Amy checked her watch. "We don't want to be late."

Mitch raised an eyebrow. "Wasn't it us who picked *you* up? Perhaps you should thank us for saving you from a dinner of lab solution."

Amy smirked. "There are plenty of vending machines in all the wings. I'm sure I would have managed just fine."

Mitch chuckled. "It kills you too much to say thank you, doesn't it, McConnell."

"Fine, thank you."

"Behave children." Charlie held a full tray. "I wouldn't want to put you in a time-out."

"Meghan wouldn't let you. She likes me too much." Mitch grabbed two sandwiches and a large bag of chips. "She's gonna be our boss someday."

"I'm not going to be your boss." I ladled chili into a bowl, my cheeks heating at Mitch's comment.

Charlie gave me a sympathetic shoulder pat. "Oh yes you are, you just don't know it yet."

"In other words, Meghan, you can fire them both on your first day, or just Mitch." Amy gave Mitch a wink.

"Ah, I'm your favorite, right, Megs?" Mitch put his arm around my shoulder and squeezed.

I waited until the squeeze was over before extracting myself from his massive limb. "Of course, Mitch. I'd miss your t-shirts too much to get rid of you."

Mitch's bark of laughter turned a few heads.

"Don't mind him," Charlie murmured to those watching us. "He doesn't get out much."

The four of us returned to our seats and wolfed down dinner before hurrying to the Inner Sanctum. A steady trail of researchers headed the same way.

We opted to enter the Kazzie's entertainment area through the researcher's direct access which allowed us to bypass the cells. However, by the time we arrived, dozens of employees were already in front of us. I tapped my foot as we waited. We only had thirty minutes until the State of the Union address.

A scratchy feeling rubbed the back of my mind. I opened myself up to Sara. *I'm trying to get in.*

So you're not in yet? She groaned. *It's going to start soon.*

I know. Trust me. I'm trying to hurry.

I checked the clock again. Twenty-two minutes until it started. *I should have gone by myself to Davin's cell and gone in that way.*

Just get in here as soon as you can.

It was five to seven by the time we finally donned suits and passed all the checks.

Mitch chuckled. "Keep your pants on, Forester. We'll make it in time."

I just gave him an irritated glare as we *finally* entered the entertainment area.

The first time I'd seen the entertainment rooms, I'd been speechless. True to the Compound's style, everything was huge, no expense spared. The multi-leveled library that we entered into was architecturally stimulating. Everything about the tiered levels and open design beckoned tranquility and serenity. Large skylights adorned the ceiling. Natural sunlight streamed from them as clouds drifted by. Tall bookshelves were packed with books. Random chairs and couches were strewn about. It put the Sioux Falls public library to shame. Obviously.

"Every time I come in here, I'm amazed at how nice it is." Amy surveyed the room through her hood's viewing shield.

"We do spoil them," Charlie agreed.

We reached the elevator and ascended to the second level, where the TV and billiards room was located. All of the Kazzies and a few dozen researchers were already in the large room when we entered.

Straight ahead, six huge, plush couches, with stadium

seating, were stationed in front of a large, movie-sized screen. A kitchen was in the back, stocked with snacks and drinks. Next to that was another sitting area.

Three couches were arranged in a horseshoe pattern, meant for those who just wanted to sit and chat. A few researchers currently sat on them, talking about who knew what before the speech.

To the left of the stadium seating was another room with two pool tables, arcade games, darts, and other grown-up toys.

Everything about the Kazzies' entertainment rooms was luxurious. The exercise rooms were no exception. They contained a basketball court, large pool, soccer field, weight and dance room, and a running track. In other words, humungous.

And in reality, not entirely necessary for a facility that could only ever contain twenty Kazzies. Yet, if the Compound was to be the Kazzies' home forever, I agreed that spoiling them was the least we could do. After all, they weren't criminals.

I searched for Davin but didn't see him.

"I think I see Gerry." Amy stood on her tiptoes. "I'll catch up with you later." She lumbered off in the huge suit before I could say anything. Charlie quickly did the same. That left me and Mitch.

"Meghan!" a voice called.

Sara strode toward me, the researchers parting like the Red Sea as she passed. They all stared. Her blue skin always got a person's attention, but I imagined it was the large grin on her face that really got them curious.

"Hi," I said when she reached me.

"I was debating if you'd make it."

"Yeah, Amy and I were a bit distracted in the lab. Luckily,

Mitch came to the rescue."

Sara glanced at Mitch. I felt his hovering presence over my shoulder. She didn't smile or say anything to him, instead, she looked back at me. "Come sit with us. We have the best seats."

She grabbed my hand and pulled me away. I felt Mitch follow.

I looked down the stairs to the couches that were quickly filling. My eyes connected with Davin's bright, blue gaze. He was staring right at me. Those eyes moved to Mitch, a questioning expression in them.

"He's been waiting for you," Sara murmured. "Not very patiently I might add." She waggled her eyebrows.

My cheeks heated. It wasn't the first time Sara had teased me about Davin. The screen suddenly turned on, making the room grow quiet. "Come on, let's go." Sara's thin, blue fingers pulled me gently down the stairs.

"Is there a seat for me too?" Mitch didn't seem bothered by Sara ignoring him, but I knew he'd be hurt if I snubbed him.

"Of course, come sit with us."

I grabbed Mitch's hand, since I knew he'd never ask for help. The last thing we needed was a researcher plummeting down the stairs in a bulky suit.

Everyone else was finding seats by the time we reached the other Kazzies.

The Kazzies had reserved the front two couches. Each couch could easily seat six people. The one in the front row held Sophie, Sage, Victor, Garrett, and Dorothy. They all turned to greet me.

Davin sat by himself on the one behind them. The researchers crammed together as best they could in the four behind that and whatever seats that were left up by the kitchen.

The bulky biohazard suits made that awkward.

An ever-present flash of annoyance coursed through me. *We've all been vaccinated. We don't need these suits!*

Davin watched me until I reached his side. I smiled and had to stop myself from touching him. We'd been waiting for this moment for so long. I wanted to hold his hand but knew that was not something a friend would do.

Instead, I said hello.

"Hi," Davin finally said, his tone flat.

His gaze flickered to my hand that was still clasping Mitch's, his expression dark.

I pulled my hand from Mitch's and sat beside Davin. Mitch plopped down on my other side. Sara curled up on the end, winking at me.

Mitch's arm lifted to rest on the couch behind me. I inched forward, so his arm wouldn't 'accidentally' fall onto my shoulders, in a typical gesture only Mitch could pull off.

"I'm not sure if you've ever been formally introduced?" I said looking between Davin and Mitch. It was no secret Davin ignored all Makanza Survivor Research Group scientists, even though Mitch had been studying Davin for seven years.

"Davin, this is Mitch."

"Nice to officially meet you." Mitch grinned. He held out his hand. "Finally."

Davin didn't take his hand, but he managed a, "you too," through clenched teeth.

After seven years in which Mitch subjected Davin to testing against Davin's consent, it wasn't surprising Davin had yet to forgive him. Of course, that non-consensual testing all stemmed from Dr. Roberts' orders.

Davin sat back on the couch, his hands moving to his knees.

"I can't believe tonight's finally here." I eyed Davin. From the way his thigh muscles tightened, he seemed tense.

"Yeah. We've been waiting for this night for a while."

Despite Davin's normal reply, I still caught the edginess.

I was about to ask him if he was okay when the lights dimmed. A hush fell over the room as an image flashed to life on the screen. It was President Morgan, sitting behind her desk in the Oval Office.

Davin's jaw tightened. I wanted to nudge him and ask him what was going on, but before I could, Mitch's arm fell onto my shoulders. His fingers brushed Davin's bicep in the process.

Davin didn't turn, but his nostrils flared. And then it dawned on me. *Is he acting like this because of Mitch?*

Shrugging Mitch's arm off, I pushed those thoughts aside as the president smiled and folded her hands in front of her.

President Morgan's shoulder-length blond hair was perfectly groomed, and her eyes bright. She began her speech by thanking everyone for all of their courage, perseverance, and strength for not giving up as our nation faced its most difficult time in its history.

"And I want to thank all of the scientists at the Makanza Research Institute. Without their dedication and hard work, we wouldn't have a vaccine today. And lastly, I want to thank the Kazzies—the people who survived *Makanza*. Without their help, the vaccine would have never been possible."

I eyed Davin again.

He still wouldn't look at me.

I put my hand over his, squeezing.

His eyes met mine. He smiled briefly, distantly, before turning back to the screen and pulling his hand away.

My heart thudded as I gripped my hands together in my

lap. He was definitely upset. Whether that be about Mitch or something else, I wasn't sure. Regardless, annoyance flashed through me that he was acting this way. This moment was huge for us. A part of me wanted to shake him and yell, "Haven't we been waiting for this ever since the vaccine breakthrough? Aren't we supposed to experience this together?"

Of course, I did nothing like that. Instead, I crossed my arms and focused on the speech.

The president continued, but try as I might, my attention kept wandering to Davin. Three inches separated my knee from his. Those three inches felt like a mile.

It was only when the president reached the part in her speech about what our representatives and her had decided, that I gave her my full attention.

"We've come to a decision on what is to become of the Kazzies, now that the vaccine has been administered to everyone in this country. It wasn't an easy decision, and we want you all to know that. Regardless of how everyone feels about the verdict, we ask that you support it and allow our country's rebuilding to continue."

Silence filled the room.

The only sound I heard was my own breathing within the hood.

Davin leaned forward in his seat, his shoulders tense. The Kazzies in front of us did the same.

"We've decided that the Kazzies will be allowed to leave the Compounds," the president said.

Sage let out a whoop of joy, the others soon following. Applause erupted from the researchers.

"But," the president added. That one word stopped all of the celebrating. "It will be under certain conditions. It was decided, for the safety of the public, that the Kazzies will not be allowed to return to society completely free. We'll be asking all survivors of *Makanza* to cooperate with this compromise. All of them will be moved to the Cheyenne River Reservation in South Dakota which is hundreds of miles away from any occupied city.

"Those infected with *Makanza* will be allowed to live there freely, however, their movements will be restricted to the reservation. Visitors will be allowed in but not allowed to stay. As you all know, our country's resources are stretched thin. Since the reservation will be isolated from cities and states, tax payer dollars will fund it. So while family and friends will be permitted to visit, they cannot live there. It would be too costly.

"Also, to appease the worries of those who fear contamination, all visitors leaving the reservation will be subjected to three weeks of quarantine to make sure he or she hasn't contracted *Makanza*. It was felt all of these measures are the safest way to ensure the Kazzies are free while also keeping the public safe."

I stared at the screen, unable to believe what I was hearing. The Kazzies would be allowed out of the Compound, but essentially, they'd just be moved to a different facility. Granted they'd be able to move around freely and go outside, but they still wouldn't be free. Not really.

I swallowed sharply at something else she'd said. *Visitors will be allowed in but not allowed to stay.*

And that was the nail in the coffin. As long as Davin was contained within the reservation, we could never be together.

Never.

I turned to Davin, wanting to know how he was taking this, but before I could ask anything, he stood and disappeared up the stairs. He did it as his speed so turned into a blur.

"Davin!" My voice shook, but he was gone before the word left my mouth.

Mitch put his arm around me again. "Megs, it'll be okay."

Davin abruptly appeared at the top of the stairs. I had no idea where he'd whizzed to and come back from.

Our eyes met. His gaze shifted to Mitch's arm, draped around me. I tried to shrug Mitch off, but before I could, something in Davin's face changed. I couldn't quite tell what it was.

Anger. Pain. Regret. It all seemed jumbled into one.

Without a backward glance, he left the room.

6 – REJECTION

It was awkward trying to stand. The damned suit again. By the time I finally got to my feet, Davin was long gone. Everyone was busy talking, the room a buzz of conversation. It was only then I realized how crowded it was. People were everywhere.

My heart fluttered. The room felt like it was closing in.

Mitch had turned, talking to the researchers behind us, so he was completely oblivious to my reaction. The Kazzies in front of me all huddled together, whispering and conversing in voices too muffled for me to hear.

I had no idea how they were taking the news. They would be free, but not really. Instead, it would be an entirely different kind of imprisonment, but they'd still be in prison.

A prison with no walls.

Only Sara seemed to notice my panic. She stepped closer as her scratchy feeling entered my mind. I opened up to our mental link. I didn't try to speak out loud, since I knew she was communicating this way to keep our words private.

Why don't you go check on Davin, she said. *He's completely shut me out.*

I knew she was referring to the mental link she shared with him too. Walls didn't stop that connection, not even distance did, but if one of us wanted her out, we could keep her out. Permanently.

I nodded tightly.

She gave my arm a brief squeeze and smiled reassuringly. *You'll be okay. Just breathe.*

I walked away, lumbering up the stairs awkwardly. Nobody paid any attention when I passed them or gently nudged someone to move.

Reaching the elevators, I took a deep, shuddering breath. The nearest person was now over ten feet away. My head began to clear.

I debated where to go. My gut told me Davin would return to his cell. If he was going to go anywhere, it would be somewhere no one would bother him.

I took the elevators down to the main floor and stepped out, walking toward his room. The walk seemed to take forever. I cursed the stupid suit the entire way. When I finally reached his door with the large number six, I typed in my MRI code into the keypad. With a hiss, the door slid open.

Davin sat on his bed, his head in his hands, his back to me.

I stood there for a moment, watching him. Sergeant Rose sat in the watch room. Since he was here past five, he'd obviously stayed late to hear the verdict. My heart went out to him. He cared as much as I did.

When Sergeant Rose saw me, he nodded sympathetically and pushed a button on the control panel, turning off his speaker before he swirled his stool around, his back to us, essentially giving us complete privacy.

A burst of gratitude shot through me. I could always count on him.

Davin had to know I was there, but he didn't turn when I approached.

I stood behind him, watching his back rise and fall with each breath. I longed to reach out and touch him, to comfort him, but then I remembered his rejection in the theatre.

He doesn't want your touch.

I took another deep breath and walked to the other side of his bed, pulling his chair over. He still didn't look up, not even when I sat directly in front of him.

"Davin?" I said softly.

His head hung in his hands. His muscled forearms were taut and covered in rope veins. Everything about him was so sexy. I snapped my eyes away. Those thoughts would get me nowhere.

"I'm fine, Meghan," he finally said, still not looking up. "You don't need to be here."

I flinched. His words hurt more than him pulling away in the theatre. He'd always welcomed me here. No matter what.

"I just wanted to check on you."

He looked up sharply. His blue eyes blazed into mine. They were lined with anger.

I flinched again.

His rage seemed almost directed at *me*. But that didn't make any sense. I hadn't done anything wrong.

"I'm fine," he said.

"I know you said that, but I also know that wasn't the news you wanted to hear."

He just stared at me.

I leaned forward, wanting to touch him but stopped myself. "Once everyone has a chance to calm down, I'll go back to D.C. I know I won't be the only person who will fight this. You *will* be free Davin. Completely free. Someday."

He smirked. "Right. If you say so."

"Davin," I said sharply. "Don't give up on this. Don't give up on *me*. I'll fight this for years if I have to."

He met my gaze again, except now the anger in his eyes was gone. All that filled them was pain. "You can't fight for me forever, Meghan. You have your own life too. A life that has nothing to do with me."

I pulled back as if burned. A life without him was not a life I wanted. "Don't say that," I whispered fiercely.

"Why can't I say it? It's true. You heard the president. Nobody's allowed to live on the reservation. Only us. Only Kazzies. That's it. You and I . . ." A muscle in his jaw ticked as he looked away. "You and I will become a thing of the past. Even though we . . ." He shook his head. "No. There's no use talking about it. It can never be."

My heart pounded in my chest as his words sank in. *Did he just hint at wanting to be with me? Or am I reading into things? Imagining it because I want it so much?*

Forcing myself to not dwell on that, I said, "I made you a promise last year, that if it was the last thing I did on this earth, it would be to get you out of here. I intend to keep that promise."

A shadow fell over his face. "You've done enough for me. You don't owe me anything. You should go, get back to everyone else. I'm sure they're all waiting for you. Amy's probably wondering where you are, and Mitch—" The muscle in his jaw ticked again. "He's probably looking for you too."

"Why would Mitch be looking for me?"

Davin gave me a look, as if I should know, but what he was suggesting was preposterous. I didn't have feelings for Mitch. I never would.

I opened my mouth to tell him that, but then he shook his

head. "Just go, Meghan. I'm fine."

A part of me wanted to protest. This was all so absurd. I didn't want Mitch! I wanted *him!* And it seemed Davin may want me too.

But then Davin's words came back to haunt me. *It can never be.* And with a bone-crushing sense of realization, I knew . . .

He was right.

We could never be together. Not as long as he wasn't allowed out of the Compound or the reservation the president spoke of. And seeing him now, I knew, that he'd never consider a life with me, not even the possibility of it, until he was free.

Making myself stand, I blinked back the tears that threatened to fall. Davin still sat on the edge of the bed, his elbows on his knees, his head hung in his hands. My heart broke into a million pieces as I stared down at him. *It can never be.*

But that wasn't a reality I was willing to accept. Not yet. Not ever. "Okay. I'll talk to you later."

I turned and walked out of his cell.

NOBODY WAS LOOKING for me back in the Kazzies' entertainment rooms. Just like I knew they wouldn't be. Davin sometimes failed to see that I wasn't the by-all and end-all at this place.

Essentially, I was just another researcher who happened to make a big discovery about the vaccine. But here, at Compound 26, that novelty had worn off months ago. Amy, Mitch, and Charlie liked giving me a hard time and joked that I'd be a Director one day, but I knew a huge reason for that was simply because they liked watching me squirm.

I hurried through the crowds. Once again, the panic began

as bodies shoved into me. Pushing me. Choking me. I just wanted to go home.

I knew I could have exited through Davin's containment room, but then I would have faced Sergeant Rose. I was barely keeping it together as it was. If I had seen the guard's sympathetic gaze, I would have burst into tears.

When I finally reached the researcher's containment room, removed my suit, hurried to my wing, and got through security to the parking lot, I took a deep gulp of warm, humid air. The evening star peeked through the clouds as crickets chirped. It was a beautiful summer evening, but I barely noticed.

Tears wanted to spill down my cheeks, but I held them back. *It can never be.*

The drive back to my apartment was a hazy blur. Once in my bathroom, I stripped my clothes and climbed into a warm bath. I cranked the music up on my ancient iPod, but no matter what I did to distract myself, I still saw Davin's face in my mind. I still heard his words, telling me to go.

Taking a deep, shaky breath, I sank into the water.

THE SCRATCHY FEELING from Sara woke me the next day. Pushing hair from my eyes, I slowly sat up and opened our mental door. *Sara?*

Hi, did I wake you?

Yeah, what time is it?

Just after six, I—

Crap! I slept in! I scrambled out of bed. It then occurred to me that Sara had contacted me at six in the morning. She usually never woke up that early. *What's up?*

It's Davin.

My stomach plummeted as I hurried along the carpet to the bathroom. *What's wrong? Is he okay?*

He says he is, but I don't believe him. I think he's taking the news harder than any of us.

My hair was a sight in my bathroom mirror. I squeezed a glob of toothpaste on my toothbrush and began scrubbing my teeth.

Have you talked to him? I tried to keep the catch from my voice.

He finally told me he was fine last night but then he shut me out again. He still hasn't opened up.

I spit into the sink and rinsed my mouth as my stomach sank even more. *He wouldn't talk to me last night.*

I felt Sara's surprise. *Are you kidding me? He always talks to you.*

I know.

You need to go see him, Meghan. Maybe he'll listen to you today.

But what can I tell him? I'm going to fight to stop the reservation, but he didn't want to hear that last night. He told me to leave him alone. My hands stilled on the towel I'd been using to wipe my mouth. It hung limply from my hand. *He told me I have my own life to lead.*

Sara sighed. *You know how he gets. He doesn't mean it. That guy cares about you more than anybody. And I don't for a second think he wants you to forget about him and move on.*

I didn't argue with her, but I also didn't tell her about the change I'd sensed in him last night. Something had shifted between us. I'd felt it. Like a crack in the sidewalk—at first, that crack seems small and inconsequential, but as time passes, the crack widens until the sidewalk crumbles apart. I hated to think that's what had started, but deep down, I knew Davin was giving up on me. He was giving up on us. I could feel it.

I'll go to the Inner Sanctum first thing when I get to work.

Sara's relief billowed into me like the warm breeze outside my window. *Thank you. Let me know how it goes.*

SERGEANT ROSE SAT at the control panel when I stepped into the watch room. Davin was sitting on his bed reading the newspaper. The front headline was so large it was impossible to miss. *Plan for Kazzies to move to Reservation.* Davin thumbed a page but stopped when our gazes met.

He nodded at me but didn't smile like he usually did.

My brow furrowed as I gazed through the thick, four-inch glass into Davin's cell. "How's he doing this morning?"

Sergeant Rose crossed his arms and sighed heavily. "Not good. He's barely said two words to me."

"Really?" A year ago, that would have been normal. Now, I knew Davin considered Sergeant Rose a friend. For Davin to be closing himself off to me, Sergeant Rose, *and* Sara meant things were worse than I'd thought. "Will you help me suit up?"

The guard jumped from his stool and opened the containment room door. We were about to enter when Davin's voice sounded through the watch room speakers.

"There's no need for you to come in, Meghan."

I jumped. Sergeant Rose seemed startled too.

On the other side of the glass stood Davin. He'd moved at his speed which meant it looked like he appeared out of thin air.

I frowned and turned back to the control panel. Clicking the microphone on, I leaned down. "Not come in?" Davin had always welcomed me into his cell.

"Yeah. I'm fine."

Swallowing tightly, I approached the glass. "Are you? Sara and I are worried about you."

Davin's gaze was steady, but tense lines tightened his mouth. "You don't need to be. I'm fine."

Sergeant Rose and I shared a look. The guard cleared his

throat. "I'm going to grab a cup of coffee. I'll be back soon."

When it was just me and Davin, I sat down on the stool and leaned forward. "Davin, you're not going to the reservation. We'll find a way to fight this new law so you can be free."

His brow furrowed. "I thought I told you to not worry about that."

"Do you honestly believe that I'm going to listen to you? Do you really think I'd give up that easily?"

An emotion flickered in his gaze, but just as quickly, it disappeared. "You have your own life to lead, Meghan."

My heart pounded in my chest. I could feel the crack in the sidewalk widening. It was exactly as I'd feared. He was pushing me away.

"Are you really going to give up?"

"I'm not giving up. I've simply accepted that some things will never be."

"But it doesn't have to be that way! This isn't the end. I'll return to D.C. There are a lot of people who will fight for you. We'll keep trying. Just give it a chance!"

He shook his head tightly. "There's no point in arguing. It won't matter what you do. They'll keep me locked up."

"You don't know that!"

"Yes, I do." He stepped away from the glass, his jaw tight. "Can you open the back door panel?"

I hesitated. More than anything, I wanted to grab his shoulders and shake sense into him, but he didn't want me in his cell. He wanted to leave.

"Of course." With stiff movements, I pushed the button on the control panel.

Before the back door had fully opened, Davin turned into a blur and was gone.

I sat in silence on the stool, staring into his empty cell. *Maybe he just needs time to process it all. In a few days, he might turn around.* I clung to that hopeful thought as I bit my lip. *That's probably all he needs. I'll come back tomorrow and try again.*

But my stomach still sank as I stood and walked away.

I RETURNED THE next day, and the day after that, and the day after that, but none of it mattered. During the next two weeks, nothing changed. Davin continued to push me further and further away.

No matter what I did, the rift between us grew. Just like I feared it would. After a week of my daily visits, he was either distant or left as soon as I appeared. The crack in the sidewalk was now at least a yard wide.

Worst of all, I had no idea how to bridge the gap between us. The normal, happy Davin, who always had a smile for me, had vanished. Now, he was distant and withdrawn. In his mind, we'd already been separated. Like so many people in his life, I was as good as dead.

To make matters worse, the few times we actually had conversations, he encouraged me to pursue Mitch. Never mind that I wasn't interested. Never mind that dating between co-workers was against MRI policy. My words fell on deaf ears.

Amy eventually noticed the toll it was taking on me, despite me trying to hide it. Mitch and Charlie noticed too. I knew it had to be bad if those two picked up on it.

"Why the sad face, Megs?" Mitch asked one day after lunch. It was just the two of us in our lab. "I don't think I've seen your smile all week."

I made myself smile at him, but I knew it didn't reach my eyes. "Sorry, I'll have to work on that."

He just frowned. "How about we get a drink after work?

On me." His expensive smelling cologne filled my nose.

I smothered a shrill laugh. *Wouldn't Davin love that.*

I shrugged Mitch's offer off. "You really don't want to see me drunk. Alcohol and I don't mix." I'd learned that the hard way the first time Amy had taken me to Sean's Pub. It was the one and only time I'd ever been intoxicated.

"Whoa." Mitch put his hands up in surrender. "Who said anything about getting you drunk? I wouldn't want to be charged with taking advantage of you."

I cocked my head, meeting his gaze. Mitch had to know that dating me could get us both fired, but like other MRI employees, he didn't seem to care about the policy. Amy and Ben certainly didn't.

And then Davin's words came back to me. *You should be with Mitch. You have your own life to lead.*

So the words flowed from my lips against my better judgment. Maybe it was frustration. Maybe it was anger at how easily Davin gave up on me. Whatever it was, I said, "Um, yeah, okay, whatever. A drink sounds fine."

He grinned. "Two beers only for you, though, little Megs. You'll probably be unconscious under the table with more than that."

I rolled my eyes, but a genuine smile streaked across my face. Mitch was always teasing me about my small frame. "Yeah, fine. Two drinks only."

Mitch winked before ambling back to his bench.

Forcing myself to focus on my latest project, I did my best to concentrate, but as the minutes passed my thoughts inevitably drifted to Davin, like they had every day since the president's address two weeks ago.

I couldn't help it. Despite agreeing to a date with Mitch tonight, a date I didn't really want to go on, I missed Davin.

Terribly.

It was as simple as that.

He was my best friend, and now, he was gone.

Tears stung my eyes, but I blinked them back. Sighing heavily, I pulled up analysis data on my computer. *Thank goodness for work.* Sometimes, it was the only thing that kept me going.

I WAS ABOUT to wrap up for the night, when the phone rang at the end of my lab bench.

"Dr. Forester?" I immediately recognized Sergeant Rose's voice. "I think you better come down here."

With a snap, I closed my laptop. "Why? What's wrong?"

"Uh . . . Just . . . can you come to the Inner Sanctum?"

Puzzled, I nodded even though I knew he couldn't see it. "Sure, I'll be right there."

I ran into Mitch on my way out of the lab. "Where you headed?" He glanced at the clock. "It's almost seven."

"I know. I'll be back in thirty minutes, or if you prefer, I can meet you at Sean's."

"No, I'll wait."

With a quick nod, I hurried through security, my mind a jumble of reasons for why Sergeant Rose had summoned me. He'd never done that before. Ever. Not to mention he was still here. His shift ended at five. He was two hours into overtime.

There had to be a reason.

When I finally reached Davin's hall, I was relieved to see Davin unharmed sitting on his bed. His back was propped against the headboard, his legs stretched out in front of him. He was breathing. In other words, he was alive and fine.

"What's up?" I asked Sergeant Rose when I stepped into the watch room. He and the night guard both stood there, watching Davin.

"Well." Sergeant Rose rubbed the stubble on his cheeks. "That," he said, pointing at Davin.

I peered into Davin's cell again. "What do you mean? He looks fine."

"Meghan, he's been sitting like that for four hours. He hasn't moved once. Not even when I've spoken to him. It's like he's not there anymore."

My eyebrows knit together in a tight frown. "Have you tried anything to get his attention?"

"Yeah, we've flashed the lights, played music, spoken to him repeatedly, everything we can think of. But no matter what we do, he doesn't move."

I was already halfway to the containment room, my heart pounding. "Help me suit up, will you? I'm going in."

Sergeant Rose let out a relieved sigh. "I was hoping you'd say that."

7 – EXPOSED

When I entered Davin's cell, he still sat on the bed. He didn't stand or greet me or help me to his chair.

My heart rate increased the closer I got. His chest rising and falling was his only movement.

"Davin?"

He didn't respond. Not a look. Not a twitch.

Nothing.

"Davin?" I reached his side and bent down as best I could in the damned suit.

He didn't appear injured, but again, he gave no response.

My heart thumped painfully as he stared, unseeing, unmoving. *Something's wrong. Really wrong.*

"Should I call medical?" Sergeant Rose asked through the speaker system.

"Yes!" I tried to stop my rising panic as I scanned my memory for any medical reason that could explain this. *Stroke? Catatonia? Paralysis?*

Nothing I came up with helped me feel better. "Davin." My voice rose. "Davin, please, look at me!"

I thought I saw a faint twitch in his cheek. Straightening, I shook his shoulders, but the damned suit made that difficult. "Davin!"

Nothing.

I shook his shoulders again. "Davin!"

Still nothing. I stared down at him, my heart pounding so hard now I thought I'd faint. "Davin? Please, talk to me!" My voice broke.

Do something!

I needed to get through to him. I needed to help him. *Do something, Meghan!*

And then something happened that had never happened before.

It was like a distant part of my brain took over. The instinctual, animalistic side of my mind that was normally kept under lock and key. The side everyone had but only accessed in extreme circumstances.

The side that ran purely on instinct.

It felt like I watched above as I unclicked my gloves and stripped them off. Warning alarms sounded in my hood as my wrist light flashed red.

I barely noticed.

Yelling sounded in the speakers all around me. The guards. Their voices grew thick and heavy, like muffled sounds traveling under water.

I twisted my hood and it unclicked.

Air from Davin's cell entered my mouth. I inhaled. *Makanza* particles flooded my lungs.

I reached down, unbuckling the rest of my suit, letting it fall to the floor. I stepped out of it and reached for Davin, touching him on his chest.

Finally, touching him.

How long have I dreamed of this?

"Dr. Forester, stop! Please!" the night guard yelled.

I ignored him and crawled onto the bed beside Davin. Wrapping my arms around him, I put my head on his chest. His heartbeat was strong and steady. *Thank God.* I quickly assessed the rest of him, paying particular attention to his head. There were no bumps, abrasions, or injuries that I could find.

"Davin," I whispered. "Please, come back to me."

I gazed at his face. Tears filled my eyes. *This can't be happening.*

Davin was my rock. He'd been the one, solid thing in my life since becoming my friend. Regardless of how he'd acted during the past few weeks, I would still do anything for him, and I knew he would do the same for me, even though he'd been pushing me away.

I searched his eyes for recognition. Nothing.

I called to him again.

Nothing. Just blankness.

He still stared unseeing at the bottom of his bed. I placed my hand on his cheek. Rough stubble, like coarse sandpaper, grazed my palms. I inhaled. I could smell him. Soap, a hint of aftershave, and a tang that was all Davin. He smelled so good.

"Davin," I said again. "Please, come back to me."

He flinched, then blinked.

"Davin?"

He looked up, his hand resting on my palm as his eyes widened. His large palm easily covered mine.

"Meghan!" His head snapped back, focus clearing his gaze.

"Davin, thank God!"

He looked around, panic coating his face. "What the hell are you doing here? Why aren't you in your suit?"

I cried in happiness at his very authoritative, very-Davin-like tone. "You're okay," I whispered. "You're okay. Thank God, you're okay!"

"Yeah, I'm okay." He scrambled back. "But you need to stop touching me! You need to wash your hands and hose yourself off. Now!"

His response took me a minute to process. When I finally did, I said softly, "Davin, I've been vaccinated. I'll be fine."

He shook his head, panic evident in his expression. Looking around, it was like he realized where he was for the first time. "Meghan, you need to get out of here! You don't know that you won't get it. You *could* get it, and you could die!"

I'd never heard Davin as anything but in control. Except for the few times Dr. Roberts had been able to goad him into a reaction, Davin had *always* been in control, but now, he looked on the verge of a breakdown.

"Davin," I said slowly. "Do you know what you've been doing for the past four hours?"

He came off the bed and sailed across the cell so fast he was a blur. He positioned himself against the wall, as far from me as possible. "Meghan, please. Stop touching my things, and whatever you do, don't touch your face. Please, Meghan. Please!"

Slowly, I pushed to standing from his bed. I'd never heard him like this before.

"Davin, I'm fine. I'll be *fine*. But I need to know if you remember the last four hours?"

He stood against the wall, his confused expression growing, as the medical team arrived. They strode into the watch room. One of them did a double take when he saw me without a suit on.

Sergeant Rose appeared again in the watch room window, on the heels of Dr. Fisher, the lead physician. The guard leaned down and spoke into the microphone. "Meghan, what the hell is going on?"

I met his gaze sheepishly. "I had to get through to him. I didn't know what else to do."

I didn't hear him sigh, but I saw it. "I'll have to tell Dr. Sadowsky you've been exposed."

"I know."

"He won't be happy." Sergeant Rose glanced at Davin. "Is he okay now?"

I shrugged helplessly. "I honestly don't know. He doesn't seem to remember the past four hours. He needs to be checked out."

Sergeant Rose nodded. "Both of you go to the Experimental Room. Since you've been exposed, you might as well join him."

"Right." I glanced at Davin who was listening to the entire interaction as if he didn't know what planet he was on.

"Come on, Davin." I approached him slowly and held out my hand, like he was a wild animal who could be easily spooked. "Let's go."

DAVIN INSISTED ON walking several feet away from me. I wanted to tell him that it didn't matter. My skin and clothes were coated with every germ, cell, and particle that had been on his body. *Makanza* virons were already inside me. Nothing could be done to change that.

But I knew that was the last thing he needed to hear, so I did as he requested and walked a yard to his side.

"Meghan, what's going on?" he asked as we drew nearer to the Experimental Room. We walked in the back curved hallway behind the cells.

"You really don't remember anything that's happened in

the past four hours, do you?"

"What do you mean?"

I explained how Sergeant Rose had called and told me his concern while I was working in the lab. "I came down to the Sanctum right away and entered your cell, fully suited up, but it was like you weren't there. You didn't see me. Your look was blank. You wouldn't respond. You stared unseeing at nothing."

"I did?" His brow furrowed.

His answer chilled me to my core. I stuffed my shaking hands into my pockets. "Yes. So, I did what I needed to do to get through to you. When I touched your cheek, with my bare skin, you finally snapped out of it."

"So it's my fault you've been exposed?"

"No! It's *my* fault. You didn't make me do anything. And besides, I never would have taken my suit off if I actually thought harm would come to me. I'll be fine. You'll see, but in the meantime, we need to do a few tests on you. To make sure you're okay."

"Hmm." The guilt on his face told me the last thing he cared about was himself. I knew, in the extremely unlikely situation, if anything *were* to happen to me, he'd never forgive himself.

"Come on, Davin, let's get you looked at."

He just followed me, his frown growing deeper.

We entered the Experimental Room. For the first time, instead of being in the large watch room with its floor to ceiling windows overlooking the room, I was *in* the room.

The Experimental Room consisted of four medical beds with robots around each one. The robots were like giant, spidery octopuses. Their arms stretched and extended with hinges like synovial joints. When Kazzies were back here, the robots took samples and did whatever work a human would normally do.

I looked at the large windows. I could see the control panel in the watch room. It stood at waist height and ran the length of the room. It put the control panels in the Kazzies' watch rooms to shame. It was filled with so many buttons, levers, touch screens, and switches that a dozen technicians were employed to run it when all four beds were occupied.

A dozen chairs sat behind it, most of them empty at this late hour. Only two of those chairs held technicians. I waved hello to Marsha and Andrew. Their responses were mouths agape.

The door to the watch room opened and Sergeant Rose, Dr. Sadowsky, Dr. Fisher, and the rest of the medical team strode in. Dr. Sadowsky's expression was grim. I hoped he'd understand why I'd done what I did, but honestly, I wasn't sure.

"Dr. Forester," he said through the speaker system. "Care to inform me what the hell is going on?"

I almost laughed. *What the hell is going on*, seemed to be the expression of the day. Keeping my face neutral, I quickly filled him in. "Sergeant Rose can verify Davin's strange behavior. I'm sorry for doing what I did, but it seemed the only way to get through to him."

Dr. Sadowsky grumbled a reply. Probably along the lines of how I constantly broke MRI policy and needed to follow the rules better.

If my brother were alive today, he'd be shocked at how many times over the past year I'd not followed policy. Prior to meeting the Kazzies, I'd been an adamant rule follower. Ironically, it was probably one of the reasons the MRI hired me. Of course, all of that changed when my priorities switched from following the rules to helping the Kazzies. Luckily, that gamble had paid off. We got a vaccine out of it.

"You do realize that since you've been exposed, you'll be placed in quarantine?" The Director put his hands on his hips.

"What?" My eyebrows shot up. Dr. Hutchinson never placed any of her employees in quarantine.

Dr. Sadowsky continued. "With the coming changes for the Kazzies, the new law states any person exposed to *Makanza* needs to be put in quarantine for three weeks."

"Oh," was all I managed. I hadn't realized the three week quarantine the president had spoken about in her speech was already in effect.

"Yes." Dr. Sadowsky drummed his fingers against his crossed arms. "So as of now, you'll have to stay in the Sanctum. Cell number seven is being readied for you."

"*Oh.*" Shaking my head, I told myself that was something I could contemplate later. Right now, Davin was priority.

The medical team took over.

Davin lay down on one of the beds as the robots swung into action. I stood by the wall, giving any support I could. After the robots took samples, Dr. Fisher said he wanted to do more tests. Davin spent the rest of the evening getting MRI's, CT's, and numerous amounts of bloodwork. It was almost midnight by the time they finished.

Dr. Fisher said he'd review all of the tests and get back to us by tomorrow.

Dr. Sadowsky took off his glasses and pinched the bridge of his nose. "Dr. Forester, I'll speak with you tomorrow about what happened today. Right now, I think it's best if everyone gets some rest. Cell seven is ready for you. I've had several days' worth of clothes brought in as well as toiletry items. Can I trust that you'll do as I ask from here on out?" There was an edge to his tone. I knew at times he found me exasperating, but I also knew he respected me immensely.

It was my one saving grace.

"Yes, sir. I'll do whatever you ask."

He sighed. "Good."

Davin joined me, and we walked back to the cells. During the entire walk, a frown marred his features, and he seemed lost in thought. But he didn't distance himself from me this time. A few times, our fingers brushed against one another's.

Each time, it sent a shiver up my arm. I couldn't tell what it did to him. His movements were stiff, his breath shallow. When we reached his cell, he walked past it, coming with me to cell seven as if on autopilot.

At my door, he stopped and turned toward me. The dim, nighttime lighting from the hall sent shadows across his face. Pain rimmed his eyes, and he opened his mouth, like he wanted to say something, but then he closed it.

"Are you okay?" I asked. "I mean really, are you *okay*?"

He guffawed. "It's more like, are *you* okay? Do you feel anything? Fever? Aches? Fatigue?"

My heart broke at the anguish in his tone. "Davin, I'll be fine. You'll see."

He looked down and said so quietly, I barely heard him, "I'll never forgive myself if you're not."

Before I could reply, he turned and walked away.

8 – QUARANTINE

It was weird going to sleep in the Sanctum. The strangest thing of all was knowing Davin slept in the adjacent cell. A wall of concrete separated us. That was it.

Surprisingly, it didn't take me long to fall asleep. I was exhausted, physically and mentally, but sleep was anything but refreshing.

Odd, scary dreams plagued me. I dreamt of dying from *Makanza*, Davin's anguish, the Kazzies' shock, my co-workers' realization that our vaccine didn't work at all. A Third Wave started. It was the end of the human race.

I woke with a start, bolting straight up in bed, sweat pouring down my face. It took me a moment to get my bearings. When I did, I peered around the cell. I had no idea what time it was. Without windows, it was impossible to tell.

Dim, nighttime lighting illuminated the glass hall. *It must still be night, or rather, early morning.*

A quick glance at the watch room, and I saw I wasn't alone. A guard, who usually worked with Garrett, sat in the watch room, appearing to be doing a puzzle of some kind.

So he's been pulled in to do overtime for me.

I didn't need a guard, so to speak, but I did need someone to control all of the mechanics in the cell. Garrett's guard apparently got assigned that duty, for the time being at least.

I coughed and then coughed again. For a moment, I thought my dream had come true. *The vaccine doesn't work. I'm already showing symptoms.*

But then my rational side kicked in. Even if the vaccine didn't work, I wouldn't show symptoms this early. It was probably just the dry air in the cell. Humidity ran rampant outside at this time of year, but the manufactured air in the Compound was stale and dry.

So this is what the Kazzies live with.

The guard glanced up. He smiled and leaned forward, pressing a button. "Good morning."

I nodded. "Good morning." I cleared my throat. My voice was hoarse. "What time is it?"

"Almost five."

So, it's still early.

I lay back in bed and turned my back to him. I had no idea if he watched me or went back to his puzzle. *Can't there at least be curtains on the windows?*

I felt so exposed. So . . . dissected.

It was not a comfortable feeling, and I hadn't even been here twelve hours. I tried to fall back asleep, but I couldn't. I think it was knowing that someone sat just outside my room, able to watch my every move. It was creepy, even though Garrett's guard was nice. I'd only talked to him a few times, but he seemed decent enough. Still . . . *Creepy.*

I pushed the covers off and padded into the bathroom, thankful Dr. Sadowsky had the foresight to bring in clothes for me, including pajamas. I had no idea where he found the clothes. They weren't mine, but they fit well enough and were clean.

Behind the half wall that shielded the bathroom, I sat on the toilet. I couldn't see the guard, which meant he hopefully couldn't see me either. Regardless, it was uncomfortable. After relieving myself and brushing my teeth, I returned to bed.

The guard was fully alert now, a smile plastered on his face. Technically, I was his boss, since I outranked him in the MRI, but in the current situation we were in, I felt anything but his superior. I was at his mercy, literally. He had the ability to gas me to unconsciousness if he chose to and there would be nothing I could do about it.

Now you're just being crazy. Those barbaric practices stopped when Dr. Roberts left. He'd be fired if he tried anything like that.

Still, he *could* if he wanted to. I think that was why it was so unnerving.

"Are you up for the day?" he asked.

I sighed. "I guess so."

"Would you like some breakfast?"

I bit my lip. *This is so weird!* "Um, sure. Thanks."

"What should I have sent down for you?"

"Toast and coffee's fine."

He nodded, looking pleased to be useful.

I lay back on the bed, wishing again for curtains. It was only five in the morning, and I'd only been awake fifteen minutes, but already I was wondering what to do for the day. I couldn't work. I couldn't sleep, at least not at the moment, and I'd never been a TV watcher.

Sweat again popped up on my brow as a suffocating feeling engulfed me. I was trapped in here. *Trapped.* And this was just the beginning. For the next however many days, I'd be a prisoner in this cell. My breath came faster, my heart rate increasing. The room felt like it was closing in.

No, not here. Don't panic here!

A scratchy feeling entered my head. I opened the mental link to Sara.

Meghan, are you okay? I got a jolt of panic. It woke me up. I knew it had to be you.

I took a deep breath. Sara was very forgiving about my receptive mind. Still, I knew it wasn't easy on her. It wasn't the first time a strong emotional surge from me had broken through the door that separated us.

I'm just . . . I don't know, I said.

Davin told me you're staying in the Sanctum. He also told me what happened.

Oh, right.

Are you okay? She sounded worried.

I . . . It still felt like the room was closing in. I began to shake.

I felt her mulling, and then she said, *Hang on. I'll fix this.* She shut down the connection and once again, I was alone in my head. A few minutes passed, and then a beeping sound came from the back of my cell.

Garrett's guard leaned over the microphone. "Davin's outside your door. He wants to come in. Is that all right?"

"Yes." My voice was tight and high. My breath came too fast. It felt like my throat was closing.

I can't breathe!

The door opened, and Davin strode in. All he wore were pajama pants. That was it. His bare, hard chest gleamed in the dim lights. Scars littered his abdomen. Disheveled hair covered his head, and another day's worth of beard speckled his cheeks.

He took one look at me and covered the distance between us in one of his blurred moves. Without saying a word, he sat beside me and hauled me into his lap. Yes, hauled.

One second I was sitting against the bedframe, my breath so shallow I thought I'd pass out, and the next I was cradled in his arms, his heartbeat steady against my ear.

"Give us some privacy, will you?" he yelled at the guard.

I didn't know if it was Davin's tone, or that the guard felt entirely uncomfortable witnessing this, but he didn't protest. His stool practically bounced off the wall in his haste to exit the watch room. Thank goodness *that* policy had changed. Under Dr. Roberts' rule, the guards had been forbidden to leave their stations.

When we were alone, Davin leaned down, his scent and breath surrounding me. I closed my eyes.

"Breathe, Meghan, just breathe," he whispered.

I did as he said, concentrating on my breath. *Deep inhale, slow exhale. Deep inhale, slow exhale.*

These panic attacks were becoming out of control. They'd only started in the last few months, after we'd developed the vaccine, and so much extra responsibility, pressure, and public attention was put on me. Prior to that, I'd simply had anxiety but never panic attacks.

"That's it. Keep breathing," he murmured. His presence and calm words worked their magic.

My heart rate slowed. My breathing returned to normal. After a minute, I felt okay. "Thank you," I whispered.

He just nodded.

I waited for him to say something, anything, but he didn't. It took a second for me to register that he was touching me, holding me. His arms were steel, his scent intoxicating. Nothing had ever felt so right, so complete. I'd dreamed of this moment for so long. I thought it would never come.

Before I could stop myself, I melted more into him. My

entire body softened against his like warm butter. Every hard inch of him seemed to fit perfectly against me.

His hand roamed up and down my back, lightly caressing me. It sent tingles down my spine.

Closing my eyes, I savored the feel of him. To be pressed against him was heaven. Laying my head against his chest, I heard his heartbeat within. It beat strong and steady.

I had no idea how long he held me. My breathing had returned to normal minutes ago, but I was loath to let him go. Instead, I wrapped my arms around him and let him hold me.

He seemed to sense the change. That I was no longer needing him for anxiety. He grew less relaxed. Stiffer. Harder.

When I shifted closer to him, his sharp intake of breath followed. Something else grew harder against my stomach. When I realized what it was, my eyes flashed open.

Davin abruptly pushed me back. In a blurred move, he sat on the edge of the bed, his back to me. His shoulders were tense and rose up and down with every breath.

My own heart responded. *He's aroused. He grew aroused holding me!* I almost squealed with glee, but my excitement abruptly vanished when he turned toward me. His bright blue eyes were guarded and dark. His words from after the president's address drifted through my mind.

It can never be.

I swallowed sharply.

He kept watching me, but he didn't say anything. With every passing second, my excitement dimmed more. I picked at a loose thread on the bedsheet unable to meet his gaze. When I finally found words, I asked the most interesting question I could think of. "Um . . . So . . . how did you sleep?"

"Fine," was his gruff reply.

I bit my lip and peeked up at him. The tension was still so

thick between us I could practically taste it.

His eyes are so blue! It was the first normal thought that entered my head. For the first time, I was aware that I saw them with my own eyes, not through some viewing hood, not through a glass wall.

I'd felt him, smelled him, *touched* him, and all I wanted was more. Yet, he'd pushed me away.

It can never be.

I clasped my hands tightly together.

"Are *you* feeling okay?" His voice still sounded weird. Strained.

I nodded. "Yeah. I'm fine."

"You don't . . . feel sick?" Fear lined his words.

I shook my head, completely confused by his reactions. For the past two weeks, he'd distanced himself from me to the point where I questioned if we'd remain friends, and then, he'd grown aroused holding me. And now he looked so scared and worried at the thought of me being sick that I felt the need to comfort and reassure *him*.

None of it made sense.

"Davin, I'll be fine. You'll see."

He continued to stare.

I cleared my throat. My voice was still hoarse, probably from the few hours of sleep. "So . . . we're talking again?" I asked cautiously.

He abruptly glanced away, taking a deep breath. "Yeah, I guess so."

I played with my fingers, my stomach twisting and turning into knots. "Can we talk about . . . what's been going on with you?"

I held my breath. Every other time during the last two weeks, when I'd tried to broach this subject, he'd refused to answer.

An aching minute passed.

Finally, he sighed. In that sound, I heard the weight of the world. "I was trying to give you space. Let you lead your own life. Once I'm on the rez, our time is up."

I suspected as much. Pushing me away seemed to be how he was dealing with the new life he'd lead. Still, I was surprised by the intense anger his admission sparked. I tried to stop it, but it bubbled out of me before I could stop it.

"Does that justify you giving up on me?"

He glanced over his shoulder. "I don't want you wasting your life on me. Why is that so hard to understand?"

"And I don't get any say in how I *waste* my life?"

He turned to face me. "Meghan, you're healthy. You're whole. You have your whole life in front of you. You can do whatever you want, go wherever you want. You don't need me tying you down. I could never ask that of you. I *won't* ask that of you."

I sat up straighter, my voice rising. "And what about what *I* want? Did you ever think that maybe I want to stay by your side? That maybe I *want* to help you? Did you even think to ask me before you made this grand decision all on your own?"

"You don't owe me anything."

"No, I *don't* owe you anything, but I *want* to do this! Don't you see that? Do my feelings on this count for nothing?"

His magnificent chiseled chest rose and fell in the dim lights. "Have you ever thought that maybe you haven't thought this through? Do you know what staying by my side means? You'd be neglecting yourself, what you could do with your life, what you could accomplish. It would be limited, everything."

"And what if I *want* that?"

"Why would you possibly want that?"

"Because . . ." *I love you and I can't imagine my life without you!* I almost said the words. Almost. Luckily, I stopped myself just in time. "Because you're my best friend. That's why. Isn't it obvious I care about you?"

He turned so fast it was a blur. One second he was facing me, the next he perched on the edge of my bed, his elbows resting on his knees with his hands clasped together. He sat there, staring at his hands, not saying anything. At least a full minute passed before he said, "You're my best friend too."

His voice sounded quieter, less angry, more like the Davin I knew.

Regardless, my heart still pounded. I'd almost told him how I felt, *really* felt, when it was so obvious now that was the worst idea ever. The past two weeks had shown that. He'd chosen to push me away versus giving us a chance.

I wouldn't forget that.

Taking a deep breath, I tried to calm my racing heart. "So now that I'm in here do you promise to not shut me out?"

He played with his thumbs, flicking them back and forth. The movement turned into a blur. I didn't think he knew what he was doing. "Yeah. Yeah, of course."

He stood in another blurred move. "I should get back to my cell. Call me or Sara if you have another panic attack. I know what these walls can be like."

And with that, he was gone.

9 – THE SANCTUM

Garrett's guard returned ten minutes later, telling me he was heading home and another guard was coming in. I felt a little sheepish when I met his gaze. He'd seen me at a low point. A vulnerable point, but he acted professionally and didn't comment. Thankfully.

Before Garrett's guard left for the day, he ordered me breakfast. To pull my tray from the system in the wall and eat at the desk with the new guard watching my every move was surreal to say the least.

It didn't sink in until I was showering that I was living *here*, in the Sanctum, literally, for the next however long. That realization made me sink to the floor and wrap my arms around my knees. The water cascaded down on me, yet I barely felt it.

I live here. This is what the Kazzies live like every day. This is what my friends live like.

It was mid-morning when the medical team arrived. "Dr. Forester?" Dr. Fisher stood in the watch room. "Would you like to accompany us to Davin's cell? We have the results of his tests. The rest of your team is convening there."

I hastily stood. "Yes, of course. I'll head right over."

In a way, it was comforting to fall into my old role, the role I knew: Makanza Survivor Research Group scientist, MRI employee.

On the other hand, my heart raced for *why* the medical team was here. Davin had been catatonic yesterday. He'd had a multitude of tests last night. And now, we'd hear those results.

I swallowed uneasily. *What if the results are bad?*

Walking on wooden-like legs to Davin's cell, I kept telling myself that Davin was fine. He'd *be* fine. But then I wondered if they found something. *What will I do if something happens to him?*

Once in Davin's cell, the first thing I noticed was that Dr. Fisher stood in Davin's cell in a biohazard suit.

The second thing I noticed was how crowded the watch room was. Not only was the medical team present, but so were Dr. Sadowsky, Sergeant Rose, Amy, Mitch, and Charlie. And on top of that, the watch room was full of medical residents and various other members of the medical team.

Full house.

Amy waved when she saw me. So did Charlie. I darted a peek at Mitch. His hands were on his hips, his mouth grim. I knew I needed to apologize to him, for missing drinks last night, but that would have to wait.

"Dr. Forester, please have a seat." Dr. Fisher nodded at Davin's bed.

Davin sat on his bed in gray sweatpants and a white t-shirt. Even in bland clothes, he looked sexy as hell.

I settled beside Davin as everyone else in the watch room crowded closer to the glass. It felt strange to be in cotton pants and a long-sleeved shirt while all of them wore work attire. I felt underdressed. Exposed. Like everyone had crashed into my living room at home unannounced.

It wasn't a feeling I liked.

Naturally, my usual anxious response kicked in: the rapid breathing, the sweaty forehead, and icy palms. *Just breathe, Meghan.*

Davin's fingers crept closer to mine, making the barest hint of contact, nothing noticeable to those watching. It was a small gesture, which I knew he meant as reassurance. I brushed his fingers in return before folding my hands in my lap. Just that small movement helped. My palms warmed.

Dr. Fisher pulled some images from a folder he carried. He had to be in his fifties, with balding hair and a paunch belly. Nothing about him screamed health and well-being, but if there was anything ever wrong with me, I'd want him for my physician. His wealth of knowledge about diseases and conditions surpassed the latest round of medical students graduating these days.

Not only had lives been killed when *Makanza* struck, but so had talent and the leading minds of innovative science. Dr. Fisher was one of those few, surviving minds from the time before *Makanza*, when advances in medicine were still being made.

"Well," Dr. Fisher began, "the good news is that we can't find anything wrong."

I exhaled in relief.

Davin just nodded, as if he already knew that.

The doctor shuffled the papers back into the file. "However, that doesn't mean yesterday's event isn't cause for concern. I'd like to run a few more tests, just to be sure. If those come up negative, I'm fine with monitoring you for the time being to see if anything additional happens. Does that plan sound all right with you?" His gaze stayed on Davin.

It took a minute before Davin replied. "You're asking me this?"

"Yes."

"Ah, yeah, that's fine."

I could tell from Davin's tone that he was shocked to be included in his medical plan. For almost seven years, he'd been subjected to tests and studying in which he never consented. I still got mad every time I thought about it.

"Good. I'd like you to refrain from eating past midnight tonight. We'll do the tests tomorrow morning." Dr. Fisher handed the file to Davin. "This is your copy, in case you're interested in what the findings were."

Davin's eyes widened in surprise.

"May I be there for the tests too?" I straightened. "I mean, if it's okay with Davin."

Dr. Fisher frowned. "I know Compound policy has allowed researchers to join their Kazzies for all testing, however, since this is in regards to Davin's personal health, I believe it would be best if I met with him alone. Patient confidentiality is important."

I smiled. "Yes, of course. I completely understand."

Dr. Fisher discussed a plan with Davin and Dr. Sadowsky before he retreated to the containment room. Once back in the watch room, his troop of physicians and eager interns followed him out.

I breathed a sigh of relief. *Davin is okay. Dr. Fisher will take care of him.*

Amy stepped closer and leaned down to the microphone. Everyone else seemed preoccupied talking to one another. Her voice was quiet through the speaker system. "Are you doing okay?"

I shrugged. "As good as I can be, considering the circumstances."

"How are the clothes? Dr. Sadowsky had me run out to buy them last night."

My eyes widened. "So that's why they fit so well."

She smiled from the control panel. "I've been around you long enough that it was easy to guess your size."

I grinned. "Thanks. You did a good job."

She nodded and stepped to the back of the watch room to talk with Charlie.

Mitch took her place at the microphone. "You still owe me a drink, Forester."

"Yeah, I'm really sorry I missed last night."

Davin stiffened.

Mitch shrugged. "Considering what happened, I think it's understandable."

"I hope you didn't wait too long for me?"

"Only an hour." He winked. "I came looking for you after that. The guards at the Sanctum told me what happened, but you were in the Experimental Room by that point, so I went home." Disappointment lined his tone.

"I'm sorry." I glanced at Davin. He was now as stiff as a board. I knew I was playing with fire, but I still turned back to Mitch and said sweetly, "I'll make it up to you when I get out."

He grinned. "I look forward to it."

Davin abruptly stood and with a blur disappeared into the back of the cell. The movement rustled the hair hanging around my face.

I glanced over my shoulder but couldn't see him. That meant he'd retreated to the bathroom, the one area he had privacy.

A sudden flash of guilt filled me that I'd goaded a reaction out of him, but then I pushed it down. He'd said he wanted me to move on. *It's your own doing, you stubborn man!*

The speaker clicked on overhead again silencing my childish internal conversation with myself. Now, Dr. Sadowsky was leaning into the microphone in the watch room. "Dr. Forester, I'd like to meet with you and your lab group to discuss the next few weeks. Since you won't be able to work, we'll have to divvy up your projects amongst Dr. McConnell, Dr. Hess, and Dr. Wang. After that, I'd like to speak with you, *alone.*"

I swallowed. All thoughts of Davin and Mitch disappeared. I knew this was coming. "Right."

My lab group and the Director stepped out of the watch room, presumably to head to the watch room attached to my cell next door.

I inched to the back of the room. Davin still hadn't returned. I found him leaning against the wall in his bathroom. He stared at the ceiling, his expression dark. When he saw me, he straightened.

Forcing myself to not feel guilty, I said, "Um . . . I'm going back to my cell."

He stiffened. "Okay."

"So . . . the news looks good, about what the doctor said about your results."

Davin nodded, his dark hair falling across his forehead. His eyes blazed cobalt as he watched my every move.

"And hopefully those tests tomorrow will also be clear." I had the ridiculous urge to fidget as I stood there. I'd never seen him so guarded.

"I'm sure I'm fine." He moved in a blur to the sink. The faucet hummed when he turned it on. He proceeded to wash his hands. "You better go see what your lab group needs. I think they're waiting for you."

"Um, right. I'll see you later."

I RETREATED TO my cell to meet with my group. It didn't take long to figure out how Amy, Mitch, and Charlie were going to spend the next few weeks. We agreed that any conceptual work could be given to me. Even though I was in the Sanctum, I still had the ability to think. However, as it happened, most of our work right now required computers.

Dr. Sadowsky said he would work on getting me a laptop. He also stated on the days I didn't work at all, it would be counted as vacation time. Considering I hadn't taken one day off since I started, I had plenty banked up. I agreed that was a reasonable plan, especially since I was the one responsible for my exposure.

"I'll come back later today, to see how you're doing and say goodbye," Amy said as we wrapped up. "I need to meet with Gerry now or I'd stay longer." She paused. "You're still not feeling any symptoms, right?"

"No, I feel fine." Other than coughing when I'd woken up, I'd felt normal.

"Guess you're the first guinea pig in our group to be exposed." Charlie waggled his eyebrows. "Let's hope you make it."

I chuckled. "I'm *fine.*"

Dr. Sadowsky waited patiently until Mitch, Amy, and Charlie left. When we were alone, he sat across from me.

It was weird, sitting in my cell with him in the watch room. Normally, we met in his large office for meetings. The only similarity between here and there were the floor to ceiling windows in the hallway, although his weren't four inches thick, bulletproof, and shatterproof. And his view was that of the beautiful South Dakota prairie, not stark white sterile-looking walls.

"Dr. Forester, I need you to tell me exactly what happened yesterday and why you chose the actions you did."

His voice was level, but I heard the disapproval. Once again, I'd broken policy. The last time I'd done that, I'd been fired by Dr. Roberts. Granted, this incidence wasn't MRI official policy, only Dr. Sadowsky's policy, but still, I'd broken the rules. Funny how good I was becoming at that.

I took a deep breath and told him everything. How Sergeant Rose had called me concerned, and how I'd tried helping Davin when I was fully suited up, but I'd become so worried that I felt human contact was necessary to better assess him.

Yes, I'd done it impulsively, but in the situation, time felt of the essence. Of course, I left out the part how I'd nearly panicked at the thought of losing Davin. While there wasn't an official policy on dating Kazzies, I had a feeling there *would* be if anyone learned of my romantic interest in one.

"All right," Dr. Sadowsky said when I finished. "I won't put you on probation, since I agree the circumstance was extraordinary. However, I hope this is the last time anything like this happens."

"I'm sure it will be."

"Make sure it is." From his tone, I could tell he wasn't convinced.

We said goodbye, and when I was alone in my cell, I sighed in relief. At least I wouldn't be out of a job.

TEN MINUTES LATER, the day shift guard was still gone. I sat on my bed, waiting for him. It was crazy how vulnerable I felt. I wasn't able to leave or do anything. I was truly a prisoner. I tried to imagine what it would be like, living like this for seven, or in some cases, nine years.

I laid back on the bed, clasping my hands behind my head. The pillow was flat and hard, not like my fluffy pillow at home. The ceiling and walls were all dull gray, boring, and bland to look at. The air was dry, the only smells from my own skin. It was silent, unnaturally so. My breathing sounded loud, echoing almost, as I scanned my surroundings. Overall, these cells were oppressive and confined.

I hated it.

In my apartment, things were constantly changing, so interesting in a way I'd never appreciated. If I opened the window, humid air swirled in with smells of rain or freshly cut grass. Birds chirped or the sounds of a passing car or distant lawn mower filtered through.

In fall, wood smoke hung heavily in the air, and sounds of the breeze whipping through trees or the rumble of thunder in the distance penetrated the quiet. Voices carried from the sidewalk as people walked by, enjoying an evening stroll.

My apartment building also had a life of its own. The hum from central air, the groan of pipes, the rattling from my shower rod. Things were alive, changing, ever evolving, or growing.

But here, nothingness.

It was silent.

Absolute silence.

I thought there might be distant humming or creaking, from the mechanics of the giant Compound, but there weren't. Perhaps it was from how thick the walls were or how deeply we were buried within the Sanctum. The only sounds were my breathing and the faint *lub-dub* of my heart. I'd never been aware of my own sounds before. They seemed magnified.

It was strange.

Movement to my right caught my attention. A guard stepped into the watch room, a coffee in hand. I sat up, envy filling me. I knew scents of hazelnut and cream would be wafting around him right now. I wished I could smell it.

The vents circulating through the Kazzie cells ran faster than any other area in the Compound. The smells from the breakfast I'd eaten, including the delicious smells of my morning coffee, had long disappeared.

"Sorry I took so long." He leaned down to speak into the microphone. "I was just notified by Dr. Sadowsky that you were alone in here." He wasn't a guard I recognized. He had olive skin, dark hair, and looked young. His cheeks were still round, his skin smooth. I guessed him to be around eighteen.

I brushed my long brown hair behind my shoulder. "That's okay. Are you new here?"

He nodded. "I'm Private Rodriguez. Just started three weeks ago. I graduated from MRRA training last month." He looked almost embarrassed when he added, "This is my first day on my own."

"Oh." I didn't know what to say to that.

He continued grinning. "I've wanted to work here since I was a kid. This place is something."

"Yeah. I guess it is."

"And the Kazzies." He whooped and sat down on his stool. "Man-oh-man, talk about weird shit!"

I raised an eyebrow.

He quickly straightened. "Ah, I mean. I just had no idea what some of the strains did. Have you heard that Sage can throw lightning bolts?"

So much for keeping that a secret. "Yes, I did."

"I mean, of course you did, since you're a researcher. Hey,

aren't you the one who discovered the breakthrough for the vaccine?"

"Uh, yes, that would be me."

"No kidding." He shook his head. "You must be really smart."

I shrugged.

"Oh, yeah, I mean of course you're smart. How could you not be?" He took a sip of coffee and then said, "Say, did you ever . . . oh wait, hold on . . ." He glanced down at the control panel, his brow furrowing. His hand hovered for a minute, as if unsure what to push. He touched something and leaned back down to the microphone. "Ah, Sara and Sophie are outside your cell. They'd like to come in."

I perked up. "Sure, send them in."

Private Rodriguez frowned. It was obvious he was trying to remember *how* to do that. I bit my cheek to hide my smile.

A minute passed before the door to the back of my cell slid open.

The twins barreled in.

"Meghan!" Sara squealed. She ran headfirst into me and wrapped me in a big hug.

I hugged her back, a little awkwardly at first. It was the first time we'd touched.

"I've been wanting to do that for months," she said, letting go. Her eyes were bright, a smile on her face.

Her affection took me completely by surprise. Besides Davin and his mother, I still wasn't entirely comfortable touching people. "It *is* a little strange, to not be in the suit."

Sophie hung back, her hands behind her. "It's nice to see you without it on."

I shuffled my feet and stuffed my hands in my loose cotton pants. "It's definitely more comfortable."

"I couldn't believe it when we heard you were exposed and staying here!" Sara grinned, her white teeth flashing against her blue skin. A floral scented shampoo wafted around her silky blond hair. "What are you doing today?" She grabbed my hand. "Do you want to get out of here?"

I glanced at Private Rodriguez. His eyes were as wide as saucers. I imagined seeing two blue women and a trapped researcher was the most entertaining thing he'd seen in a while.

"That would be great, but I'll have to come back later and work. I'm not off the hook just because I'm in here."

Sophie giggled while Sara pulled me to the back door. "Let's head over to the arcade room. Everyone's meeting for games of pool this morning."

We waited at the back door until Private Rodriguez figured out how to open it. He kept uttering apologies and expletives when he repeatedly opened the wrong mechanics. The twins were giggling uncontrollably by the time the door finally opened.

I DIDN'T THINK in my entire twenty-three years that I'd ever had girlfriends my age. The twins were now twenty-three, the same age as me. They'd had a birthday a few months ago.

Since Sara and I shared the mental link we'd become quite close. And while Sophie was shyer and harder to get to know, she still seemed comfortable around me and readily spoke if I asked her something.

In a way, it made me more comfortable to be around someone who also felt awkward with others. At least with Sophie, my anxiety didn't matter. She had her own problems to contend with that made mine seem minimal.

All of the Kazzies, except for Davin were in the arcade room when we arrived.

"Meghan Forester! The woman of the hour!" Sage boomed when we stepped inside.

My cheeks immediately flushed.

"I heard that you're now one of us, but I didn't know if I believed it." Sage waggled his eyebrows. "Welcome to the dark side."

Sophie smothered a laugh.

"It's so good to see you in normal clothes," Dorothy said. "You're even prettier without that hood on."

My cheeks heated. "Um, thank you."

"You do look pretty hot," Sage added. "But you already knew I thought that about you."

Victor rolled his eyes. "Does that sweet talking crap actually work on women?" The red skinned Kazzie did not look impressed with Sage's wooing. As usual, Victor wore an irritated expression.

"Used too." Sage shrugged.

"I think it depends who the woman is." My comment got a bark of laughter out of Victor and Dorothy.

Everyone stepped forward, crowding around me. Normally, that would have made me step back, but with the Kazzies my usual anxious response faded.

Dorothy picked up a pool cue. She wore workout shorts and a t-shirt. My guess was that she'd exercised again this morning. The woman was hell bent on losing weight and proving us all wrong. The brown shorts matched her eyes. Gray streaked through her dark hair. At forty-eight, she was the oldest one here. "So it's really true that you're stuck in here since you were exposed?" she asked.

"It's true. I'm officially quarantined for three weeks."

"Does that mean you're going to play pool with us?" Garrett's quiet tone drifted my way. Dark smudges covered his fingers. I figured he'd been doing more charcoal drawings lately.

When I turned to address him, his large eyes blinked. Since they were as big as eggs, it was hard not to stare. I shrugged. "Sure, but I've never played before so I'm not sure how good I'll be."

"We'll teach you." Sage winked.

"Where's Davin?" Sara twirled around, the movement as graceful as a dancer.

"He said he was busy." Victor picked up a pool cue while Dorothy racked the balls with the triangle.

"Busy?" Sara raised an eyebrow. "Since when are any of us busy? Is he feeling okay today? You know, after whatever happened to him yesterday?"

Victor shrugged. "He said he felt fine."

"Maybe they're doing research on him." Sage stood by the pool table. He shot an electric bolt from one hand and caught it in the other. A loud *zap* filled the room.

"He didn't seem very happy when I left his cell earlier." I crossed my arms over my chest.

"Why? What's up?" Sara asked.

Heat filled my cheeks. I knew my face turned red despite trying to prevent it. I couldn't exactly admit what had happened. *Um . . . well . . . I'm totally in love with Davin, and I think he has feelings for me too, except you know, we can't be together because of the virus and the government's rules, so you know . . . He's been pushing me away, telling me to hook up with Mitch as a way to distance himself. So I agreed to a date with my co-worker, never mind that it's against policy, cause you know, I wanted to give Davin a taste of his own medicine.*

Yeah, definitely couldn't say that.

I settled with, "I'm not sure."

Sara watched me, a glint in her eyes. I knew I didn't fool her.

"Should one of us go find him?" Sophie asked, oblivious to her sister's more in-tune reaction.

Sage stopped throwing electric bolts and shook his head. "You know how he likes to be alone sometimes. Let's leave him be. He can find us if he wants to."

The group proceeded to divvy up teams for the pool game. I tried to get into it, but without Davin there, it wasn't the same.

AFTER WE FINISHED three games of pool, I bowed out. "I have to work. Really, I do."

A few loud protests followed which only made me smile. The group seemed genuinely sad to see me go. My insides warmed.

"Do you want me to walk back with you?" Sara stepped forward. She'd just beaten Sage at two games, and the Canadian didn't seem happy.

I knew a part of the reason she wanted to walk was to ask me about Davin. However, I wasn't ready for that conversation. "No, I'll be fine. Besides, I think Sage wants to redeem himself."

Sage perked up. He tossed an electric bolt up from his palm, a loud *zap* emitting around him before it sank back into his hand. "Third time's a charm, Sara. Unless you're afraid I'll beat you."

Sara snorted. "Please. I could beat you in my sleep."

I left as the bantering continued and opted for the stairs to the lower levels.

When I emerged into the back hallway that lined the Kazzies' cells, the only sounds were the tapping of my canvas shoes on the concrete. It was eerily quiet in the vast gray corridor.

Before, I'd always been in my suit. Inside that, my breathing was present and sounds echoed in the hood when I spoke. But now, without it, there was nothing.

When the hall curved to door six, I paused. It was closed. I had no idea if Davin was inside.

I hesitated.

A part of me knew that I should carry on, leave him alone, but the other part of me hated this new dynamic between us.

Before I could change my mind, I pushed the button to the side of the door and glanced upward at the camera. Sergeant Rose's voice sounded through the speaker. "Good morning, Meghan."

"Hi, is he in his cell?"

"He is. He just finished lunch."

My stomach grumbled at the mention of food. *Right, lunch. I really need to stop forgetting to eat.*

Before I could ask to be let in, the door slid open. Davin waited on the other side.

His presence only two feet away startled me. He was so tall and so strong looking. My gaze traveled up his chest. As always, defined pectoral muscles were visible through his t-shirt. My gaze continued its upward journey. A strong neck, square jaw, firm lips, high cheekbones, and eyes so blue they put sapphires to shame regarded me with a veiled look.

Without the hindering biohazard suit, my neck kept bending, and without the added height of my suit's boots, I realized how small I felt next to Davin. I cocked my head and said the first thing that came to mind. "How tall are you?"

He cocked his head. "Um, six-two. I think."

That would explain it.

"Sorry to interrupt your meal," I managed. Despite Davin being the most comfortable human being I felt around, he could also be the most nerve wracking. Already, my heart hammered in my chest.

He shrugged. "I'm done."

The urge to wring my hands lessened as one thing became obvious. Davin didn't seem as distant as he'd been this morning. *Maybe he doesn't like this new dynamic between us either.*

"What are you doing?" His voice was deep as he again watched my every move.

"I was on my way back to my cell. I'm sure there's work waiting for me."

He put his hands on his hips. I tried to ignore how that made his shoulders bulge. "When was the last time you took a day off?"

"Day off?" That concept was completely foreign to me. "I can't remember."

"That's what I thought." He stepped into the hall and nodded goodbye to Sergeant Rose. The door slid closed behind him.

With stiff movements, he turned. "Follow me. I want to show you something."

10 – SECRETS

I followed Davin to the elevators. Both of us walked stiffly. When my hand accidentally brushed his, I jumped while his breath hitched.

A strange, unspoken vibe emanated between us. Like both of us were aware that we had entered new territory. We were now together, physically, and it had never felt so apparent.

Once in the elevators, Davin stood ramrod straight as we ascended to the top floor.

"I didn't know you could get up to the fourth level," I said awkwardly when the doors slid open.

"That's because you're not supposed to be able to."

My eyebrows rose.

His lips quirked up. "Just follow me. Trust me. It's fine."

I stepped cautiously into a wide hallway. Like the research corridors in the Compound, this hall was bright white, harshly so. I shielded my eyes from the fluorescents. Our feet tapped on the floor as I followed Davin.

My curiosity grew. It didn't appear there was anything up here, other than an empty hallway, which put me at ease.

Hardly anything top secret.

"Just a little farther," Davin said.

The hallway widened. Only a wall waited after the corner we just passed. It looked like a dead-end. I slowed. "There's nothing back here."

"Yes, there is."

A few feet from the end of the hall, Davin stopped and pointed up. "See?"

It was only then I noticed the windows. Just below the ceiling were three. Each was small, only twelve inches high and about eighteen inches long.

Davin smiled. The expression stopped my breath. He looked almost boyish in his excitement. "Look out them."

I stood on my tiptoes but wasn't nearly tall enough. Each window base was at least eight feet from the floor. Davin chuckled and with a flash of movement, I was sitting atop his shoulders.

I gasped in surprise, not just from the abrupt position change but from the way his strong hands felt holding my thighs on his shoulders.

Perhaps I imagined it, but his hands seemed reluctant to let go of my thighs before moving to safer territory. He settled his large palms against my shins, steadying me. "Can you see it now?"

I nodded mutely, still reeling. "Uh, yeah."

"What do you think?"

The view was similar to the view from Dr. Sadowsky's office. Prairie grass stretched forever. Wildflowers bloomed in a sea of color. It went as far as I could see. "It's beautiful." And I meant it.

"I think so too," he said quietly.

"How are you able to see it?"

He lifted me from his shoulders, his hands clamping firmly just under my rib cage until I slid against his body to the ground. The intimate touch made my head spin. Again, he did it as if I weighed nothing. He didn't strain or groan. Strain 11's effect on him was mind boggling. It was like he possessed the strength of ten men.

When I stood on the floor beside him, his hands lingered on my waist. With a start, he abruptly cleared his throat and stepped back. "I'll show you."

With an inhumanly fast jump, he gripped the lip of the window. Flexing his biceps, he lifted his chin up to the window's ledge and hung there in a paralyzed chin-up.

My mouth dropped. "*That's* how you look out?"

"Yep, it's not like there's anything to stand on." As the minutes ticked by, he didn't seem tired or strained, even though he hung from the window's edge. There couldn't be more than an inch of trim to hold onto, but it didn't seem to faze him.

"Um, how long can you do that?" I played with a strand of my long, brown hair and tucked it behind my ear.

"I think the longest I've ever looked out is around an hour, maybe two."

"And you stay like that the entire time, just . . . hanging by your fingertips?"

He let go and dropped back to the ground, landing as gracefully as a cat. "Yep."

I shook my head. "I really need to learn to *not* be surprised by this stuff."

He chuckled.

"How did you find this place?"

"By accident. For a long time, the elevator wouldn't come up to this level. I'm not sure why it does now, but one day, I pressed the button for this floor, when I meant to press three, and it took me up here. Must have been a glitch in the system that never got caught. I've been coming up here ever since."

"And no one knows about it?"

"Nobody except me and the other Kazzies. We all come up here sometimes to look out. It's the only way any of us have seen the outside in the last seven years."

That statement made my heart fall. "That's awful."

"You could say that."

"So there must not be security up here?"

He shook his head. "No cameras. It's like a forgotten corridor. This place is so big, there are probably lots of forgotten areas."

"But how do the others look out? I'm guessing nobody can hang from there except you?"

"I lift all of them like I did you, and let them look outside until they've had their fill."

"And you don't get tired?"

"Nope, never."

I just shook my head, happy that we once again seemed to be enjoying each other's company. With hesitant words, I peeked up at him through my lashes. "Are there any other secret places you've discovered?"

"There are a few." His look turned sly.

I smiled. "Lead the way."

WE SPENT THE afternoon touring the entertainment rooms' massive enclosures. I knew I needed to work, but I couldn't pull myself away from the fun we were having. It felt like old-times, like how we used to be when we hung out. Only now a new subtle undercurrent of energy shifted between us, as if we were both more aware of each other physically.

A few times our hands brushed, or his body bumped into mine, or I accidentally leaned against him. Each time, we both stiffened.

The tense energy flowing between us made heat cascade to the junction of my thighs, but as much as I wanted to squirm, I made myself stay still and keep acting like it was just another normal afternoon in which we hung out.

After the forgotten corridor, Davin showed me a closet in the locker room by the pool that he guessed was supposed to be locked but never was. Inside were chemicals and cleaning agents.

My head cocked as I stared down at them. "Who uses these? I thought the robots cleaned all of these rooms?"

"They do. I think these are left over from construction."

Davin then told me how he, Sage, and Victor had joked over the years about making a bomb and breaking out of the Compound. I knew he wasn't serious, but from the dark way he described it I wondered if a part of him *would* consider doing something like that.

Imprisonment could do strange things to people. People would do things they never thought they were capable of before confinement. That much I'd learned in my time at the Compound.

"Have you ever tried breaking out?" I asked as Davin shut the cleaning closet.

He latched the door and moved a bucket back in front of it. His knack for detail was obvious. Nobody would ever know we'd been in there.

"Yes, once."

My eyes widened. "You did? When?"

"After a particularly bad treatment with your former boss a few years ago." Davin rested his palm against the closet door as his mouth turned grim. He rarely referred to Dr. Roberts by name. It seemed even saying his name brought back too many painful and rage-filled emotions. "But it didn't work. We got caught by two guards before we left the Sanctum."

"*We?* How did you . . . and whoever . . . try to escape?"

"Victor and I found a vent that was big enough to crawl through. What we didn't account for was how loud it would be with us moving through it. The guards at an access point heard us."

I swallowed tightly. "Were you punished?"

"Of course."

He said it so matter-of-factly. My gut burned.

Davin crossed his arms and leaned against the closet door. A dark look again flashed across his face. "We haven't tried since even though we could probably breakout now with Sage's power, but he would never do it."

"Why not?"

"Do you know how Sage was caught?"

I nodded. "Yeah. He somehow crossed the border from Canada and jumped from town to town in northern Washington until the MRRA picked him up."

"So you probably know how many people died from his actions?"

It hit me what he was implying. "You're saying that Sage feels guilty for all of the people he exposed? That since they all died, because he ran and tried to avoid getting caught, he won't try running again?"

"Exactly." Davin pushed away from the closet and pulled me into a walk. When our hands touched, it was like he caught himself in the familiar gesture. He let go and cleared his throat. "He never speaks about that time, but he always refused to try to escape, no matter how bad it became in here. All he would say is that innocent people would die if we got out."

Our feet tapped on the linoleum. It was the only sound in the hall. "He's right," I said. "Before the vaccine, you most likely *would* have killed people if you had escaped. Even if you tried to avoid people or cities, inevitably somebody would have caught *Makanza* from you and died."

"I know." His eyes clouded over. "That's why we didn't try again."

"And now?"

He smiled playfully, the dark look vanishing. "And now that we have a vaccine would we try escaping if they don't let us out?"

"Yeah." I held my breath as I waited for his reply.

"No." He opened a door to a stairwell.

I stepped inside and waited for him to join me. He nodded to the ascending stairs. I jogged up them as he continued.

"If I were to escape, I'd spend my life on the run. I'd never be able to see my mom or have a normal life." His words grew quiet, reminding me of how separate our lives would be once he was forced to move to the reservation.

My breaths turned shallow. *I need to stop the reservation from happening!*

Davin pushed the door open on the second floor. Bookstacks appeared. We were in the library. He led me to a bookshelf. After one look, I realized every book on it was dedicated to medicine.

I raised an eyebrow. "Have you read these?"

"Yeah. All of them."

"*All* of them?"

He crossed his arms again and leaned against the shelf as I pulled a book out. "When I first arrived here, seven years ago, I wanted to know more about my condition. Unfortunately, modern medicine had never seen a virus like *Makanza*, as you know. So these textbooks did little to help." He pushed away from the stack and shrugged. "But it didn't stop me from wanting to learn about viruses and what can be done to stop them. It helps that I like science."

My heart warmed when he said that. Given my background, I obviously had an interest in science too.

"Now where?" I asked after putting the book back.

"Wanna see a place Sage and I found?"

"Sure."

He led me to a walkway between the soccer field and weight room. About halfway down the hall, he stopped and glanced up. When he didn't say or do anything, I cocked my head curiously. "What are you looking at?"

"The security camera's still scanning this area. We need to wait . . . four, three, two . . ."

He squatted to the ground. It wasn't until he started picking at something that I realized a panel of some kind was screwed to the wall. Moving too quickly for me to really see, he unscrewed all eight screws that were holding it in place. With a careful lift of his hands, he removed it, revealing a tunnel within.

My heart pounded. "Davin, what are you doing?"

"Don't worry. Follow me."

He crept into the tunnel on all fours. My stomach twisted into knots, but I still squatted down and cautiously followed. I imagined this was definitely against the rules, but while I may have grown somewhat comfortable breaking the rules to help the Kazzies, that didn't mean I wanted to break *all* of the rules. Besides, I still worked here. I could possibly get fired for doing something like this.

"Davin, I don't think this is a good idea."

He carefully lifted the cover back into place. A sliver of light peeked through the side since it wasn't fully sealed. It didn't leave much light to see.

"Do you trust me?" I felt his breath against my neck. It smelled fresh, like him. I shivered.

"Yes."

"Then follow me."

"But what if we get caught?"

"We won't get caught. I've been doing this for years."

He didn't seem the least bit perturbed that we were in some tunnel, in the wall, that couldn't be taller than three feet.

Reluctantly, I crawled on all fours after him. I had no idea where we were going. I couldn't see a thing. Away from the panel with its crack of light, it was absolute darkness.

I followed Davin's shuffling sound, bumping into him every now and then. I muttered an embarrassed apology each time it happened.

A few times, I sneezed. It was dusty and smelled like mildew in here.

It felt like we'd been crawling forever when the walls of the tunnel turned from pitch black to dull gray. My eyes instantly recognized light coming from somewhere.

"Almost there," Davin said.

The light grew as we carried on. Sounds also emerged, faintly at first but then louder. Knocks, mechanical groans, and hisses. As the sounds and light escalated, I was able to work out the maze of pipes that ran above and to the side of us. A few minutes later, it was bright enough that I was able to sense something ahead.

Davin stopped, and I saw what appeared to be an opening to the tunnel over his shoulder. He turned his feet around and hopped down into some room.

Grinning, he peered into the tunnel at me. His hair was disheveled and a bit dusty from grazing against the tunnel's ceiling.

I didn't want to know what I looked like. Holding out his hand, he beckoned me closer.

I took his hand as I awkwardly sat on my butt and shimmied forward so I was feet first. He helped me inch to the edge and then, putting his hands around my waist, pulled me out, setting me down gently beside him.

Once again, his hands lingered.

To cover up my reaction, I glanced around. "Um . . . where are we?"

He shrugged and let me go. "I have no idea."

It was a mechanical room of some kind. It was huge and loud. The groaning and hissing sounds I'd heard earlier came from large machines. The mechanics knocked and rumbled as they supplied who knew what to various areas in the Sanctum.

"How big is this room?" I peered around.

"It runs about twenty yards that way and about ten the other. We've tried to find another way out through here, but all of the other tunnels either get too narrow or don't have any panels, like the one we crawled into. Sometimes, we'll come back here, just to get away from the ever-present cameras."

"And no one's ever noticed that you're missing?"

"Not yet. We never stay gone long, so if we disappear from a room and someone starts looking, we pop up eventually. That seems to have kept the guards happy since they're always able to find us."

"Huh. So this is what you get up to in your spare time." I guessed if I lived in a confined area, I'd probably explore every inch of it too.

"It's not much, I know, but it's some place different and

hidden from the guards."

I glanced up at him. Once again, he watched my every move. "I'm glad you showed me."

"You're not going to tell on us, are you?" he teased.

I plucked my hands on my hips and gave him a stern look.

He just chuckled. "Come on. I'll show you some more places."

He led me back to the tunnel entry and easily pulled himself into it. Reaching down, he lifted me up since the opening was at my eye level—not exactly easy to hop into. In the process, his hands brushed the sides of my breasts.

Stiffening, for a moment he didn't let go. In the dark enclosure, it was impossible to read his facial expression, but once again, I became acutely aware of how close we were.

His face hovered inches from mine. Each of us stayed that way, looking at each other, assessing each other, as if unsure of what the other would do. In the dark light, it was hard to tell, but it seemed that his gaze dipped lower, settling on my mouth. I licked my lips.

I swear he stopped breathing.

Feeling the energy grow more charged around us, I hesitantly leaned forward only to shriek when a loud *bang* erupted behind me.

Davin caught me as I lunged against him. A rumble shook his chest again.

"What was that?" I asked, wide-eyed.

"One of the mechanics. That one can be particularly loud and never gives a warning." The rumble against me continued until I realized he was silently laughing . . . at me!

I slugged him in the shoulder which only made him laugh harder. It was only then I became aware of his arms. He was holding me, almost like he didn't know it.

Shifting in his embrace, before I could think twice about how wise my actions were, I rubbed against him. His laughter died, as if he'd been doused with a fire extinguisher. Stiffening, his gaze dropped when my breasts rubbed on his chest.

My gaze lowered to his mouth. His beautiful, sexy, perfectly shaped mouth. I licked my lips again.

He abruptly pulled back, effectively putting a yard of distance between us. Taking a deep breath, he raked a hand through his hair. Even in the dim light, I could see his chest rising and falling rapidly with each breath.

"We better get back. They're bound to notice." In a blurred move, he turned.

My heart pounded as I crawled behind him on all fours. Davin wasn't the only one affected by the game I was playing. I wasn't entirely sure why I was acting how I was. *It can never be.*

As always, those words haunted me. Maybe my subconscious had taken over and was making me act so brazen as payback for him throwing away any chance at our future. I knew on some level he wanted me, but I still didn't know how *much* he wanted me.

Regardless of our uncertain future and his stubborn resolve to keep me at a distance, my body ached with need for him.

The light from the mechanical room quickly faded as the tunnel turned to tar. The complete blackness helped dampen my desire. It was creepily scary in here.

"How do you not get lost?" My voice echoed in the confinement.

His breaths were harsh ahead of me. A bit too harsh to only come from crawling. It seemed I wasn't the only one warring with desire.

Finally, his response came after he took a few deep

breaths. "I've memorized the steps, but mostly, I just wait for the light peeking in from the panel. It helps when Garrett's with us. Since he can see in the dark, he just crawls ahead and lets us know when he sees it."

"Oh, of course." Next to the Kazzies, I was like a kid crawling behind a superhero. Funny how I'd never thought of them that way before, but in a way, they were.

When we reached the panel, we left the same way we'd come in. Davin peeked out first to check the camera. When it was turned away, he crawled out, pulled me with him and then screwed the panel back in place before the camera swung toward us again.

"Seems like a handy skill," I commented as he pushed the screws back in at light-speed. No normal human could move as fast as him.

"It is quite useful. I won't pretend it's not."

Standing, he made sure to keep several safe feet between us before nodding in our next direction. He proceeded to show me a dozen other hidden areas in the entertainment rooms. My mental map of the rooms grew and with it came the realization that the Kazzies led a secret life that none of us knew about.

By the time we returned to the cells, it was late afternoon and my stomach was howling in protest.

"Didn't you eat lunch?" Davin asked after it gave a particularly loud rumble.

"No, I came to your cell instead."

"Meghan . . ." he growled. He promptly returned me to cell seven and told Private Rodriguez to order my supper immediately.

It only took three wrong buttons and one episode of all of the lights going out before Private Rodriguez finally figured out how to use the phone.

"I'll see you later?" Davin asked as the back door panel opened.

I nodded. Amy would probably be arriving any minute. Luckily, I hadn't forgotten that she was stopping by before she went home for the day.

"Do you have more secret places to show me tomorrow?" I whispered.

He grinned. "Of course."

11 – LIFE INSIDE

Amy arrived shortly after six. I had just finished supper when she stepped into the watch room. We told the night guard, Sergeant Appleton, to grab a coffee while we visited.

He didn't seem to mind being asked to leave. His grin and, "Well, okay then!" told us exactly how he felt about an unexpected break. I doubted that ever happened when he was on duty with the Kazzies.

"I'll come find you when I leave," Amy called to his retreating form. She turned back to me. "Let's hope he comes back."

I laughed and settled into the chair I'd pulled up to the watch room window.

"So what'd you do today?" She propped her elbow onto the control panel and cupped her chin in a hand. Her wild red curls flew around her head.

I thought about what Davin had shown me. My breath caught. "Um, not much. Just got out into the entertainment rooms for a while."

"No work?" She raised an eyebrow.

I ducked my chin. "I'll do that tonight."

She just grinned. "And you're still feeling okay? No mild symptoms as your immune system fights the virus?"

I shook my head. "Nope, nothing."

"That's good." She fluffed her hair behind her shoulders as a frown covered her face. "I've got something else to tell you. Dr. Sadowsky received news from the president this afternoon. There's a big building crew heading out to Cheyenne River. The reservation construction is officially underway, and they plan to move the Kazzies this fall."

My movements stilled as she continued.

"They need to get a wind station up and running, build stores and stock them with goods, build houses for the Kazzies and the MRRA soldiers who will be stationed there, and build everything else that's needed to get a town functioning again."

It took a second before I could get the words out. "But they're not building a wall around the reservation, right? It'll stay as it is? Just open land?"

Amy cringed. "I wish, but unfortunately no. They're building a perimeter fence."

My cheeks grew hot. "Are you kidding?"

"I wish I was. It'll be topped with barbed wire and have watch stations every hundred yards. The whole works."

My chest rose and fell so quickly I felt lightheaded. "How is that any different than a prison? Any different than their life in here?"

"You're preaching to the choir, sister. I don't agree with it any more than you do."

I slumped back, crossing my arms. My mind grew abuzz with all the ways I could fight this. "We need to return to D.C. And I *need* to talk to Dr. Hutchinson." I looked at the bedside table and grumbled. Still no phone.

Amy followed my gaze. "I'll have one installed tomorrow. Oh, and they've renamed the reservation. It's no longer Cheyenne River."

"It's not? Then what is it?"

"Reservation 1."

"Reservation 1," I repeated. "As in, the first reservation with possibly more to come?"

It was how the government had named the Compounds. The first Compound 1, the second Compound 2, the third Compound 3, and so forth.

"It's happening again." My stomach fell. "It's happening all over again."

"No, it's not." Amy leaned forward. "Don't jump to any conclusions just yet, Meg. There are still only twelve hundred Kazzies in the country. That won't change, and the reservation is plenty big enough to accommodate that small number of people. They shouldn't need to build another reservation."

I could only hope she was right.

She pushed to standing from her stool. "I better go. I probably won't get home till seven."

We said our goodbyes before she went in search of Sergeant Appleton. He returned a few minutes later, still chewing whatever food he'd been snacking on.

I barely noticed. All I could think about was Davin and the Kazzies being transported from one prison to another. Reservation 1 didn't seem much different than Compound 26.

AFTER AMY LEFT, I ventured to Davin's cell even though I knew I needed to work. If I wasn't so worried at what Amy had told me, I'd probably be fluttering in anticipation of seeing him again. As it was, when his door slid open and Davin stepped out, my shoulders sagged.

He frowned. "What's wrong?"

"I got some news today, and it's not what I wanted to hear."

We started walking toward the entertainment rooms as I told him about the government's plan. "They'll be a fenced perimeter, with barbed wire on the top, and watch towers to keep you all in. How is that *not* a prison?"

"Will there be guards?" His voice was flat, his expression stone.

"Yes, MRRA soldiers who will also be your guards."

"Hmm." A muscle ticked repeatedly in his jaw.

When we reached the movie theater, some of my anxiety lifted when I saw that everyone else was there. Sara bounced up from the couch when she saw me and raced over.

"Meghan! I was hoping you'd join us." She grabbed my hand and pulled me to the sofa.

For once, I could sit on it while also being able to stand back up.

"Why do you look so upset?" Her eyes searched mine. "Are you feeling okay?" I opened my mouth to reply, but she added, "I mean, I know symptoms don't show up until three weeks after exposure, but is it the same way with the vaccine?"

I shook my head as my thoughts drifted away from Reservation 1. "No, my immune system already has antibodies to fight *Makanza* so that's what it's doing right now."

Davin sat on my other side. I could feel him listening so continued. "If you're vaccinated, your immune system responds immediately when it detects the virus, as it would with any disease you've been vaccinated against. That's the whole point of a vaccine, to have antibodies already in your system that recognize a foreign attacker and to kill it before it does actual damage. So, right now, as we speak, I'm assuming my immune system is hard at work, even though I can't really tell, not yet at least."

"How have other people reacted?" Dorothy leaned against a pillow, her plump arm resting on the couch's back.

Garrett, Sage, Victor, and Sophie all turned to listen since they sat on the couch in front of us.

"Most of the researchers that have been exposed do get a little sick." I angled myself against the sofa so I could see everyone better. "All that means is their immune system is working so they may feel tired or have a few symptoms, but nobody's moved beyond the second stage of the virus. Everyone's returned to normal after a few days."

"Good." Sophie cupped her chin in her hand. "Then I won't worry about you." She smiled shyly.

"I heard my guards talking about what they're going to do with us." Sage's skin looked silvery in the dim light, the scaly reptilian-look somewhat shiny. "Something about moving us this autumn?"

I nodded. "You heard right."

"So that's a good thing, right?" Garrett turned more. "We'll go live on that reservation and be free."

"If you mean free, as in we can't leave that area of land, then yeah, we're free." Anger laced Davin's tone. "It's exactly what they did to my ancestors."

As the last remaining Lakota Sioux, I wasn't surprised at his response. I almost covered his hand with mine but stopped myself. "It won't be that bad. You'll be treated much better."

"Is that why they built a fence?" His gaze met mine.

"A fence?" Sophie's voice rose. "So we'll be locked inside?"

"Are you kidding me?" Victor's nostrils flared, his red skin stretching with the movement. I could practically see his temper rise.

I tried to calm the rising energy in the room. "Yes, but you should be treated very well. It's not a prison. None of you have done anything wrong."

Sophie's guarded demeanor didn't change. "But they've never treated us as equals. Why would they start now?"

I wanted to convince them that it wouldn't be like that, but since I was so upset about it too, I couldn't find the words to reassure them. All I managed was, "I'm going to fight this new law. You all know that, right?"

Victor nodded. Since he wore a long-sleeved shirt and pants, the only skin that showed was his red face. It was as red as a tomato. It grew brighter which meant he was pretty angry. It also increased his resistance to heat—something his researcher's had discovered under Dr. Roberts' rule.

"I know you'll fight for us, Meg. You're the only one that does," he grumbled.

"That's not true. There are a lot of people on your side on the outside, you just don't know it."

Garrett raised an eyebrow over a large eye, not looking convinced. "If you say so," he said in his typical quiet tone.

"Can we start the movie now?" Sophie was twisting and turning her hands.

"Sure, I'll go start it." Sara rose from her seat in her usual gracefulness and glided up the stairs. She'd been strangely quiet, but I'd seen her picking at her fingernails nervously as she listened.

Dorothy stood too. "I'll get the popcorn." She hurried off, her wide bottom bumping into Garrett on her way to the stairs.

The movie turned on as the lights dimmed. Popping sounds and fresh popcorn smells permeated the room as the menu on the DVD popped up.

"A comedy?" Victor complained.

"Would you prefer a romantic-comedy?" Sage asked sweetly. "I know how you love Sleepless in Seattle."

"Oh yuck." Victor gagged. "How about The Bourne Identity? That's always a good one."

Dorothy returned carrying three buckets of popcorn. "It's my turn to choose, remember? And this is what I want to watch."

"Just eat your popcorn," Sophie said gently to Victor.

He grumbled but reached a huge red hand into the bucket.

Davin passed our row's bucket of popcorn over for me to hold, since I sat in the middle between him and Sara. I settled onto the couch beside Davin, his heat warming my side. Normally, that would have caused shivers to race through me, but tonight, all I could think about was fences, barbed wire, and watch towers.

AFTER THE MOVIE finished, we all ambled back to the cells. Our group grew smaller and smaller with each door we passed. Davin and I were the last ones since we were in cells six and seven. He walked me to my door.

When we stood in the hall, I eyed the camera. A brief flare of annoyance surged through me. "I'm starting to understand your rage." I watched the camera moving slowly back and forth.

He nodded. "I've never gotten used to them, watching everything we do."

"I never really appreciated how intrusive it is."

"Life is very different in here."

"I'm starting to see that."

He stuffed his hands in his pockets, his muscled forearms

peeking out. A frown covered his face. "Have you felt okay today?"

It seemed to be the question of the hour. "Yeah, I'm completely fine, I swear. It's you I should be asking that question to." It was only yesterday he'd been catatonic. "Whatever happened to you really scared me."

He shrugged. "I don't really know what to say about that. Honestly, I haven't really thought about it."

"But Dr. Fisher's doing more tests tomorrow?"

"That's the plan."

"Hopefully, it was just a fluke."

"I'm sure it was."

A moment of awkward silence passed between us. More than anything I wanted to stand on my tiptoes and kiss him goodnight, but from the stiff way he stood, I knew he wouldn't reciprocate despite his body betraying him today.

It can never be.

Running a hand through my hair, I shuffled from foot to foot. "Um . . . goodnight, then."

He abruptly took a step back and cleared his throat. "Yeah. Goodnight."

It took all of my willpower to walk into my cell without brushing against him, and this time it wasn't to drive him crazy or make him jealous. I simply wanted to touch him.

THE NEXT DAY, Amy, Mitch, and Charlie appeared in the watch room just as I finished breakfast. I grinned when I saw them. Since Davin was gone all morning with Dr. Fisher, I knew I'd probably spend the time wondering if they'd found anything. Work was exactly what I needed.

Mitch put his hands on his hips and winked at me. It was only then I remembered I'd given him the impression that I

I also shivered intermittently, but I did my best to keep working. It was normal to have a reaction to the virus, even after being vaccinated. It didn't mean anything sinister. Besides, most researchers worked right through it, only feeling mildly ill. *Surely, this is normal. No reason for me to stop.*

I was reading a research paper I was drafting when the lines blurred together. *Strange.* I hadn't heard of that happening. I glanced at the clock. Eleven in the morning.

That's it? Only eleven in the morning?

I was so tired I could barely keep my eyes open. Another cough rattled my chest just as another shiver struck. *Maybe I should lie down for a while. Just for a little bit. I'm sure I'll feel fine then.*

Standing, I barely made it to the bed before I collapsed. Everything ached. *Everything.* And I felt so cold. I pulled the covers over me, shivering uncontrollably. *I'll just sleep for a little while then I'll go back to work.*

The rest of the morning passed in a blur. By mid-afternoon, my fever was 104.

12 – SICK

Everything was a fog. A thick, oppressive fog. I was burning up.

Amy came into my cell late that afternoon in her biohazard suit. I croaked a hello. Even through the viewing hood, I could see her eyes bright with worry, but she smiled reassuringly.

"I heard you're sick."

"Hmm," I mumbled.

"Going through the stages, huh?" She pulled over the desk chair and sat at the bedside. "Thirsty?"

"Very."

"Can we get some water in here?" she called to Private Rodriguez.

I barely saw as he fumbled around on the control panel. *He must have returned when I was sleeping.* I hadn't noticed him.

A moment later, the panel in the wall that delivered my trays opened. Amy stood clumsily in the suit and returned with a large glass of ice water. It even had a straw.

"Is this service or what?" she joked.

I laughed, but my eyes were glued to the water. Nothing

had ever looked so delicious.

She sat again and leaned over, helping to get the straw in my mouth. "I've never played nursemaid before. Let's not make a habit of it."

"Ha ha," I managed before greedily sucking from the straw. The water disappeared like a lake draining from an opened dam. A loud slurping sound echoed in the cell when I finished.

"I think we'll need another one of these." Amy jingled the empty glass, the ice cubes clinking.

Private Rodriguez fumbled with the controls again as I closed my eyes. I could hear the rustling from Amy's suit as she moved back to the panel to retrieve another glass of water, but I didn't bother to watch. Just keeping my eyes open was tiring.

I'd had the flu before, bad colds, even meningitis once when I was a kid, but nothing compared to this. I was hot, everywhere, but when I'd been sleeping, freezing chills had startled me out of delirious dreams.

I knew it was my body's immune response to the virus. If anything, it was promising that I was reacting this quickly. It meant my body detected *Makanza* immediately and determined it was an intruder. It was fighting it effectively. If it wasn't, I wouldn't be having symptoms.

Or at least, I kept telling myself that.

"Here you go." Amy reappeared with another glass.

I opened my eyes just as she leaned over, placing the straw in my mouth again. I'd emptied about half the glass when a loud banging sound startled me.

Private Rodriguez shakily spoke through the speakers. "Um, Davin's outside your cell. He wants in."

Amy's eyebrows rose. "Subtle, isn't he?"

"Let him in." I greedily drank from the straw again.

The panel in the back slid open just as I finished.

Davin stormed in, his shoulders tense. He took one look at me and bolted to my bed.

"Meghan." He leaned over me. His movements were so fast I hadn't processed any of it. One second, he was at the door, the next he was just *there*, worry so apparent in his eyes, I could have drowned in it.

"I'm fine," I whispered.

"No, you're not." He looked at Amy accusingly. "Do something!"

She held her hands up in surrender. "There's nothing we can do, Davin, other than supportive care. We need to let the virus work its course while her immune system fights it."

He growled. "Tell me what to do." I knew he was speaking to Amy even though his eyes darted around my clammy skin.

"Keep her hydrated. Help her to the bathroom. Make sure she sleeps and if she's able, eats." Amy leaned forward, tentatively placing a hand on Davin's shoulder.

He flinched back as if burned.

She dropped her hand. "We can move her into the Experimental Room if need be. We have technicians who will take care of her twenty-four hours a day. She'll receive the best care as the virus works its course."

"No," he replied, his voice so low I barely heard him. "I'll take care of her."

"Only if that's what Meghan wants." Amy directed her gaze at me. "The other Kazzies have been asking about you too. They'd all like to visit."

"No," Davin said before I could reply. "They'll tire her out."

Amy bristled. "I believe those are Meghan's decisions."

I smiled, not being able to help it. Amy was not one to be intimidated, even by Davin.

"I'd rather not," I croaked. "Davin's right. I'm really tired. Honestly, I just want to sleep, and it's fine if he wants to care for me, really."

"All right," Amy said matter-of-factly. The worry was still in her eyes, but she smiled anyway. "And I think sleep is a good idea." She stood and gave me another overly bright smile. "You're going to be fine."

I grimaced. *Why do I have the feeling she's saying that more to reassure herself, than me?* "I know. Everyone gets a little sick the first time they're exposed."

"Exactly." Amy smiled again before leaving, as if convinced optimism would cure all.

Davin and I were quiet until she exited. "I want to take you to my cell." Davin shot a look at Private Rodriguez. "We'll have more privacy there."

"That's fine." Arguing took too much energy, and besides, I didn't really care where I slept. I just wanted to *sleep*.

Davin addressed the guard. "I'm moving her to my cell."

Private Rodriguez's eyes bulged. "What? Move her? Um, I don't think you can do that."

"Really? Meghan, did you hear that? He doesn't think we can do that."

I rolled my eyes. The testosterone was flowing. I knew Davin was spoiling for a fight. I'd felt his edginess since he'd entered my cell. He was scared, and that wasn't something he was used to feeling. Poor Rodriguez was gonna get an earful if I didn't intervene.

"I'd like to move, Private." I tried to sit up but lay back when it hurt too much. "Could you please open the door?"

"Um, well . . ." he stammered.

"She's your superior, remember?" Davin advanced toward the glass.

"Just do it," I said sternly, which thankfully, stopped Davin in his tracks.

"Of course. Whatever you wish," the guard replied.

"Thank you." I did my best to smile.

Private Rodriguez nodded in return but then glanced at Davin. He whipped his gaze to the control panel, searching for the buttons to get me out.

For not the first time, I felt sorry for the new guard. He was young and so unsure of himself. Having Davin's hostile attitude to deal with obviously didn't make his job any easier.

"Should I come with you?" the guard asked when the door finally slid open.

Davin opened his mouth to reply so I quickly cut in, "No, that's all right. If your shift doesn't end for a while, you can stay here. Sergeant Rose should be able to manage everything just fine."

"Okay." He eyed Davin warily before dropping his gaze again. It didn't take a genius to see who the alpha was in the room.

In a hurry to get next door, I stood too quickly and the room spun. Davin's form blurred and then he stood at my side, steadying me. In a way, I was glad I'd almost fallen. It had taken Davin's attention off Rodriguez.

It was still embarrassing, though. I'd never had anyone take care of me when I was sick, and I'd certainly never been sick like this at work before. I may have thrown up a few times before presentations, from my ever-present anxiety, but that was in the privacy of a bathroom, not in a cell on display. The Kazzie's private quarters resembled a fish bowl. Everyone could easily see my humiliation.

"Are you okay?"

The anguish in Davin's voice trumped my own thoughts. He hovered over me.

"Yeah, I just stood up too fast."

It took more effort to walk the fifty feet to Davin's cell than I wanted to admit, but that was to be expected. *Right?*

Sergeant Rose smiled when we entered, but once our eyes met, his expression turned stricken. "I heard you were sick."

"Yeah, I've been better."

Davin helped me to his bed. I sank onto it, reveling in his scent that clung to the sheets. It was only when he pulled up the covers that my eyes flashed open as a thought struck me. "But where are you going to sleep?"

"Don't worry about me." He settled the covers around my shoulders. "Just rest."

I tried to protest. I *meant* to, but I was so damned tired that it was a struggle to keep my eyes open. Before I knew it, darkness surrounded me.

THE NEXT FEW days passed in a haze of sleep, heat, guzzling drinks when I was awake, and eating when I could manage. Davin was at my side the entire time. He looked as bad as me, if not worse. He slept on the floor by the bed, in intermittent shifts, despite my protests that I could return to my cell or stay in the Experimental Room.

He also helped me to the bathroom every time I pushed to standing, but thankfully he left me in peace to do my business. Every time I was thirsty, a drink was instantly at my lips. If I got too sweaty, he wet a rag and wiped my face. And when I had a rare spell where I was awake for more than a few hours, he read me stories.

Essentially, he was the perfect nurse, if a little hovering at times.

If anyone thought it weird that a Kazzie was taking care of his researcher, no one commented. It almost seemed that everyone was too concerned to do anything that may disrupt my recovery. Perhaps the brave smiles and worry filled reassurances were more bravado than actual belief that I'd be okay.

At times, I wondered if I *would* be. Most people only experienced a mild reaction for a day or two before feeling well again. But then I remembered the researcher at Dr. Hutchinson's facility who'd moved into the second stage of symptoms. It seemed I was another lucky one in that boat.

On the fifth day, my fever broke. Davin was asleep when it happened. I woke in a bed of sweat, but for the first time in days felt healthy. Good, even.

The night guard was in the watch room. The clock read 4:45. Sergeant Rose would arrive any minute.

I stood which got the guard's attention. I put a finger to my lips so he wouldn't wake Davin. Padding to the bathroom, I dipped behind the half wall and stripped my sodden, sweaty clothes.

I'd lost weight. I could tell just from glancing down.

My hip bones stuck out, and my abdomen was hollow. I grimaced and looked in the mirror. The sight wasn't pretty. My hair was a mess of dark snarls that stood six inches off my head. Shadowy smudges lined my tired-looking hazel eyes. My face was thinner than it had been just five days ago.

In other words, I looked amazing.

Starting the shower, I stepped under the spray and sighed in contentment as hot water washed away days' worth of grime, sweat, and sickness. I shampooed my hair twice and scrubbed every inch of my body.

When finished, I toweled off and dressed. Sergeant Rose grinned when I emerged. Since it was just after five, he must have just come on.

I waved and made a spooning movement to my mouth. He nodded and through the watch room window, I saw him call up to the kitchen.

MORNING CAME AND went. Davin still slept. I wasn't surprised. He'd barely slept for the past five days since he'd hovered continuously over me.

I ate a mountain of food while I waited for him to rouse. It seemed no matter how much I ate, I wanted more. I blamed it on the last five days where I'd barely eaten anything.

Davin finally stirred mid-afternoon. He groaned when he lifted his head, probably from the uncomfortable angle it rested at on the floor. He seemed groggy at first as he pushed himself up, but when he noticed the bed was empty, he shot to standing.

"I'm over here," I said before he could panic.

He whirled around, his hair in much the same state as mine this morning.

I smiled. I couldn't help it. He looked confused, like he was trying to figure out if he was still in a dream or had just woken from one.

"You're up?" he finally said.

"Yes, and I feel fine, better than I have in days."

A whiz of movement and he was at my side, his hand to my forehead. "Your fever's gone."

"Yes, and I've eaten enough to feed a small country—"

He crushed me to him. It came as such a surprise that my words left me.

His arms wrapped so tightly around me that I could barely

breathe. His ragged breaths filled my ears. "You're not dead. You're okay." His chest rose and fell heavily.

After the shock of his sudden embrace began to wear off, something else became apparent.

Davin was terrified.

"Hey," I said softly. I tentatively reached up and rubbed my hands up and down his back. His entire body still trembled. "Davin . . . it's okay. Really, it is. I told you I'd be okay."

He didn't respond, but his grip didn't lessen.

"Davin?" His muscles were steel beneath my hands.

"I thought . . ." A deep shuddering breath filled his chest. He still clung to me as if I'd disappear into thin air. "I thought you were going to die."

My heart ached at the anguish in his voice. And then I remembered what Sharon had told me, how Davin had been on the reservation with his brothers and sisters when they all died. He never spoke of that time. Never. But he'd been with his family when they all passed away from the virus. I knew that much.

Pulling back, I met his gaze squarely. Tears shimmered in his eyes. So much emotion swam in them that my heart went out to him. I cupped his cheeks tenderly. "*Makanza* can't kill me. I'm not going anywhere."

It took another moment before those words seemed to fully sink in. When they did, he abruptly let go and raked a hand through his hair. "Right. Sorry . . . I see that now."

I wanted to say more, to reassure him that his reaction was fine and that I understood, but he suddenly seemed embarrassed.

After taking a deep breath, he rubbed his hands over his cheeks a few times before his gaze became clear. Offering me a smile, he looked me over before saying, "You've lost weight."

"I know. Trust me, I'm trying to make up for it."

He eyed the empty food trays. "Anything left for me on there?"

"Sorry, no."

He took another deep breath, and the panic on his face eased more. His mood was shifting like the dawn sun rising after a cold dark night. Whatever had terrified him was fading away.

Davin turned to the watch room. Sergeant Rose was watching us, his brow furrowed.

"Do you want to order me my usual?" Davin asked.

The guard nodded, a look of relief filling his face. "Sure. I'll do it right now."

13 – EXPERIMENTAL ROOM

Davin and I spent the afternoon and evening together. It was a little bizarre. I felt amazingly fine while he struggled to keep his eyes open. Thankfully, he no longer seemed afraid that I'd die—that intense moment between us had passed, and I didn't bring it up. I got a distinct impression the past five days for him had been a nightmare that he didn't want to remember.

And I knew, despite his twelve-hour slumber, he still felt exhausted. Since he still hadn't suffered another strange catatonic state, I tried to feel reassured that his tiredness had nothing to do with that. After all, five days of little to no sleep could exhaust any person, even a Kazzie with Davin's unique abilities.

During my sick time, he hadn't met with Dr. Fisher, but now that I was well, I'd overheard him quietly set up a time with Sergeant Rose to have the doctor visit again.

When he returned to my side, I asked, "What's that all about?"

His head tilted. "What's *what* all about?"

"You're meeting with Dr. Fisher again? Is he doing more

tests?"

"Oh." He raked a hand through his hair. "No tests."

"But you're seeing him again?"

He turned so I couldn't see his face. "Yeah, we're meeting. Say, I'm going to shower. Be back soon."

I stared at his broad shoulders before he turned into a blur. The sound of a shower starting came from the back corner. Sitting down on his bed, my eyebrows knit together. *He doesn't want to tell me why they're meeting.*

I nibbled my lip and tried not to worry.

A FEW HOURS later, I bid Davin goodnight and returned to my cell. Night had arrived according to the clock, but without the sun, I had no idea what time it was. Regardless, I thought I'd fall into a deep sleep, given all that had transpired, so I was surprised when the exact opposite happened.

I slept fitfully.

Dreams plagued me. Horrific dreams of my friends being held captive on the reservation, wasting away into people I no longer recognized. In one nightmare, I clung to the fence that surrounded the reservation shouting Davin's name as I searched frantically for him within. But I never found him. He'd been so deeply buried in its interior that we were forever apart. Never to be together again.

Sweat drenched me when I woke. Pushing damp hair from my forehead, it was like a lightbulb went off. Now that the virus had worked its course, I knew what I needed to do.

I have to get out of the Sanctum. I need to call Cate. We need to convince our government that the reservation isn't needed. It's the only chance Davin and my friends have to be free.

Biting my lip, I straightened more.

The new law required people exposed to *Makanza* to stay in quarantine for three weeks. They were monitored during that time. If three weeks passed, and an exposed person remained healthy, they'd effectively detected the virus and fought it off.

However, that hadn't happened to me. The virus had begun multiplying before my body defeated it, which was why I'd moved into the second stage of symptoms. That meant *Makanza* had been active at one point inside me. The MRI now needed to make sure no traces of it remained.

The three week quarantine essentially doesn't apply to me since I exhibited extreme symptoms. We know I've gone through the stages already. So if they test me, and my samples are clean, there's no logical reason to keep me in here.

Bounding out of bed, I raced to the watch room window. The night guard was still on. It had to be early. I banged on the window which made him jump. He'd been reading a book with his back to the glass. Swirling his stool around, his wide eyes met mine.

"Dr. Forester?" His voice sounded surprised through the speaker system.

"How many days have I been in here?"

"Um . . . about a week. I think."

One week. That means two more weeks before I'm out of quarantine unless I can convince them to test me and release me sooner.

"Will you call my lab group? I need them to come in here."

He checked the clock. "Um . . . It's only 4:30 in the morning. I doubt they're here yet."

My reflection stared back at me in the watch room glass, and I understood why his tone sounded so wary. My hair stood out on all ends. I wore pajamas. And I stood barefoot in front of him, appearing as if my life depended on his answers.

Only it's not my life. It's Davin's life. Sara's life. All of the Kazzies who live in here. And the twelve hundred other Kazzies throughout the country.

Running a hand through my hair, I took a step backward so I wasn't right against the window.

"I'm going to shower and dress. Will you order me breakfast? Coffee, toast, and eggs."

"I'll do it right now." He sat his book down before he called up to the kitchen.

I retreated to the bathroom. My lab group would arrive in a few hours. *So that gives me a few hours to work out a plan to convince the MRI that it's safe to let me out.*

"YOU RANG?" MITCH'S voice boomed through the speaker system.

My head snapped up from the research paper I'd been reading on my laptop. A smile spread across my face when Amy, Mitch, and Charlie all peered at me through the watch room window.

Mitch seemed to interpret my smile as something other than what it was. He winked, a knowing look in his eyes.

Crap. I really needed to find a way out of the mess I'd dug myself into with him, but now wasn't the time to figure that out.

"What's up?" Amy pulled out a stool.

Private Rodriguez was nowhere to be seen. I guessed he'd excused himself when they all appeared.

"Yeah," Charlie chimed in. "We all received emails from your nighttime guard saying it was *dire* that we all race down here." He cocked his head. "*Dire.* I can't remember the last time someone used that word."

Pushing back from the desk, I joined them at the watch

room window. "I need to get out of here."

"Can't wait any longer for our drinks, huh?" Mitch grinned wolfishly.

Smiling wanly at him, I addressed Amy. "I've been exposed. I reacted. It's obvious my immune system detected *Makanza* and effectively fought it. I know the law says three weeks in quarantine, but test me. Take samples from me. I'm sure they're viron free."

"Is it really that bad in here?" Amy frowned, looking genuinely concerned.

A flash of Davin filled my mind. "No, it's not bad, but I can't do anything in here to fight the reservation."

Mitch crossed his arms. "How are you going to fight it?"

I shrugged. "Go to Washington D.C. to protest? Start a petition? Raise awareness about the vaccine's effectiveness? I don't know. How are laws changed?"

Charlie raised a finger. "Probably all of the above."

"So that's what I'm going to do. Hence, why I need to get out of here. And logic deems that if all of my samples are *Makanza*-free then I safely *can* leave here."

Mitch drummed his fingers on his arm. "Makes sense. I wonder what the MRI's rule is on that."

"There probably isn't a rule," Charlie said dryly. "The three week quarantine law was only made last week. Meghan's the first scientist to be restricted to the Sanctum."

Amy nodded. "But she's right. If she's viron free, there's no reason for her to stay in here." Her green eyes grew bright. "Okay. Let me see what I can do."

THREE HOURS LATER, I was on my way to the Experimental Room. Amy had met with Dr. Sadowsky and explained my request. After his call to top MRI officials and

Compound 26's attorney, it was agreed that if I was viron-free, there was no need to keep me in the Sanctum.

My situation was unique. Essentially, the law didn't apply to me since my exposure had happened within a Compound, not on the reservation, and I was held in a facility that was able to test my samples.

When Amy relayed that information, I breathed a sigh of relief. Thankfully, my colleagues still based decisions on science and facts versus fear and hysteria.

Now if only we can convince our government to be so logical.

When I passed Davin's cell on my way to the Experimental Room, I was about to knock on his door, but then I remembered he was meeting with Dr. Fisher this morning.

Sergeant Rose's voice made me jump. "He's not in, Meghan. He's with Dr. Fisher right now."

The camera above had swung my way. Sergeant Rose had obviously seen me standing outside of Davin's cell.

I peered up at the camera. "When will he be back?"

"Probably not until early afternoon."

"Thanks. I'll stop by later."

Biting my lip, I once again wondered what Davin and Dr. Fisher were up to before hurrying down the hall into the Experimental Room. I donned scrubs and entered the massive enclosure.

Two technicians sat at the Experimental Room's control panel. Alison and Nate were on duty today. Nate picked up his headpiece so he wouldn't need to use the microphone.

"Dr. Forester, good morning."

"Good morning," I replied.

"Can you please lie down on Bed Two?"

I did as he said, having to hop onto it since it was so tall.

The robotic arms stationed around the bed were quiet and still, like dead soldiers waiting to come to life, their bayonets and weapons ready. I took a deep breath as my heart rate picked up. The anxiety that constantly plagued me geared up a notch.

If I want to get out early, this is the only way. Just breathe.

"We're going to take a few samples." Alison's voice sounded through the speakers. "Mostly blood but a muscular biopsy too."

The robotic arms suddenly spun to life, waving and flapping above me. I just nodded, lay still, and folded my hands over my stomach. It was everything I could do to keep myself calm.

I closed my eyes and practiced my deep breathing exercises as best I could. I could still hear the robots, though. They made a swishing movement as they sliced through the air. I didn't dare look at them again.

So this is what the Kazzies feel when they're back here.

"Can you extend your arm?" Alison asked.

I straightened it. The bed shifted, a portion of it mirroring my movement. I could feel it beneath me as the bed elongated so my arm rested perpendicularly on it. I opened my eyes to slits and darted a glance at my arm just as a robot descended, wrapping a rubber band around my bicep so quickly, it was done before I closed my eyes again.

The pressure in my arm increased, the blood pooling in my forearm and fingers.

"You'll feel a little prick," Alison said, "when the needle's inserted."

Something cool washed across my inner elbow.

"That's the alcohol," Alison explained. "Here comes the poke."

I didn't have time to ready myself. A sharp sting traveled

up my arm when the needle went in.

A moment later, the sting vanished, leaving a dull ache in its place just as the rubber band snapped off. "The blood work's done." Nate's voice sounded through the speakers. "Now, we'll take some muscle. Do you have a preference for where we take it?"

I opened my eyes when the swishing sound stopped. The robots hung frozen above me. They looked like a gigantic spider ready to descend upon me for lunch.

"Um, wherever," I mumbled.

"The thigh's a pretty easy place." His quick suggestion made me guess he usually dissected from that area.

"Sure."

The robots sprang to life, and I squeezed my eyes shut again.

MY ARM FELT sore when I left the Experimental Room. My leg however was numb. A stark, white bandage covered the hole where they'd taken the biopsy.

I felt strangely empty when I returned to the cells. Used, almost. Not human anymore. It was a sickening feeling. I told myself that the technicians were just doing their job. The MRI needed to know that *Makanza* no longer circulated in my blood and body before they discharged me from the Sanctum.

If they discharge me.

Even though I was now symptom free, I could still pass *Makanza* to others if I carried it. Which, in theory wouldn't matter, since the entire public had been vaccinated, but our government seemed hell bent on feeding the public's irrational fears.

Still, the way Nate and Alison had done their jobs, stoic faced and devoid of emotion, as if on auto-pilot—*that* was what bothered me. They were my colleagues, people I'd worked with for almost a year, but it no longer felt like I was one of them. I felt like a Kazzie. A body. A sample that needed to be taken.

The twins, Sage, Victor, and Dorothy had lived like this for nine years, ever since the Compounds opened two years after the First Wave. The first two years of the First Wave, they'd spent living in makeshift quarantine facilities. That was before the Compounds had been built. However, since Davin and Garrett had contracted *Makanza* in the Second Wave, they'd only been in the Compound for seven years, but that was still seven years of being subjected to the Experimental Room. My stomach twisted as bile rose in my throat.

A fuzzy feeling entered my mind. I opened the door that connected me telepathically to Sara.

Hey, she said. *Where are you?*

Walking back to my cell.

Her voice grew curious. *I heard your fever broke. So you're feeling better?*

Much, I feel back to normal.

I'm so happy to hear that. Do you want to come up to the library and join me? I'm by myself up here.

I nodded internally. *Sure, I'll turn around.*

I FOUND SARA sitting alone on a couch. She was in the corner of the library on the top, tiered level.

"You're up early," I commented. The twins usually slept till nine or ten.

"I felt your anxiety," she said.

I grimaced and sat beside her. She curled her slim, blue, muscular legs beneath her to make room. Had the First Wave never occurred, I could picture the twins becoming dancers.

They naturally had ballerina physiques. Lithe, long, and graceful. Everything about them seemed to flow.

"Sorry. I'll try to keep it more in check next time."

She shrugged. "I'm not mad. I know you can't help it." She smiled cheekily.

I giggled. "The curse of being so *receptive*, huh?"

"Yep." Sara's gaze alighted on the bandage on my thigh. Her eyebrows knit together. "What happened?"

I tried to pull my shorts over it, but it was no use. "They took a biopsy. It occurred to me this morning that if I'm viron-free, I can leave the Sanctum."

Her face fell. "You're leaving us?"

"Only if my samples come back clean and only so I can fight the new law." I waved at the massive walls. "In here, my hands are tied. I can't do anything."

"Is that why you were anxious? Because you were in the Experimental Room?"

I sighed. Heat flushed my cheeks. "Yes. Stupid, isn't it?"

"Are you kidding me? The first time I went back there, I was fifteen. Even though Kyle was really nice and stayed in the watch room the entire time, I was scared out of my mind. I hated it, every minute of it." She looked away. "I still do."

"I understand that now."

She met my gaze, her blue eyes as bright as her skin. "It's kinda like you're one of us now. I mean, you've always felt like one of us, but now it's like you really *are*. You live back here. They take samples from you. You're infected—well, kind of." She cocked her head. "Is it weird?"

I pictured my cell, Davin, the Kazzies who had become better friends to me than anyone in my life. I felt even closer to them than Amy, and I counted her as a good friend.

"Yeah, it is. I never appreciated how horrible it is in here."

Sara cocked her head. "So if your samples are clean, when are you leaving?"

"Hopefully soon."

WHEN I RETURNED to my cell it was early afternoon. I knew Davin would be looking for me. Sure enough, he was in my cell.

"He let you in?" I mused, nodding toward Private Rodriguez.

Davin grinned wickedly. "I think he's scared of me."

I smothered a smile. "How was your meeting with Dr. Fisher?"

Davin's grin vanished. "Fine."

My stomach flipped. I studied Davin's profile while he looked down, fiddling with something on his shirt. The straight nose, high cheekbones, and long eyelashes. He was striking.

"And?" I prompted gently.

"And what?"

"What did he say? Are they sure you're okay?" An image of him in that catatonic state popped into my mind. He'd seemed fine since that incident, but the thought of something actually being wrong with him . . .

"Yeah, I'm fine." He inched closer. "You look good, like your old self." I knew he was changing the subject, but I let him. He obviously didn't want to talk about whatever he and Dr. Fisher had discovered.

I'll leave it alone. For now.

As his gaze traveled down my length, his expression darkened. He lifted my arm, his eyes glued to my elbow. I'd forgotten to take off the bandage where they'd drawn blood. His brow furrowed as his eyes raked the rest of me. When his gaze alighted on the bandage on my thigh, his jaw tightened.

"What did they do to you?" Anger dripped in every syllable.

"Nothing." I pulled my arm back. "I went to the Experimental Room this morning so they could draw blood and do a biopsy. It wasn't a big deal."

"They cut into you?"

"A little."

Davin's gaze whipped toward Private Rodriguez. The young guard swallowed. I hadn't realized the guard was watching us. "Did you know about this?"

Apparently, the speakers were on and Private Rodriguez had been eavesdropping because he stammered, "Ah . . . um . . . I had nothing to do with it."

I sighed and grabbed Davin by the arm. "Davin, stop. I requested this. It's the only way I can leave the Sanctum."

"Leave the Sanctum?"

I sighed and pulled him toward the back panel door. I tried to ignore the feel of his forearm muscles bunching beneath my fingers or how his breath sucked in when I touched him.

"Come on. We're leaving." I glanced over my shoulder at Private Rodriguez. "Has anyone from my group or the Director stopped by?"

"No."

"Are you able to find me in the entertainment rooms, if they do?"

"I think so."

"Ask Sergeant Rose if you can't figure it out. It's imperative I know when my samples have been processed. Would you please open the back door?"

Private Rodriguez nodded emphatically and pushed a button. The door slid open immediately. *At least, he's finally figuring out the control panel.*

I pulled Davin out of the cell. He resisted, but I still got him moving.

"He's always got that speaker on, you know that?" Davin seethed when the door closed behind us. We stood in the back hallway. "He eavesdrops on everything we say."

"I know. I'll talk to him about it."

"Sergeant Rose would never do that. At least he has the decency to——"

"Davin, stop. It's fine. I'll talk to him."

Anger strummed from him in dark waves, like a fierce storm at sea. He closed his eyes and took a few deep breaths, looking remarkably similar to how I probably looked when I practiced my deep breathing.

I stood quietly. After a minute, I asked, "Are you okay?"

He took another deep breath before opening his eyes. "Yeah, sorry . . . it's just . . . seeing that they cut you . . . and then hearing that you may . . ." He looked at his feet, his brow furrowed.

I grabbed his hand. "Let's go to the track. Do you want to run? I need to burn off some energy."

"You really feel up to exercising? Even though you've been so sick?"

I pictured Davin, the Kazzies, my friends on a reservation—trapped, imprisoned forever. And then I thought about how I was trapped in here, unable to do anything about it. My life was out of my control.

"Yes, I need to run."

I BEGAN RUNNING after Jeremy died. Running was what I needed when things in my life became too overwhelming or too chaotic. Right now, that was how it felt. Something may be medically wrong with Davin, yet he wouldn't tell me about it. I was stuck in the Sanctum and despite now feeling fine, I couldn't leave. And on the outside, plans were being made to imprison my friends in a new location.

I couldn't let that happen.

My feet pounded against the track as I ran lap after lap. The canvas shoes weren't ideal. My shins hurt from the impact, but I didn't stop.

Davin kept in stride at my side. I'd never run with anybody before. He easily kept up and never breathed heavily or seemed fatigued. A few times, I caught him watching me as my ponytail whipped around my face.

"What?" I finally asked when we stopped. I breathed heavily. Sweat poured from my face. I walked in circles around him to cool down.

He raised his hands in surrender. "*What* what?"

"You keep looking at me." I lifted a hand to my face. *Oh, no . . . do I have food on my cheek or something in my teeth?*

"I'm just . . . surprised. You're in really good shape."

His dark hair which curled at the ends brushed his ears. He didn't seem the least bit winded or tired. Only a light sheen of sweat covered his brow. He stood watching me, his hands on his hips, his shirt accentuating his chiseled chest.

It was obvious my vigorous run had felt like a Sunday afternoon stroll to him. I walked another circle around him as my heart rate slowed.

"I've been running since Jeremy died."

He nodded knowingly still watching my every move. "Right. That's good. That's a healthy way to deal with it."

Planting myself in front of him, I studied him. His beautiful blue gaze traveled across my face. I felt it again. That energy that strummed between us. It was like we both wanted the other to be okay. To be happy. Yet, that happiness was never a life in which we were together.

It can never be.

Taking a deep breath, I again remembered him in that catatonic state.

In a quiet voice, I asked, "So what were the results of those additional tests Dr. Fisher wanted to run?"

I knew I was pushing him to tell me, but seeing him standing there, strong and unyielding . . . I needed him to stay that way. The thought of something happening to him terrified me.

Davin's finger tapped against his hip. He shrugged. "They're fine."

"So all of your tests turned out normal?"

"Yeah."

"Then what happened?" I practically screeched.

His gaze, once again, wouldn't meet mine. His finger still tapped his hip. "Should we head back?"

I sighed and could feel my brow furrowing. *He doesn't want me to know. Whatever the cause of him being in that state, he doesn't want me to know why.*

Taking a deep, shuddering breath, I said, "Davin, do you promise to tell me if you're ever sick? Or if something's actually wrong? Will you *please* not keep me in the dark?"

His finger stopped, but he looked away again and cleared his throat. "Yes, if something's actually wrong with me, I'll tell you. Can you drop it now? I'm fine, seriously, I am."

I knew he wasn't telling me everything, but I also knew whatever he and Dr. Fisher discussed wasn't really my business. Dr. Fisher was right. It was Davin's personal health information. There was no reason I needed to know about it if it didn't affect the virus that inhabited his body.

I still hated not knowing.

"Dr. Forester?" a voice boomed in the field.

I jumped.

Davin chuckled. "You did ask him to call you." He glanced upward until he found the camera. "Yes, Private Rodriguez?"

"The Director is here to see Meghan. He'd like her to return to her cell. The results from her tests are back."

14 - SAMPLES

Davin and I hurried to my cell. I was still a sweaty mess and my anxiety over what was to come only made it worse.

If the results showed that *Makanza* still inhabited my body, I wouldn't be able to leave the Sanctum. Possibly ever. Because if the virus was still active inside me, it meant I was now a Kazzie, even though I'd never Changed. That hadn't happened to anyone exposed, so I knew I was being irrational.

Still . . .

If for some reason that *had* happened, I'd be able to infect others. According to the new law passed over the weekend, I'd be moved to the reservation like the rest of the Kazzies. And worse, I knew it would be the end of my friends ever being free since it meant the vaccine wasn't as effective as we claimed it to be. Cate and I had vehemently denied the government's concerns that someone could carry *Makanza* after being vaccinated. I hoped we were still right.

I shuddered, not because I abhorred the idea of living with the Kazzies or being labeled as one, but at knowing that I'd never be able to help them again.

My palms were clammy when the back door slid open to my cell. Davin and I strode in.

Dr. Sadowsky waited. He wore a navy blue suit, a crisp white shirt, and a red patterned tie. He stood in the watch room. My lab group flanked his sides. Amy waved when she saw me.

I hurried to the window.

"Well? What are the results? Am I still infected?"

"Whoa, Forester." Mitch chuckled. He wore jeans and a typical comedic t-shirt. *I'd be unstoppable if not for law enforcement and physics.* "It's nice to see you too."

Davin tensed.

"Sorry. I'm a little edgy." I wrung my hands. "I'm sure you can guess why."

Amy's red curls were in a high ponytail today. She leaned over the microphone. "You're in the clear. No active virons were detected in any of your samples."

Private Rodriguez smiled. "So that must mean she'll get outta here soon, huh?"

"Something like that." Amy drummed her fingers against the control panel.

Dr. Sadowsky put his hands on his hips. "I'd like to run one more set of tests, just to make sure."

I swallowed. *That means I'm going back to the Experimental Room.* "Okay."

"By the way, I didn't forget about your phone," Amy said. "It'll be installed this afternoon when they're getting those samples. Although, I'm not sure if you'll need it. You could be out of here by tomorrow."

Which means I can go to D.C. soon. "Good, thanks. How about we get those samples taken?"

I RETURNED TO the Experimental Room after my lab group departed from the watch room. I clenched my hands tightly during the walk there.

"Do you want me to come in with you?" Davin strode beside me. Every day I realized more and more how big he was. I barely came to the tip of his shoulder.

"No. I can do this."

"You're sweating, Meg. And you're so tense I could see it a mile away."

I tried to relax, I truly did, but the thought of those spidery machines cutting into me again made panic flutter in my chest.

How am I going to face D.C. again if I can't handle the Experimental Room on my own?

I gritted my teeth. "I can do it by myself. I'll be okay."

Davin pulled me to a halt. His intense blue eyes searched my face. "We're all scared in there. It's nothing to be ashamed of."

My shoulders relaxed under his gentle words. "Really?"

"Yeah, so don't beat yourself up."

Despite me telling Davin I'd be fine, he insisted on standing by my side while they took additional samples. I could tell Davin's presence made the technicians nervous. Baron and Wendy were at the controls this afternoon. Both seemed uneasy when Davin positioned himself against the wall. He didn't interfere, and he didn't hover, but his presence was like a menacing cloud on the horizon. I knew at any minute, a storm could be unleashed.

They took more blood this time, as well as saliva and another biopsy. Both technicians smiled apologetically when the robots cut into me. That made me feel a little better. At least they felt *something* about what they were doing.

Two incisions now marred my thighs. I knew I'd have

scars from both. It was still nothing compared to Davin's scars. And even though I wasn't a vain person, I still grumbled when we walked back to my cell. It seemed like overkill to take samples *again*, but that was the MRI for you.

When we reached my door, neither of us hit the button to let Private Rodriguez know I'd returned. Instead, we turned and faced one another.

Tilting my head back, I smiled sadly. "I could be leaving soon."

He nodded silently.

"It may be weeks before I return."

He took a deep breath and hung his head. "I know. It'll be . . ." He cleared his throat. "It won't be the same without seeing you every day."

I swallowed thickly. "I'll still call."

"Yeah. Yeah, I know." He raked a hand through his hair. "Well, I suppose I'll head back to my cell. I know you have a lot to do." When he dropped his hand, it brushed against my arm. For the briefest moment, his fingers enclosed around mine. He squeezed. "I'll see you later today."

His touch sent tingles to my toes, yet it made my heart feel heavy when I punched in my MRI code to enter my cell. Forever, Davin would be in here or trapped on the reservation. Despite my exposure, our lives were still separate.

I knew I needed to talk to Dr. Hutchinson about my wishes to return to the nation's capital. We had so much to plan, but Davin's words haunted me.

It can never be.

It felt like those words would haunt me forever.

A new phone greeted me when I reached my bedside. Seeing it helped kick me back into action.

I sat on the edge of my bed and addressed the young

guard. "Do you want to grab a coffee? I'd like to make a call in private."

"Oh, sure." Private Rodriguez stood hastily and retreated.

When I was sure he couldn't hear me, I picked up the phone, dialing one of the only numbers I ever called. Dr. Hutchinson was next on the list, but first I needed to talk to someone else.

"Hello?" Sharon said.

"Hi, Sharon?"

"Meghan? Is that you?" Her voice sounded hopeful.

"Yes, it's me."

She sighed. "I've been worried about you. Davin told me what happened."

I knew her son would have informed her of my exposure and illness. It was the only reason I hadn't stressed too much about calling her before today. Funny how I'd never once thought of contacting my own parents since becoming sick. Come to think of it, they probably had no idea I'd been exposed or what I'd gone through over the past week. Normally, we didn't speak more than once a month. I bit my lip, feeling a little guilty that my first call to the outside had been to Davin's mother and not my own.

"I figured Davin would keep you informed," I said.

"He has. But you're okay now, right?"

"Yes. I'm fine."

"How much longer do you need to stay in there?"

"Probably another day maybe two." It was funny how that statement created conflicting feelings within me. A part of me was anxious to leave and fight for the Kazzies while the other part ached at not seeing Davin every day.

"Would you like me to visit this weekend?"

I smiled. Sharon was willing to drive to Sioux Falls to see

me. She'd never done that before which only confirmed how much I meant to her.

"I wish you could, but if I have any say in it, I'll be in Washington D.C."

"About the reservation?"

"Yeah, I'm going to fight it tooth and nail. There's no reason they need to stay confined."

Her voice grew quiet. "All of my babies, except for Davin, died on that reservation. And they're going to make him live there. He'll be reminded of it every day."

My mouth went dry. "You're right. I hadn't thought of that." I gripped the phone tighter. "I'm going to do everything I can to make Davin and all of the Kazzies free. Nobody should have to live like they do."

"Thank you, Meghan. I hope you can."

15 - LEAVING THE SANCTUM

Two days later, Dr. Sadowsky deemed me safe to return to society. No traces of *Makanza* remained in any of my samples, unlike the Kazzies, who'd carry the virus until they died.

Since I never had any personal belongings, there was nothing to pack. My heart hurt, knowing that in a few hours, I'd once again be separated from Davin and my friends. It could be weeks before we'd see each other again.

Dr. Hutchinson and I had worked out a plan. We'd fly to D.C. and speak with the president about the new law. We would bring more evidence and data—science was on our side. If that didn't change things, we'd begin a campaign to sway the public. Cate had already begun recruiting other MRI employees and members in the public who wanted the Kazzies free. There was power in numbers, and if that was the route we'd have to go—we'd do it.

Luckily, Dr. Sadowsky was supportive of our plans. He granted me a leave of absence so I wouldn't need to worry about missing work.

An hour before I was due to be discharged from the

Sanctum, Davin and I took the elevator to the fourth floor and walked to the end of the forgotten corridor. In a short time, I'd be leaving. This was the last time I'd see him for who knew how long.

We sat cross legged on the floor.

I sat opposite him. The cold floor seeped in through my pants as I tilted my chin upward toward the small patch of sunlight streaming in through the windows above. Neither of us made any attempts to look out them.

It was funny that in all the time I'd lived in the Sanctum, the only time I'd seen the outside was that day I sat on Davin's shoulders and peered out the above windows. How quickly I'd become detached from the outside. In here, that world did not exist.

Davin played with his fingers in his lap. He'd been strangely quiet all morning. He clasped his strong hands together and met my gaze. "What will you do when you leave?"

"Dr. Hutchinson and I are heading back to D.C. tomorrow afternoon. We have a meeting with the president scheduled in two days."

His eyebrows shot up. "The president? As in, President Morgan?"

"Yeah, crazy isn't it?" I tucked a stray wisp of hair behind my ear. "Dr. Hutchinson has a lot of power within the MRI. She was able to arrange the meeting. I'm sure if I'd asked, they'd have laughed at me."

He made a disgruntled sound. "Don't discredit yourself. You've done a lot for this country. Without you, the vaccine would have never been discovered."

"No, without *us*."

He rolled his eyes.

It was a bit ironic. Any time I tried to give him credit for the vaccine, he brushed it off and said it was all me. Even though we both knew why his sample had been stable enough to generate a vaccine, we'd never spoken about it.

Love stabilized the virus.

Whether that be platonic love or romantic love—it didn't matter. All that mattered was that the person infected with *Makanza* be in a peaceful state feeling a strong surge of love. If they were, the virus would be stable enough to use traditional DNA methods to extract the genome. Dr. Hutchinson's theory of mind-body genomics had proven correct.

I'd never asked Davin if he'd felt platonic love or romantic love that day I took his sample. I hoped more than anything that it was romantic love, and sometimes when he looked at me a certain way, I felt certain he loved me as deeply as I loved him, but . . .

It can never be.

We'd never spoken about that day. Not once. A part of me wondered if we ever would. After all, an invisible barrier separated us regardless of how we felt for one another. I lived in the outside world. His life was ruled by the MRI.

We could never be together in our current circumstance.

And since it had now been many months since that day I took his sample, I didn't have the guts to bring it up. So like a lot of things in my life, I swept it under the rug and didn't think about it. Or tried not to think about it.

"This place won't be the same without you." He smiled, but the smile didn't reach his eyes.

My breath caught in my throat. *I'm really leaving, and it may be weeks before I see him again.*

"I know. It'll be strange to leave here. Even though I've only been here a week, it's started to feel like home in a weird way."

"Have your parents been worried?"

I ducked my head. "They don't know I'm here."

"What?"

"I know. I know. It's just been so busy . . . with me getting sick and then planning for what I need to do when I leave—"

"Meghan, you should call them."

I sighed. Davin was always trying to repair my relationship with my parents for me. "But they're not like your mom. They don't care like she does."

"How can they not care? You're their only child now."

I flinched.

Davin swore under his breath. He reached for me, as if instinctually, but dropped his hands at the last second as if aware of what he was doing. He shook his head. "I'm sorry. That was insensitive."

"No, it's fine." Already the pain was evaporating, but Davin didn't know that. I'd grown stronger over the past year. I no longer pretended that my brother was alive. I no longer had imaginary conversations with him. I'd made a lot of progress.

"No, it's not. That was a dick thing to say."

I tentatively laid a hand on his arm. His muscles clenched underneath and his breath stopped. "Jeremy's dead and gone. Nothing will change that. I need to learn to not react every time it's brought up."

His fingers brushed my arm. "Still . . ."

"It's fine, Davin, really it is. And, hey," I joked, "I'm doing better than I used to. I haven't hallucinated in months that Jeremy's around. I'm not completely crazy."

His brow furrowed, but he didn't say anything.

"And you're right. I should probably call my parents. For

all I know, they've tried to call my cell phone in the past week and may be wondering where I am."

His hand settled on my leg, and he squeezed lightly. The heat from him felt deliciously hot.

I stared at his large hand with his long, strong fingers. A shot of desire raced through me. "So . . ." I tried to remember what we'd been talking about, but all thoughts had left me. All of my focus had centered on him touching me.

As if sensing where my attention lay, he stiffened, but instead of removing his hand, he tentatively moved it an inch higher.

My heart raced, and I glanced up.

His gaze darkened.

Licking my lips, I inched closer.

He stared at my mouth, his pupils dilating.

I leaned forward more.

"Meghan . . ." he growled.

"Davin." My voice came out breathy. My heart was beating so hard.

He still stared at my mouth. The pulse in his neck visibly pounded. Tilting his head down, our lips grew closer until his sweet minty breath puffed toward me.

I closed my eyes. *This is really happening!*

But then a curse filled the air. A rush of air came next.

My eyes snapped open.

Davin stood several yards away.

With a stunned realization, I realized how close we'd come to kissing. But while that made my heart flutter in anticipation, it seemed to do the opposite to Davin. He paced the hallway width, his hands fisted into tight balls.

It can never be. I slumped back onto the floor.

"It's possible I'll never see you again." His voice was

harsh.

My breath stopped. "What? No, that's not true."

His pacing grew faster. If he kept it up, he'd soon be a blur, unable for me to see at all. "It *is* true. If you're going on some quest to free us from the reservation and it fails, and they move me before you return, I may never see you again."

I pushed to a stand and approached him slowly. "Davin. They allow visitors on the reservation. *Of course,* I'll see you again."

He stopped, his body rigid as skepticism lined his face. "Are you sure about that? The MRI is notorious for making promises they don't keep."

My shoulders sagged. I knew it didn't matter what I said. Davin's experiences over the past seven years had shaped his cynicism. He'd told me once that I was young and naïve, but so far, I'd proven his beliefs wrong on several occasions. I intended to keep doing that.

"I'll see you again. That's a promise."

He just nodded yet it didn't take a genius to see he wasn't convinced.

Tentatively taking his hand in mine, I squeezed. He squeezed my hand in return.

Only inches separated us. My gaze sought his. Fear and anger warred in his irises, and before I could change my mind, I stood up on my tiptoes and whispered, "I promise," before pressing my lips softly against his.

The kiss seemed to take him by surprise. He stiffened, but he didn't pull back.

I was about to put distance between us when I felt something in him change. His lips softened under mine. His mouth opened.

Feeling emboldened, I placed my hands on his shoulders

and ran my tongue along his lower lip, and in that second, I felt his control snap.

He groaned and crushed me to him, his arms like steel bands around me. The sudden shift made me gasp before I closed my eyes and let the feel and taste of him consume me.

Heat from his body pressed against mine as his powerful arms molded me against him. I felt every inch of his raw power. His strength, scent, and the feel of his lips returning the kiss created a longing in me so deep, I thought I'd die from my sudden pulsing desire.

But as abruptly as the kiss started, it stopped.

Panting, he pulled back. "Meghan . . ." He breathed harshly. "We can't."

I ran an agitated hand through my hair. I wanted to scream in frustration. My body suddenly felt empty. Cold. Not complete without him.

"We could do long-distance." The words tumbled out of me. "Just because you're on the reservation doesn't mean we can't be together. Sooner or later, you'll be free, and then—"

"No." His word was low. Harsh.

I flinched.

"I'll probably never be free, Meghan. I admire your determination and optimism, but I said it before and I meant it. I won't let you waste your life on me. It can never be."

And in those four, hurtful words—I heard it again. His resolve. His absolute and complete conviction that a world in which we existed together was never possible.

Tears filled my eyes. I turned abruptly so he wouldn't see them. It took a moment before I could speak. "Um . . . We should get back. They're sending me through the decontamination process soon."

He nodded tightly and raked a hand through his hair.

"Right. Yeah. Let's go."

We walked back to the cells, yet the tone between us had changed. What used to feel caring and playful, now felt raw and exposed.

We'd opened Pandora's Box and there was no going back.

It didn't matter that he'd reacted as passionately to me as I had to him. He was one hundred percent convinced that we'd never be together, and despite me being willing to give up everything, he wouldn't have it.

Maybe he's right. Maybe I'm a foolish dreamer. After all, what kind of life *could* we have with him on one side of a fence and me on the other?

But still, I didn't care. Deep down, I didn't care. I just wanted to be with him.

When we reached my door, he turned toward me. Regret filled his eyes.

I longed for the easiness that we'd shared only an hour ago. More than anything I wanted to reach for him and wrap my arms around him, but that honest moment had passed. For a few brief minutes in the forgotten corridor, we'd exposed how we really felt—I loved him, and I think he loved me too, but once again our reality came crashing down.

He lived in here. I was leaving. He was a carrier. I wasn't.

It can never be.

"I guess this is goodbye." His voice sounded raw.

"It's only goodbye for a few weeks." I swallowed the tears that wanted to rise.

He frowned, that simple look conveying all of the warring emotions within. "Travel safely."

"I will. I'll see you in a few weeks."

His breath hitched as he reached for my hand. At the last moment, he stopped. Once again, resolve grew in his features.

"Bye, Meghan."

THREE HOURS LATER, I was once again on the other side. The decontamination process hadn't taken long. Since *Makanza* was so unstable outside of the human body, it never lived on surfaces for more than ten minutes. However, the MRI never took chances. Even with the population being vaccinated, their strict policies hadn't changed.

Consequently, I'd been hosed down like a forest on fire with the special solution that destroyed all virus particles. It wasn't pleasant, but at least, I was out.

I headed back to my lab with everything that had happened between Davin and me swirling through my mind.

Davin wasn't in his cell when I passed it. I had no idea where he'd disappeared to after we parted ways. My heart ached to see him again, to mend whatever rift had started between us, but I knew that wasn't possible.

Only his freedom could fix that.

Knowing these emotions would only lead to a downward spiral, I shifted my attention. Concentrating on the door that opened my connection to Sara, I knocked.

She opened up readily. *Hey, Meghan, I hear you're out.*

Yeah, I'm heading back to the lab now. I nodded to a guard who admitted me through an access door. He had no idea I was carrying on a conversation with a Kazzie inside my head while my palm flashed green on the monitor.

What's the plan from here? Sara asked.

Dr. Hutchinson and I are returning to Washington D.C. We have a meeting with the president in two days.

The president? Wow, you two aren't messing around.

I laughed on the inside, or thought I did. The guard gave me a funny look. I muttered my thanks and hurried down the hall.

Once I knew the guard couldn't see me, I continued my conversation with the twin. *No time to waste. If we fail, you all move to the reservation in less than two months.*

I could feel her tense through our bond. *I know. I keep thinking about that, but I want you to know that no matter what happens, I know I'll be okay. It's just Sophie I'm worried about. You know she has this fear that they'll—*

They'll what?

Sara cursed quietly. *Nevermind. She didn't want me to tell anyone.*

I sighed. Sara tried to keep secrets from spilling, but she managed so many people in her head, she occasionally messed up. It wouldn't be the first time she'd given something away she promised not to.

Changing the subject, I said, *I've been wondering how Sophie will do with the change.*

Sophie had always been the quieter and softer of the twins. Sara was pretty tough and usually did the talking for the two of them, but Sophie was more like me. She turned inward and dealt with her problems on her own. There had been multiple times in the past where she'd stopped eating or refused to interact with anyone as she battled her own demons.

Yeah, Sara replied. *I've been wondering that too.*

A few researchers approached, walking the opposite direction to me in the hall. *I better go. I'm in the main hall and you know how my expression turns funny when we're talking.*

Sara chuckled. *Okay, I'll talk to you later. Keep me posted on how things are going, and I'll spread the word to everyone else.*

By *everyone else*, I knew she was referring to the other Kazzies.

We both closed down the connection, and once again I

was alone in my head.

I sailed down the halls, stopping at the multiple access points that admitted me through various areas within the Compound. The blazing white walls followed wherever I went. That was one thing I definitely hadn't missed while imprisoned with the Kazzies. The muted grays in the Sanctum were much more preferable.

By the time I reached my lab, at least fifteen minutes had passed. I was slightly winded since I'd walked so fast, but the sight that greeted me when I stepped onto the metal platform overlooking the lab below left me speechless.

"Surprise!" Amy yelled.

Balloons, a cake, and a large banner that read, "Congrats! You survived *Makanza* and lived to tell about it!" hung across two lab stations.

Amy, Mitch, Charlie and at least three dozen other researchers cheered and threw confetti, which really appeared to be computer paper that someone had run through a shredder.

Celebratory music followed. Mitch hit a button on his stereo and the old classic song, *Eye of the Tiger* rolled through the speakers.

My mouth dropped before I burst out laughing. It didn't matter that so many people crowded the room. It didn't matter that Davin and I had just had our most tumultuous encounter. The surprise cut through my anxiety like a sharp knife through warm butter.

"When did you do this?" I still stood on the metal platform. Everyone else mingled below me. I hastily gripped the railing and hurried to Amy's side.

A few researchers clapped me on the back when I passed. Someone had started cutting the cake and was passing pieces around. The music continued to blare while conversations erupted amidst my co-workers.

"It was Amy's idea." Charlie handed me a plate with a piece of cake. Chocolate with chocolate frosting. My favorite. "She felt the least we could do was celebrate your non-death."

I rolled my eyes at his joke but couldn't help my laughter.

"We're just happy you're back and okay." Amy handed me a drink. Lemonade from the looks of it. "You had us scared for a while when you were going through the phases."

I took a bite of the cake. Chocolate goodness coated my tongue. "Yeah, I guess I was one of the lucky ones that got to experience stage two symptoms."

"Meghan!" Mitch's voice boomed through the crowd. He shouldered his way past a few researchers. In his hand was a gift. "I bought something for you."

"You got me a present?" My surprise was evident in my tone. It also occurred to me that I still hadn't set things straight with Mitch. I set my cake down and hesitantly took the present in his outstretched hand.

"Yep, and I think you're gonna like it." He grinned as a lock of shaggy blond hair fell across his forehead.

The music switched to another classic from the past.

"What is it?"

"Ah, you generally open it to find out." Charlie raised a midnight eyebrow.

I tore open the wrapping paper, which was really newspaper since wrapping paper was hard to come by these days. There *was* a large pink satin ribbon around it, though. I had no idea where Mitch had found that.

When I pulled out what was inside, I grinned. I couldn't help it.

"Do you like it?" Mitch's eager tone only made me smile

wider.

A green t-shirt with the phrase, *Always give 100% unless you're giving blood*, with the picture of a heart behind it stared back at me.

"I know how you like my shirts." Mitch scratched his beard. "I thought you may like one of your own."

"I love it." I held it up to my torso. "I think it will fit well too."

Mitch winked and squeezed my shoulder. His hand lingered before I subtly moved, making it drop. "I thought you'd like it."

Taking another step back from him, I picked up my cake again. Amy and I quickly fell into conversation as we ate cake and drank lemonade while everyone chatted and celebrated. At times, I had to step away when bodies pressed too close. My initial surprise had worn off which meant my usual anxiety had returned.

Once, I excused myself when the room seemed to be closing in. But overall, it was an enjoyable party and a much needed distraction from what had happened between Davin and me.

"So what's the plan now?" Charlie polished off the last bite of another piece of cake. "Are we heading to Sean's?"

I glanced at the clock. It was only four in the afternoon. "Don't we need to work?"

Amy rolled her eyes. "You survived *Makanza* and lived to tell about it. I think we can all take the afternoon off and have a little fun."

With that, I was hauled up the stairs and out our lab's door. Muffled sounds from Mitch's stereo continued blasting through the lab walls behind us.

16 - NEW EXPERIENCES

For the second time in my life, I drank more than I should. The partying didn't stop at Sean's. Once we left the Irish bar, the four of us drove to Mitch's house. Both Charlie and I had the foresight to not overdrink so we could still safely drive, but once we reached Mitch's home that changed.

It was so unlike me. I kept thinking about Davin, but my co-workers were having none of it. Each time I hinted at leaving, another drink was put in my hand.

Mitch lived in a small bungalow on the southeast side of town. Hills and trees surrounded his neighborhood. The small jug of beer Sean had sent home with us quickly disappeared. And as the beer flowed, my worries fell away.

At one point, I felt Sara trying to get in touch. I opened up to her, but since I wasn't thinking very clearly, I wasn't sure how much sense I made.

It was only in the morning, when I woke up with a pounding head and dry mouth that I realized how incredibly foolish I'd been. I was leaving that afternoon with Dr. Hutchinson, we had a meeting with the president tomorrow, and my head hurt so bad I could barely breathe.

"Morning, Forester." Mitch held out a steaming mug of coffee. Amy lay sprawled on the couch. Charlie slept on the floor. Wrappers from snack foods and candy littered the carpet.

My cheeks flushed crimson.

I groggily pushed to sitting in the chair I'd apparently slept in. Mitch still held the cup out. With a downcast gaze, I took it. "Um, morning."

I brought the rich brew to my lips. Despite my pounding head, it tasted good.

"Here are some potassium pills." He held out the supplement. "To help with the hangover."

I took them. *Where the heck did he get these?* Supplements were near impossible to find.

"I've got bacon and eggs cooking. Bread's in the toaster. Want to help?"

With a wince, I stood. "I'm pretty sure you don't want me to help. I'm rather notorious for burning anything I touch in the kitchen."

Mitch chuckled. "In that case, how about you butter the toast? Can you handle that?"

"I can probably manage."

Scents from the kitchen reminded me that most people had mastered the elusive art of cooking. Since restaurants were so expensive, it was either learn to cook or die from starvation. My cooking was one step above dying.

I followed Mitch. He returned to the stove, so I opened the fridge. My eyes widened.

"Where did you get all of this?" I surveyed the impressive selection. He had three whole sticks of butter. I pulled one out.

"I've got my connections." He gave me a sly look.

Not for the first time, I wondered what his connections were. *Perhaps the same connection finds his t-shirts?* Despite searching all of Sioux Falls, I still hadn't found any stores that supplied the comedic t-shirts that Mitch wore.

When the toast popped, I spread butter over each. Mitch flipped eggs and cooked the bacon. The entire kitchen smelled like heaven.

"Last night was fun." Mitch nudged me.

Vague memories surfaced. The four of us sitting around a table at Sean's. Irish music playing in the background. Beer flowing freely. Having drinks at the pub before Sean sent Mitch home with a gallon of pale ale. The four of us piling into two cars. I drove one, Charlie the other. But after we arrived at Mitch's house, things became a little fuzzy.

I figured I'd had more than a few drinks of the pale ale.

"You look like you're about to faint." Mitch's large hand gripped the spatula. He expertly flipped an egg.

My dark hair hung around my face. I sheepishly pushed it back. "I . . . uh . . . don't remember too much about last night."

Mitch waggled his eyebrows. "You were pretty fun."

My eyes turned to saucers.

Mitch laughed. "Relax, Megs. You were perfectly well behaved and pretty darn cute last night."

Cute? I shuffled uncertainly as it once again became apparent Mitch was interested in me. My socks slid along the linoleum. "So . . . I didn't do anything embarrassing?"

"Nothing you need to worry about. You giggle a lot when you drink, and when your hair's down you're definitely sexy, but nothing happened you need to be ashamed of."

Sexy? I balked. I really needed to set things straight with Mitch but wasn't sure how. I turned so he couldn't see me as I buttered more toast.

Mitch reached over me to grab the salt as I plated the last piece of toast. His arm brushed mine.

I jumped.

He just chuckled and winked.

By the time everything was plated, my anxiety had cranked through the roof. I'd never been alone with Mitch like I was now. And outside of the Compound, a side of him was emerging that was anything but professional. I distinctly got the impression that he liked having me in his home, beside him at the stove, making breakfast together.

Thankfully, Amy and Charlie appeared a few minutes later. Both stumbled into the kitchen with disheveled hair and sleepy eyes.

"What time is it?" Amy yawned.

"Just past seven. Everyone should have time to go home to change before work." Mitch waved her toward a plate of bacon and eggs.

"Mmm, thanks." Her chair scraped against the floor when she pulled it out. She was already munching a piece of bacon before Charlie sat.

"Breakfast and coffee." Charlie rubbed his cheeks. "My kind of morning." He forked a huge bite of eggs. "Man, I can't remember having as much fun as we did last night in a long time. Maybe we should make a habit of people being exposed to *Makanza*. It's definitely a good excuse for a night out."

I was about to sit down when I slapped a hand to my forehead. "Crap! I forgot my laptop at the Compound!"

Charlie took a bite of toast, the crunching sound filling the room. "And that's a problem, *why?*"

"It has my files on it. Dr. Hutchinson is flying in early this afternoon. I was going to pack this morning and review a few presentations on my hard drive at home before she arrived."

"Ah, to lead the jet setter life." Mitch threw an arm around my shoulder and squeezed. A tinge of sweat and day old cologne permeated his clothes. His fingers squeezed my bicep before he dropped his arm and joined everyone at the table.

It wasn't until everyone was seated that I realized I wore the green t-shirt Mitch had bought me. Apparently, I'd put it on during the night. I cringed. Never in my life had I ever partied before. Never. Not even once. It felt weird, to wake up with my co-workers, all of us slightly hungover. But given how the three of them seemed more than happy to sit down for a quick breakfast around Mitch's kitchen table before heading to work, meant I was apparently the only one new to this.

I shifted again from foot to foot. "Ah, I'm going to go. I have a lot to do this morning and not much time."

Mitch frowned. "Seriously? Not even breakfast?" He pulled out the chair beside him.

My stomach flipped as my anxiety once again kicked in. If I didn't remember putting the shirt on last night, it was possible I'd done other things I didn't remember. Embarrassing things. Regardless of what Mitch claimed.

Relax, Meg. Nobody's acting weird except you. You obviously didn't do anything too stupid.

I grabbed a slice of toast. "Thanks. I'll see you guys when I get back."

Amy and Charlie waved goodbye. Both seemed too consumed with eating while grimacing in between bites. I felt fairly certain each nursed a headache.

Only Mitch seemed sad to see me go. I felt his frown follow me as I sailed out the door.

Outside, I breathed in gulping breaths of warm morning air. A sparrow tweeted from the giant oak in the boulevard.

Thank goodness my car's here.

At least I'd been sober enough to drive from Sean's.

But apparently, my sobriety hadn't lasted. With another disbelieving huff at my very un-Meghan-like behavior, I slipped into the driver's seat. My head still hurt, but it seemed like a fair reward for doing something so stupid the night before my flight out with Dr. Hutchinson.

I drove straight to the Compound. The large windmill farm north of the city, our main power source, held its usual tranquil appeal. With each mile that passed, my head cleared a little more.

Maybe I didn't drink as much as I thought.

But if I hadn't, I'd remember things.

"Ugh!" I shook my head in disgust as I turned onto the frontage road.

A scratch filled my mind as the MRRA workers swept my car. As I stood by the body scan waiting for them to finish, I opened up to Sara.

Good morning.

Morning. She sounded wary. *Are you coherent?*

A flush of embarrassment filled me as a strong breeze whipped hair around my face. *Oh no, what did I do?*

She laughed. *Nothing. Well, I mean, you were pretty silly last night when we spoke. And our connection felt wavy, like we were on one of those rides they used to have at fairs. The car . . . no, caro . . . no . . . Oh, crap. What was it called?*

The carousel?

Yes! That one. She paused. Her curiosity strummed right through our bond. *What were you doing last night?*

I grimaced. *Nothing I'm proud of.*

Her curiosity grew. *Now you have to tell me!*

I summed up my grand night of partying as succinctly as possible. I still couldn't believe that was how I acted the night before one of the biggest trips of my life.

Sara laughed. *It's okay to enjoy your life, Meg. Nobody ever said you couldn't.*

But my focus should be getting all of you out of the Compound. Not partying.

Meghan. Her tone turned scolding. *You didn't miss your flight. You're still going to the capital, and you're still going to fight for us. None of that has changed, so why shouldn't you have some fun every now and then? You hardly ever do anything fun. How many friends do you have outside of us?*

I slid back into my car as the guards waved me forward. A few gave me curious glances. I blushed as I realized my facial expressions had probably conveyed the conversation Sara and I were having. Of course, they wouldn't know that. They'd just think I was a weirdo.

You know I don't have a lot of friends, I said.

I know. That's the point I'm trying to make.

Well, thanks.

That's not what I mean, and you know it. I'm just saying that you're doing much better with your anxiety. I know you and Amy get along and you sometimes see each other outside of work. You should embrace that. She's your friend, and she cares about you.

I sighed. *Yeah, I know. It's just . . .*

It's just that you've never put yourself first and now that you finally did it feels wrong?

I frowned. I'd never thought of it like that. The blue sky shone above as I drove slowly forward. *Um... maybe.*

Sara sighed. *Ever since Jeremy died you've had one goal and one goal only—to develop a vaccine and stop* Makanza. *Well, you did that. And now you have a new goal—to free us. And I'm not saying there's anything wrong with that, but you have to remember it can't always be about everybody else. You need to take care of you too.*

I do take care of me.

Really? Is that why you work twelve to sixteen hours a day? Is that why you exposed yourself to Makanza?

I pulled into my parking spot. *Davin was hurt! What was I supposed to do?*

I know. I know, and we're all grateful for what you did, but the point I'm trying to make is that you've put everyone else before yourself for a lot of years. There's nothing wrong with putting yourself first every now and then.

I mulled over what she said as a smile came to my lips. *Since when did you become a psychologist?*

She laughed. *It just so happens that the medical section in the library has a lot of self-help books. I may have read a few lately.*

Self-help books? I thought you liked romance?

Yes, those are fun too, but I felt like a change. I'm getting a little tired of the damsels in distress as they dance in their ball gowns while enjoying the ton's parties.

I giggled as I walked toward my admittance door. *No more historical romances for you then?* Private Williams came into view. He stood straighter when he saw me.

I better go. I'm about to enter the Compound, and I'm pretty sure I've embarrassed myself enough in the past twenty-four hours. The main perimeter wall guards already think I'm weird.

She chuckled. *Will you stop in the Sanctum and say goodbye before you go? Who knows when I'll see you next.*

A flash of Davin filled my mind. It was possible I'd see him too. *Sure. I'll see you soon.*

I GRABBED MY laptop from my office before hiking to the Sanctum. The computer bag jostled at my side while my stomach flipped again and again. Despite Sara telling me I'd done nothing wrong by drinking and partying, I still felt guilty.

I should have spent last night preparing. I should have realized our meeting with the president had the chance to change history. Reviewing our data was more important than a night out.

Besides all of that, I'd said goodbye to Davin yesterday knowing it would be weeks until I saw him again. My mindset had shifted to accommodate that.

Now, I may see him.

It was crazy how giddy that thought made me. I felt like a little kid riding a pony for the first time. Excited, scared, yet exhilarated. Only Davin could do that to me.

But then I remembered our awkward goodbye and the stiff way he'd turned. *Maybe we can mend things before I go.* I clung to that hope as I strode forward.

A few of the guards gazed at my t-shirt when I passed through access doors. With scarlet cheeks, I hurried past each. I'd never worn casual clothes to work. At only twenty-three, soon to be twenty-four, I was the youngest researcher to ever be employed by the MRI. Consequently, I usually wore business suits or business casual.

I'd certainly never worn t-shirts.

I hurried into the Sanctum. In the first hall, Garrett's cell was empty. At the next cell, Sara was waiting. She nodded toward the watch room. A few steps later, I stood by her guard.

"Dr. Forester." He sounded surprised. "I heard you were going to Washington D.C. to see President Morgan?"

News travels fast.

"Yes, I leave this afternoon."

Sara motioned to the containment room. I hadn't intended to enter the Kazzies' cells but if I was quick, I guessed I had time.

"I'm going to go in for a few minutes." I dropped my bag on the floor.

"I'll help you suit up." He pushed his stool back.

I shook my head. "I've been exposed. I never need to wear a suit again."

"Oh, right," he said sheepishly. "Habit."

A few minutes later, I was in Sara's cell. Sophie was nowhere to be seen.

"It's awesome that you never have to wear the marshmallow suits again." She grinned, her teeth bright white against her blue skin.

"I know. I'm so relieved. I hated those things."

Sara grabbed my hand. "Come with me." She pulled me to the back panel, and we sailed through.

"Where are we going?"

"You'll see."

I cocked my head as the gray walls of the back hallway passed. It seemed everyone had surprises for me lately.

She led me to the library. When we stepped out of the elevator, bright sunlight streamed through the ceiling skylights.

Nervous energy emitted from Sara. She wore her typical tank top and shorts, and her long slim legs fidgeted.

"What's going on?"

Instead of replying, she once again grabbed my hand and pulled me up a set of stairs to the second tier. Large bookstacks surrounded us.

Sara's brow furrowed. She kept glancing around. "They said—"

"Surprise!"

I shrieked as the other Kazzies all jumped out. Each grinned. Sophie threw paper in the air. More confetti. Dorothy and Victor whistled and cheered.

"What the heck is going on?" I couldn't stop my smile.

"Sara said you were coming back in to collect a few things. We decided last minute to surprise you with a going-away party." Dorothy wore her workout gear. She even had a sweatband on. My guess was that she'd been in the gym again.

"A going-away party?" I felt Davin's eyes on me, but I hadn't looked at him yet. Our last encounter still hung in my mind.

"It's not a very exciting going-away party," Sage said dryly. "With only thirty minutes to plan, we could only do so much."

"Davin shredded the paper." Dorothy kicked at the confetti on the floor. "Good thing he's so fast."

I shook my head. "You guys . . . I had no idea."

Garrett's massive eyes blinked. "That was the point. We just wanted you to know that we'll miss you, Meg. It won't be the same in here without you."

As embarrassing as it was, my eyes misted over. I darted a look at Davin. He was watching me. "I'll be back."

"We know." Sara threw an arm around my shoulders and gave me a half hug. "But we still wanted you to know that we appreciate what you're doing for us. It means a lot."

"Yeah," Sophie added, "and things were so crazy yesterday with you leaving that we never got to say a proper goodbye."

My gaze shifted to Davin again, except instead of watching me, his eyes were on my shirt. It was impossible to decipher his expression.

While everyone pulled me toward a table up the stairs, he hung back. I could feel him. His presence pulled at me like the moon pulls at the oceans, creating the tides. Even though he was at least two yards away, I was acutely aware of his presence.

He wore his typical jeans and t-shirt, but outside of his cell, he wore shoes. His dark hair curled at the ends. As always, his face was a reddish tan, like he'd just been out in the sun. And his eyes were the blazing, sapphire blue that were uniquely him.

My breath grew shallow despite trying to control it.

"We didn't have time for a cake, but we do have popcorn and sodas." Sophie waved excitedly at the display on one of the library tables.

"No alcohol, though." Sage winked. "Sara told us about your partying escapades last night."

I glowered at Sara. "Sharing my secrets?"

Sara laughed. "I *had* to share your giggles and slurred words last night. I've never heard you like that before."

Everyone chuckled, other than Davin, which only made me blush.

I peeked at Davin again. He stood with his hands stuffed in his pants. When our gazes met, he smiled, but he seemed different—more stiff, not relaxed like he usually was. Our emotional goodbye yesterday filled my mind.

Sophie and Garrett dished up bowls of popcorn for everyone before handing out drinks. From there, we all headed to the next tier in the library where the large couches and chairs were located.

I inched closer to Davin. We brought up the rear.

"I didn't think I'd see you again before I left."

He nodded but wouldn't meet my gaze. "Yeah, it sounds like you had a good time last night. I'm glad you were able to do something fun before you leave."

My cheeks heated. "It was fun . . . I guess, but still kind of weird. I don't usually party."

"It's good that you enjoyed yourself, Meghan. You deserve it. That's what your life should be like, not like . . ." He cut himself off, as if knowing that we'd never agree on our future.

When I glanced up at him, I stumbled on a stair. He caught me when I swayed into his arms, but his brow furrowed when I pressed against his side. "Is that . . . cologne you're wearing?"

"Cologne?" I righted myself and sniffed my shirt. A hint of Mitch's day-old cologne clung to the fabric. Understanding dawned. "No, I mean yes, but it's not my cologne. It probably rubbed off from Mitch."

Davin stopped, his foot hanging midair over the next step. "Mitch's cologne rubbed off on you?"

"Yeah, we went to his house last night. I spent the night there, and he gave me a hug this morning. Some of his cologne must have rubbed off on me."

Davin's eyes flashed as his jaw locked. "You spent the night at Mitch's?"

"Yeah, after the bar we went to his house. Sean set us home with a jug of beer, so we . . ." My words trailed off as a dark expression grew on Davin's face.

It was only then I heard how my words sounded. I wanted to smack my forehead. *Oh my God! He thinks I slept with Mitch!* I shook my head and rushed to explain. "I mean I slept there, but I didn't—"

"Meghan! Come on! We know you have to go soon so come sit with us!" Sara waved from her chair. Everyone else was piled around the circle of seats waiting for me.

I turned to finish explaining to Davin what *really* happened last night, but he suddenly stood five feet away.

I reached for him, but he took another step back. His jaw was locked so tight now, the muscle ticked. "I should get going. I promised Sergeant Rose that . . ."

My stomach sank. I stepped forward, wanting to explain he had it all wrong, but in a blurred move, he disappeared.

The air rustled around me as a pit formed in my stomach.

"Where did Davin go?" Dorothy came down the stairwell. She looked left and right. "He didn't stay? But he seemed so happy that you were coming back into the Sanctum this morning."

I swallowed tightly as my gut churned.

Of course, he didn't stay. He thinks I slept with Mitch. He actually thinks I'd do that after everything that's happened between us!

But then I replayed in my mind what I'd said to him. *"Yeah, after the bar we went to his house."* And I smelled like Mitch. *"I spent the night there, and he gave me a hug this morning. Some of his cologne must have rubbed off on me."*

This time, I did smack my hand to my forehead. *Seriously, Meghan! Could you make a bigger mess of things?*

A stone settled in my stomach at how hurt I would be if I were Davin. Taking a deep breath, I followed Dorothy up the stairs. *I just need to talk to him. Once I explain to him that he has it wrong, then everything will be fine.*

Despite that rational thought, I wrung my hands.

17 – THE WHITE HOUSE

I tried calling Davin twice after I left the Sanctum. Both times, Sergeant Rose answered and said he wasn't in his cell.

"Can you tell him I called and ask him to call me?"

"Will do, Meghan. Have a safe trip."

We hung up. I fingered the smooth screen on my phone. I was currently in my apartment, sitting on the couch in my living room with my packed bags at my feet. In an hour, Cate would be picking me up at the airport.

I'd have to leave soon.

Everything will be fine. I just need to explain to him that I would never betray him like that.

Taking a deep breath, I tapped my phone again. There was another call I needed to make before I left.

I hesitantly tapped in the number for my parents. I didn't want to, but Davin was probably right. They deserved to know what had happened to me. Besides, sitting on my couch while mulling over what had happened between Davin and me wasn't helping.

My dad answered on the first ring. "Hello. Forester

residence."

He was the only person I knew who answered phones like that. It was so old-fashioned yet still made me smile. "Hi, Dad. It's me."

"Well, hi there, kiddo. How are you?"

He was also the only person who still referred to me as if I was three years old versus twenty-three years old. "I'm okay, but I thought I should call you and Mom and let you know what's been going on."

"Something's going on?"

Guilt followed me as I leaned back and pulled my knees up. "You could say that. I spent the last week or so living in the Inner Sanctum at the Compound."

"You were *living* in the Inner Sanctum?"

"Yes, but I'm fine now."

His voice dropped. "Meghan, what happened?"

Since my dad worked for Cantaleve Steel, the company that had built all of the Compounds, he'd know exactly what the Inner Sanctum was. Guilt bit me harder, like an alligator that clamped onto its prey and refused to let go. *Davin was right. I should have called sooner.*

I explained my exposure, subsequent illness, and release from the Sanctum as succinctly as possible. When finished, I was so thankful it was my dad I spoke to. I could only image the icy responses that would be emanating from my mother.

"Will you let Mom know too?"

"Yes, of course, but . . . why didn't you tell us sooner? Why did nobody alert us?"

Because I don't have an emergency contact number in my file with the MRI. Funny how when I'd reached that part of my application I'd glossed over it. I would have put Jeremy on there if he'd been alive. It had never occurred to me to list my parents.

"Um . . . I don't know, but I'm fine now, so it's okay."

"Are you sure? You don't have any lingering side effects?"

"Nope. None. Trust me, the MRI ran vigorous tests before they released me."

A heavy pause followed. "I wish we'd been told sooner."

I swallowed thickly. "Yeah, I should have called. I'm sorry." I then summed up that I was leaving for Washington D.C. which launched into a dozen more questions.

I answered each one honestly if haltingly. My dad and I had never spoken so candidly before, but by the time we hung up, with him promising to also fill in my mother, I couldn't help but wonder if Davin was right.

My dad really does love me, even if he has a hard time showing it.

Biting my lip, I sat on my couch for a few minutes, mulling over all that had transpired in the last twenty-four hours.

SIX HOURS LATER, we landed in Washington D.C. It was only Cate, me, and the pilots on the plane. The team that Cate had put together was busy working behind the scenes. She'd managed to rally teams in every state in the lower forty-eight. They were currently going door-to-door doing their best to educate the public about the vaccine.

I bit my lip as we taxied to a stop on the runway. My phone sat on my lap. Still no calls from Davin.

Hot summer air swirled around the tarmac as Dr. Hutchinson and I stepped out of the plane. I expected the airport to be empty, so what we encountered instead was a complete surprise.

A small crowd gathered just off the runway. Gates blocked them from stepping onto the tarmac. At least half a dozen police officers stood alongside the gate, bordering it.

Protecting it.

When the people in the crowd saw us, they started yelling, booing, and screaming at us to leave.

"What the . . ." I cleared my throat and clung to the plane's railing as we descended the stairs. "What's going on?"

Bright, late afternoon sunlight streamed overhead as the wind picked up. Cate tucked a strand of short blond hair behind her ear. "Word must have spread of what we're trying to achieve. My guess is that crowd," she nodded toward them, "doesn't want the Kazzies freed."

The angry yells and hisses continued. The group had to be at least fifty people. The sight made my stomach roll. They only stood a dozen yards away. One stepped forward. A police officer pushed him back, but it didn't stop his yell.

"Hey, Kazzie lovers! What are you trying to do? Get us all killed? Those animals belong exactly where they are, locked up and kept away from the rest of us!"

The guy had to be middle-aged. Anger lines tightened his face, making him appear ugly and hostile.

I clutched my laptop bag tightly to my side as a woman threw something at us. It fell a few feet short, but it still exploded upon impact. Red looking sauce splattered the ground. A few splashes reached my pants.

A police officer reached for her.

"Damn, Kazzie lovers!" she screamed. "If you love those virus infected scum so much then why don't you go live with them?"

I hastily stepped back as something else was thrown. Another police officer tried to intervene, but the object already sailed toward us. It landed a few feet short. More sauce.

The homemade food bombs didn't stop the anger that ignited in me.

"Those Kazzies are the reason we have a vaccine!" The

statement bubbled out of me before I could stop it.

It was a mistake to engage them. It only seemed to rile them more. More jeers and obscenities followed. Another bomb of what I guessed was a mixture of tomato sauce and vinegar from the smell of it was thrown.

A dark sedan flew around a corner onto the tarmac at the end of the runway.

Dr. Hutchinson gripped my arm and pulled me back. "Don't talk to them, Meghan. You're wasting your breath. They don't understand that the Kazzies aren't a threat to them. They're unaware of the complexities of the virus and efficacy of the vaccine."

The sedan pulled to an abrupt stop only yards away, squealing on the pavement. With it came the smell of burnt rubber. The driver stepped out and hurried to our side.

"I'm so sorry I'm late. Protesters were blocking the highway. It took me the last thirty minutes to get around them."

"That's quite all right." Dr. Hutchinson pushed her dark rimmed glasses up her nose as yells continued from the crowd. "But I think we best be on our way and in a hurry."

"Yes, ma'am." He grabbed our bags.

Cate and I slid into the open doors just as another food bomb landed on the pavement behind us. Its smell flooded my senses. The vinegar was extremely potent in that one.

The pilot taxied the plane to the end of the runway as we drove off. The crowd didn't seem to be targeting the plane, just us.

I breathed a sigh of relief at that. There were only a few jets that the MRI kept well maintained for air travel. If something happened to our plane, I'd either be stuck in Washington D.C. or South Dakota—whichever city I happened to be in when the incident occurred.

I leaned back in my seat as the driver sped away from the runway. He pulled onto the road that exited the airport and accelerated. Another crowd of protestors outside of the airport hurled objects at our retreating vehicle. The road whizzed by as the driver expertly navigated the streets.

Both Dr. Hutchinson and I sat tensed in the back. It seemed the driver was avoiding the interstates and highways. We stuck to the smaller roads in mostly abandoned neighborhoods. However, I did know one thing. We weren't going to our usual hotel.

"Where are we going?" Dr. Hutchinson leaned forward. A ring of authority filled her tone.

"The White House, ma'am."

My eyes widened as Cate's shoulders tensed.

"The White House?" Cate repeated. "I thought we were staying at the hotel until we were due to see the president?"

The driver swerved around a large pothole in the road. "The president has changed your plans I'm afraid. We've had an influx of border crossers into Maryland ever since the announcement was made to free the Kazzies. Protests have been going on all week."

"Border crossers?" I couldn't believe what I was hearing. Crossing state borders was illegal. Nobody was stupid enough to do it out in the open. "Why haven't they been arrested?"

"You can thank Senator Douglas for that. He's rallied a new temporary law that says those coming to D.C. to practice their freedom of speech rights have the ability to cross borders if they keep their protests peaceful."

My eyes bulged. "Does he call that crowd back at the airport peaceful?"

"Um . . . I can't answer for him, ma'am." His eyes met

mine in the rearview mirror. It was only then I realized how young he was. He couldn't be much older than me.

"Why haven't those protestors been arrested?" Cate demanded. "They're hardly peaceful."

It seemed Cate had the same thoughts as me.

"Probably because most of the police force is around the White House right now. The entire grounds have been ringed with angry mobs since the beginning of the week. A lot of the American public is not happy about the Kazzies being freed."

A lot of the American public? Or naïve protestors stirred up by Senator Douglas?

My stomach sank as we crested a hill. It didn't matter what fueled their fire. They were still voters.

The White House came into view. The large colonial style mansion stood proud and promising, in ever-present defiance of the battles that had been waged on this soil.

And just as the driver said, crowds lined the perimeter grounds. It was only as we drove closer and those crowds pressed around our car that fear truly grew in me.

We'd come to Washington D.C. to rally the public in our support.

It had never occurred to me that we'd have to fight the public to give the Kazzies a chance at total freedom.

IT WAS A harrowing few minutes before the police force was able to admit us through the tall gates that surrounded the grounds. When they finally did, the crowds fell back but angry yells could still be heard through the windows. Dr. Hutchinson seemed as shaken as me. I didn't think either of us had known what we were getting into.

"Are we staying here versus the hotel because of the protestors?" Her voice shook slightly before she cleared her throat.

"Yes, ma'am." The driver pulled into a parking spot and shut the motor off. "The police were concerned with the limited security options at the hotel. President Morgan said you were to be escorted here. Rooms have been readied for you."

My heart hammered in my chest. *I'm staying at the White House? The actual White House? And unruly crowds are running around the city as we speak?*

It felt like history was repeating itself. That chaos was once again ensuing. The same had happened after the First Wave. Everyone was scared. Nobody had any idea what we were dealing with, and people were dying. Mobs and unruly crowds had formed then too.

I grabbed my laptop bag as I opened my door. "So they know that we're here to appeal the decision that was made about the reservation?"

The driver turned to face us. "That's right. They want to stop any further talks of freeing the Kazzies."

Shallow breaths made my chest rise and fall. Anger and fear coursed through me at the same time. *How did we not know this was happening?*

"Why hasn't this been covered on the news?" Dr. Hutchinson demanded.

"The president is trying to keep the protests hushed. She's concerned that it could start a movement to stop the progression toward rebuilding our society. There's a lot of fear out there about the Kazzies. I'm sure you can understand that."

No, I couldn't understand that. As someone who'd been vaccinated and exposed to the virus and lived to tell about it, I knew just how effective the vaccine was. There was truly no reason to be afraid.

But the public didn't know that.

"We need to educate them more." I gripped Cate's hand as we stood by the trunk while the driver lifted our bags. "They're afraid because they don't know any better. The MRI has done such a good job at keeping the public in the dark about the virus that it's now working against us. We need to change that."

Cate's mouth tightened. "We'll need to discuss a few things with the president first and assess how bad this situation is. I'm afraid our agenda has just changed. Until we can convince the public that the Kazzies are not a threat to them, we won't stand a snowball's chance in hell at defeating Reservation 1."

We were ushered into the White House through a simple side door. Inside, we followed two men. I tried to look around and take in what I was experiencing, but my mind had focused on one thing and one thing only.

The public doesn't want the Kazzies freed. They want them to stay prisoners in the Compound.

The men walked briskly through a maze of wide hallways. Oriental rugs covered the floor. Antique canvas paintings hung on the wall. Several past presidents smiled down at us from the portraits we passed.

When we reached a broad staircase, they stopped. A different man and woman, both housekeepers I presumed from what they wore, greeted us.

"Dr. Hutchinson and Dr. Forester." The woman nodded. "The president will be happy to see you first thing in the morning. Until that time, she's ordered rooms readied for you. Please, follow us."

I swallowed tightly as my anxiety kicked in. Sweat erupted across my brow. We climbed the stairs and continued on down another wide hall. Armed guards lined this one. I felt their eyes on me.

My fingers sought my shirt collar and tugged.

"Your rooms are here." The woman stopped at the end of the hall and indicated two doors. It appeared Dr. Hutchinson and I had bedrooms across the hall from one another.

"Please, follow me." The man opened one door and waved Cate forward. She nodded a goodbye to me and stepped into her room.

The woman opened my door and beckoned me to follow. She smiled and smoothed her hair along the side of her head. A severe bun was tied at the nape of her neck. She appeared to be middle aged yet was trim and fit. Her uniform was clean and pressed. Assurance and efficiency oozed from her.

"My name's Molly Crane. I'll be here throughout your stay. May I unpack your belongings?" She held out her hand.

I awkwardly handed her my suitcase.

She took it and swiftly crossed the room to a large wardrobe. With quick movements, she emptied the two weeks' worth of clothes I'd packed.

Turning, she clasped her hands and addressed me again. "The supper meal is served at 7 p.m. Someone will return at that time to escort you. In your free time, feel free to wander around this wing. However, you're limited to this wing and this wing only. Is that clear?"

Her words were soft yet steel rang in her tone. I had a feeling she was a head housekeeper and was used to giving orders.

"Yes, that's fine. I'll stay in this wing." *Or in this bedroom.* My stomach fluttered at the thought of all of the personnel and guards I'd encounter in the halls.

"Thank you. You may use the phone by your bed to

contact me. There are instructions on the notepad for who to reach if you should need anything else."

I nodded mutely.

Molly turned on her heel and strode out the door. With a soft click, the door closed behind her.

For a moment, I just stood there. My head was still spinning from being back in D.C., the crowds we'd encountered at the airport, and this sudden change in travel plans.

The room they had me staying in was huge. A four-poster bed with an ornate canopy stood by one wall. The large wardrobe was directly across from it. In the corner was a TV surrounded by a couch and two chairs. The colors in the room were dark. Navy blues, dark browns, and deep reds. Everything was spotless and smelled fresh.

Kicking my shoes off, I padded silently on the thick carpet to the window. I pulled the curtain back. The large lawn in front of the White House stretched all the way to the perimeter. My breath caught when I saw the protestors lined around the distant fence.

There were more than at the airport. Many more. Hundreds of people stood outside the gates. Most had fists rising in the air. Several held large signs. This far away, I couldn't read the signs or hear what they were yelling, but I could guess.

And it wasn't pretty.

Letting the curtain fall, I spun away from the window. My heart hammered a hundred miles an hour. I loved the Kazzies more than anything, and the thought of others intending them harm . . .

A scratch filled the back of my mind. I sighed. Sara had no doubt picked up on my sudden and explosive reaction. I closed my eyes and imagined opening our mental door.

Our connection clicked.

Hi, I said. *Sorry, I'm fine.*

Are you sure? A wave of such intense anger and protectiveness surged through me. I thought something happened.

No, nothing happened. Not really. Things are just worse than I thought they would be.

Worse? What do you mean, worse?

I wanted to smack myself. Sara didn't need to worry about what was going on here. She wasn't supposed to know about it. The president didn't want this hateful epidemic spreading.

Nothing. Really, it's nothing. There are just a few protestors, but it's not a big deal.

Protestors? She paused. *I watch the news every morning, and I haven't seen anything about protestors.*

Exactly. There are so few of them, ANN isn't bothering to cover it. I ran a hand through my hair. I hated lying to her, but she had enough stresses right now. By the end of the summer, she could be moving to the reservation, and Sophie too.

How's Sophie?

This time Sara sighed. *Fine. I guess. She's still really quiet about being moved. I think all of us, as excited as we are to get out of here, are a little nervous too. There's . . . what? 1200 Kazzies in the nation? That means we'll be meeting 1,193 new neighbors. And considering how some of us look, we'll probably look like a giant freak show.*

I knew she was trying to lighten the mood, to alleviate her own worries about the potential change, but I still heard the catch in her voice.

We're doing everything we can so you never have to be locked away on a reservation. You deserve to live like everyone else. Nobody should live in a cage.

I felt her nod. *So when do you meet the president?*

Tomorrow.

And the hotel? Did you get another good room?

Oh, right. There was a slight change of plan. We're staying at the White House.

The White House? Her screech made me wince. *What the heck. Are you serious?*

I padded to the window again and peeked out. The protestors hadn't left. *Very serious.*

Why? What happened to the hotel?

Nothing. The president thought we'd be more comfortable here. It wasn't a complete lie. The president *did* think we'd be more comfortable here, but that was because our safety wasn't in jeopardy.

Far out. So how's your anxiety? No panic attacks?

No, thankfully. I paused. *How's Davin?*

I'm not entirely sure. He's been really quiet since you left. He hasn't said much to anyone.

I swallowed thickly. *Has he been back to his cell?*

His cell? I dunno. Why do you ask?

No reason. I knew I said it too quickly. Curiosity strummed from Sara's end, so I rushed to say, *I should probably get going. I think I'll check out this wing. I was told I could wander around it but had to stay within certain boundaries.*

I felt Sara nodding. *Okay, yeah. I think it should be an unspoken rule that whenever one stays at the White House that no excuses are needed when one wants to go and explore. In fact, exploration of the White House should be most definitely encouraged.*

Smiling, I pushed my hair over my shoulders. It was getting so long it was halfway down my back. *Agreed.*

We closed down our connection. Pulling my phone from my bag, I checked my messages. Nothing. *Maybe he hasn't received my messages yet.*

I peeked out the window again. It was only early evening so the sun wasn't high, but it had still been incredibly hot when we'd arrived at the airport. Bright green leaves on the surrounding trees fluttered in the breeze. I eyed the protestors again. They had to be hot standing under the sun with no shade.

With a decisive turn, I let the curtain fall. I definitely planned to do some exploring, but it wouldn't be within the White House walls.

IT TOOK SOME finagling, but I was finally able to find a guard who agreed to escort me to the outer door. I knew Dr. Hutchinson said not to engage the protestors, but until we understood why they were so angry, there wasn't much hope in subduing that anger. Or so I told myself.

The summer breeze rolled across my cheeks when I stepped outside. I wore pants and a short sleeved shirt. My hair fluttered around my upper arms. With a deft movement, I pulled it into a ponytail.

"You'll need to come back to this door to be readmitted." The guard stood in the door frame. He was young. Most of the staff here seemed to be around my age. I wondered if that was because the former staff had been killed in the First Wave.

"I've alerted security that you requested a short walk outside. They'll have eyes on you, however, I strongly suggest you stay away from the gates."

I swallowed uneasily. "Of course."

His cool green eyes narrowed. Before he could change his mind about leaving me unescorted on the grounds, I turned away and jogged down the steps.

"I'll be back within the hour. I promise," I called over my shoulder.

I dashed out of his view before he could reply.

I tried to act like I wasn't walking anywhere in particular, but as the distance grew between me and the White House door, I hurried my pace. The protestors became visible. I could hear their shouts now. They were no longer a hazy murmur in the distance.

Chants of, "Lock 'em up! And keep it shut!" was one of the popular ones.

So was, "The virus kills, no more fall ill!" also rang in the background.

As I strode closer to the gate, I was able to see the crowd more clearly. It seemed that the majority were men, but at least thirty percent were women. Their angry chants and glazed eyes alighted on me as I drew within their vicinity.

My gaze darted around the people gathered here. At least nothing was thrown at me. Not yet, anyways.

A few tried to engage me. Not in actual discussion but in hate spewed accusations. I wasn't surprised that they recognized me. My face had been flashed across the news. The MRI had done a good job at making me the poster child for the vaccine.

"Hey, Kazzie lover!" one man yelled. "Why don't you and your freaks both go live on the reservation? If you love them so much, why not stay with them?"

I hurried past him and made sure to keep my distance. Police officers lined the fence, but the protestors still outnumbered them. I hated to think what would happen if this mob grew out of control.

As I approached the end of the crowd, my eyes fell on a young woman. She stood near a man and woman, but she didn't appear to be yelling or jeering. Instead, a look of anxiety was plastered on her face, the same way a look of horror flashed across everyone's eyes when they knew a bomb was about to drop.

She caught me watching her. For a moment, our gazes locked. An understanding dawned in me at the frightened and horrified expression I saw there. *She doesn't want to be here. She wants no part of what's taking place.*

A police officer yelled at the man and woman who stood at her side. They'd been yelling and screaming at me since I came into view. I kept my focus away from them and sought the girl again.

When she found me watching her, she backed away. With a turn, she hurried out of the crowd and pushed her way to the side. When she emerged on the sidewalk, I ran to catch up with her even though the fence still separated us.

Her hands stayed stuffed in her pockets. Thankfully, the rest of the unruly crowd stayed where they were. More guards had appeared on the lawn, heading my way. The crowd had turned their attention on them. I could only guess those guards were coming to retrieve me.

I didn't have much time.

"Wait!" I yelled to the girl. She stood on the other side of the fence, only yards away. She had brown hair like me, but it was shorter. Fear coated her expression when she turned to face me.

"I shouldn't be talking to you." Her voice was small and hesitant.

I approached the fence and wrapped my hands around it. The metal spindles were black and felt cool. "Why shouldn't you be talking to me?"

"Because you're that researcher that wants the Kazzies free. My parents would kill me if they knew I was talking to you." Her eyes alighted back to the crowd. I guessed the man and woman she'd stood beside were her parents. However, they were so engrossed in yelling at the approaching guards, they didn't seem to know their daughter was missing.

"Please." I gripped the fence tightly. "Tell me why they're so angry. Tell me why they don't want the Kazzies free."

"Because they're carriers." She said the words as if it should have been obvious.

"Yes, but we've all be vaccinated. None of us will catch the virus."

"You don't know that." While she didn't seem infused with the hate that coursed through her parents, I still caught the fear in her tone.

They really don't know. They don't understand how effective this vaccine is.

My heart broke at how much we still needed to do. We'd never sway the public to our side if the majority thought they'd still die, even after being vaccinated.

"I *do* know that. I helped develop the vaccine. I've been exposed to the virus, just like hundreds of other researchers have been, and none of us have died from the virus. It's safe. The Kazzies are not people we need to fear."

Her gaze shifted to her parents again.

Her parents no longer seemed so caught up in yelling and chanting with the crowd. They were looking around. Most likely for their daughter.

"I need to go."

"Please!" I gripped the fence tighter. "Please go home with your parents and explain to them that the Kazzies are nothing to be afraid of. They're people, just like you and me. Some may look different from us, but they're still the same people that they were before they caught the virus. And it's not their fault they survived."

She swallowed sharply.

I couldn't tell if anything I'd said had resonated with her or not. I opened my mouth to tell her more about the vaccine, but she darted away. She reappeared a moment later within the crowd, back at her parents' side.

With slumped shoulders, I turned away from the crowd. The guards were getting closer. I knew I needed to return before Dr. Hutchinson caught wind of what I was doing. I felt one hundred percent certain she wouldn't approve.

I turned away from the gate just as a black sedan rounded a turn in the distance. It was driving toward the White House and slowed as it approached the crowds. Since it was the telltale black and had tinted windows, I knew whoever rode in it was affiliated with the government.

It slowed as it pulled closer.

I meant to turn and hurry back to the White House, but something made me pause. It was strange, I had no idea why, but I felt like I was being watched. Raising a hand to shield my eyes from the sun, I peered closer at the vehicle. It wasn't far away now, maybe twenty yards.

The back window cracked. It rolled down as the vehicle grew closer. My eyes widened as an image of something being thrown at me flashed through my mind, but just as quickly, I told myself I was being paranoid. It was a government vehicle. Whoever rode in it was on our side, not the crowd's.

A face appeared through the window just as the window began to roll back up. When the vehicle drove directly in front of me, it was only yards away. Gray, narrowed eyes stared at me for a brief second before the window fully closed, sealing the occupant's image inside.

My heart hammered.

Those eyes. I'd seen those eyes before. *No, it can't be!*

But he worked in Washington D.C. now. That was the last I'd heard about where he went.

I stared after the retreating sedan as a stone sank in my stomach. My chest rose and fell quickly with my rapid breathing. The sunshine continued to beat down on me as sweat coated my brow.

I knew without a doubt I'd just seen Dr. Roberts.

IT WAS HARD to focus for the rest of the day. I still hadn't heard from Davin, but after calling and speaking with his evening guard, I was informed that Davin had received my earlier messages. However, he was once again out of his cell.

I tried to shove down the feeling that Davin was avoiding me. He'd know the only way for me to reach him would be if he stayed by his phone. He was obviously upset.

Really upset. *And yet, this is what he claimed he wanted. For me to move on with Mitch.* It only solidified in my mind that he *didn't* want me with anyone else.

"Would you like me to tell him you called?" The guard seemed curious. I'm sure having a MRI scientist desperately trying to reach a Kazzie wasn't normal.

"No, that's fine."

We hung up, and I knew I wouldn't be able to keep calling. While the guards knew Davin and I were friendly, I'd never been in the situation in which Davin ignored me. That would definitely raise eyebrows. It wasn't wise to bring that kind of attention to our relationship.

I'll have to wait for him to contact me.

I tapped my phone and bit my lip. It had to be close to nine at night when I stepped out of my room and walked across the hall. We'd finished supper an hour ago, but we hadn't been able to speak freely due to the housekeepers. I could only hope Dr. Hutchinson was still awake.

I knocked softly on her door.

The sound of muted footsteps on the other side followed. The door opened with a flourish. I was relieved to see her still dressed in daytime clothes.

"Meghan." She opened the door wider. "Come in."

I stepped into her suite. It was similar to mine. It held a huge bed, large wardrobe, and a comfortable seating area around a cold fireplace. The moon was visible through her window as stars peeked through. A hazy red sky lined the western horizon. Being the height of summer, the sun had just set.

"Is everything all right?" she asked.

I closed the door behind me. "Yeah, I just wanted to talk to you about what I saw today."

She crossed her arms. "Do you mean the protestors? I heard that you ventured outside to talk to them."

So much for keeping that a secret. "Yes, I did, but that's not what I'm referring to."

She waved me toward the empty chairs. We both sat, me perched on the edge of mine while she leaned back and crossed her legs.

"I saw Dr. Roberts."

Her eyes widened. "Where?"

"He drove by when I was outside. I didn't get a good look at him, but I'm sure it was him." I pictured the way his sedan slowed when he passed me. I shuddered. He'd probably told his driver to slow down when he recognized me.

Cate steepled her hands in front of her face. "There have been a few rumors that he'll be in charge of Reservation 1."

My heart stopped. "What?"

Cate nodded grimly. "I know. I couldn't believe it either,

but it's not set in stone. There's no guarantee those rumors are correct."

I jumped to standing and paced in front of the fireplace. "Cate, he *can't* be in charge of the reservation. He abuses the Kazzies! How can a man like that be put in charge of their care?"

"I know. I know. Please, calm down. There have been no definitive decisions yet on the managerial structure of the reservation. It could simply all be rumors and rumors only."

I continued to pace. It once again came to mind that Dr. Roberts' record was clean. *Nobody knows how he treated the Kazzies.* The thought of Dr. Roberts being anywhere near my friends again made a burning resentment and anger fire through me. It felt like heat coated my veins. He *couldn't* be allowed into that reservation.

"That only makes it more imperative that we don't fail." I continued pacing. "Someone like that can never be allowed near them again."

Cate stood and stopped my movements. She placed her hands on my shoulders. Her cool eyes held steady as she peered into mine. "We'll stop the reservation, Meghan. I know we can."

OUR MEETING WITH the president was scheduled for after breakfast the next day. After my panic last night at the thought of Dr. Roberts on Reservation 1, I'd pulled myself back together. If we wanted to convince the president to veto the reservation bill, we'd need cool rationale and sound science to do it.

Dr. Hutchinson came to my room first thing in the morning. She was all business-like which I appreciated. Between the two of us, I definitely had a higher emotional investment in the Kazzies. Her cool and calm manner balanced my passion and determination.

It was probably why we made such a great team.

"Do you have your data in order?" She flipped through the slides in our presentation on my laptop. We'd start with hard data and facts. Only then would we bring in the emotional aspects. The backstories of who the Kazzies were. They were people. Each had a face. A name. A story to go along with their infection. They weren't a number. They weren't statistics. They were innocent people who'd been given a grossly unfair hand in life. And even though they appeared different, they were still just as human as the rest of us, and they deserved to be treated as such.

I tucked a strand of hair behind my ear. I wore a business suit. It was the charcoal gray two-piece that I'd worn for my first day at the Compound over ten months ago. In a way, it was a good luck charm.

Dr. Hutchinson flipped through the slides for a second time. "All right, to recap, I'll talk about the effectiveness of the vaccine first. I have all of the latest data. Exposures, side effects, and percentages of reactions to the vaccine. That information will be important to convey."

I studied the slides. "And I'll go into details about each Kazzie in Washington and South Dakota. Their names, their pictures, where they grew up, their hopes and dreams before the First Wave hit, and . . ."

We discussed our strategy again and rehearsed our presentation one final time. It was similar to the presentation we gave at the Summit, only now, it was the only thing that stood between the Kazzies being free or spending their lives behind a fence.

When the time finally came for us to meet the president, I

wasn't as nervous as I thought I'd be. We were prepared. We had sound data and science on our side. Any logical person would see that our argument for the Kazzies' freedom was not only a safe choice but the fair choice.

It seemed inevitable we'd walk out of the meeting smiling and triumphant.

Two guards led us out of our wing to the Oval Office. It was surreal to march down the stairs and through corridors I'd only heard of but had never seen.

When we entered the Oval Office, the president sat behind her desk. She was on the phone and waved us to a couch. With a flick of her hand, she dismissed the guards.

Dr. Hutchinson and I waited while she finished her conversation. My heart hammered. Only a few yards away was the president.

She wore a black business suit and silk shirt underneath. Her short hair had streaks of gray. Crow's feet lined her eyes. Everything about her exuded confidence and authority. It was hard to not feel intimidated.

If only Jeremy was alive. He'd love to hear about this.

The president set the phone in the cradle and stood. "Excuse me for being in the midst of a call."

She came around the desk and held out her hand. Cate shook it first. "Madam President."

I smiled meekly since I was sure my palm was embarrassingly sweaty. I had the ridiculous urge to curtsy. "Madam President."

The president waved us to the couch. "I hear you have some information for me about the reservation." She sat opposite from us and folded her hands. "I'm all yours for the next twenty minutes."

Cate and I exchanged a look that conveyed, *okay, this is it, let's not blow it.*

True to what we rehearsed, Cate swung the laptop around and brought up our slides. She launched into the science and background of the vaccine's effectiveness. In the way that only she could portray, she made it easy to understand and follow for someone who did not have a scientific background.

When it was my turn, she shifted the laptop in my direction. With shaking hands, I took a deep breath and began recanting the names and details of the Kazzies in South Dakota and Washington. I felt my voice become more animated, more impassioned as my rehearsed speech progressed. I cared so much for the Kazzies. I was sure that was evident in my tone.

As our rehearsed presentation came to an end, the president's brow furrowed as she leaned back in her seat.

"You're suggesting that we scrap the reservation all together and allow the Kazzies to return to the public, living as each of us does today?"

"Yes." I answered before Dr. Hutchinson could. "There's no reason to keep them contained. They're not a threat to us."

The president nodded. "You're right. They're not a threat. You know that, I know that, the CDC knows that, the MRI and MRRA know that, but *they* don't know that." She waved her hand to the large window. In the distance, the protestors could be seen. Their numbers hadn't diminished. If anything, they'd grown. I wondered if they'd even slept. Or perhaps they protested in shifts. I had no idea how organized they were.

"So we convince them." Cate stated the obvious. "We educate them more about the virus and the vaccine. With time, they'll understand."

"Yes, with time, they may." The president's tone remained skeptical. "But you have to understand that it's not that simple. There are many state representatives who also oppose moving the Kazzies out of the Compounds. And with this many protestors fueling the fire, I fear the riots that may break out if we deviate from our current plan. There's enough volatility right now as it is. I don't want to add fuel to the fire."

"So give us a chance to change their mind." My voice rose in desperation. "If we can educate them further, the representatives can reconvene and vote again."

The president sighed. "It's not that simple."

"Why not?" I demanded.

Cate gave me a sharp look.

The president continued. "Construction is already underway at the reservation. Most of the public has come to terms with this huge change. Obviously," she waved toward the window, "not all of them, but to change course this quickly with the reservation deadline looming isn't wise."

My mouth turned dry. "Are . . ." I cleared my throat. "Are you saying you're still going to move them to the reservation? No matter what?"

The president's expression turned regretful. "Please understand that I heard every word you said. It did not fall on deaf ears. But at this time, in our country's current state, I cannot veto a decision that was hard enough for our representatives to make. I am doing my best to maintain the peace and keep order. If the protests grow, if this fear mentality isn't kept in check, the Kazzies may be returned to the Compounds until future notice."

Return to the Compounds! That's moving backwards! "No! They need to be set free! You can't keep them in the Compounds."

Dr. Hutchinson put her hand on my knee. "We understand. You have a lot to consider right now, and we appreciate the time you've given us. Perhaps to help facilitate a successful transition to the reservation, Dr. Forester and I can begin an education campaign to better alleviate fears that the public and protestors are having."

The president nodded. "That would be helpful. I can have my staff assist you in whatever you need."

But that doesn't change their fate! They'll still be prisoners!

With that, the president stood and extended her hand. She and Cate seemed oblivious to my dropped mouth and paralyzed response.

"Thank you for what you're doing, and thank you for your contributions." The president smiled at Cate. "I know that you both played a significant role in the vaccine's development."

Cate shook the president's hand and said words that I didn't hear. When it was my turn to shake her hand, I stood on wooden-like legs and forced a smile. My mind still reeled from what our meeting conveyed.

It was only when the president turned to leave that I snapped out of my trance. "Madam President, I'm sorry but one more question."

"Yes?" She cocked an eyebrow.

A flash of gray eyes filled my mind. My voice shook when I spoke. "Has it been decided who will be the Director at Reservation 1?"

"No, not yet. That's still in discussion." With that, she left the room as aides ushered forward to escort us.

As Cate and I followed them down the hall, only one thing dominated my thoughts. The Kazzies were not going to be free. They'd be moved to the reservation and that was only *if* the public's fear didn't grow. I trailed my hand along the wall to steady myself.

I've failed.

I've failed to set my friends free. And now I have to tell them.

18 - CONFESSION

After we left the president's office, my mind filled with fog. Cate's words from our meeting haunted me as we sailed down the hall. She'd so willingly accepted moving the Kazzies to the reservation. My frown deepened as I gave her a sideways glance. Her expression remained stoic.

How can I tell Sara, Davin, Sophie, Sage, and all of the other Kazzies that I failed them? That they'll have to live on the reservation? And that's only if peace continues? Trying to tell them they'd have to stay in the Compound, and that the reservation was no longer an option due to the angry public made me physically nauseous.

It's exactly what Davin would expect.

I imagined their devastated reactions and grim acceptances that once again they'd be subjected to the government's whim.

The aide glanced over his shoulder as we neared our rooms. "The MRI plane will arrive shortly to pick you up."

I almost stumbled. *In other words, they're kicking us out of the White House.* I wasn't surprised. We'd only come to D.C. to meet the president. Now that our meeting was over, there was

221

no reason for us to stay.

In the hallway outside of our bedrooms, they left us. Cate gripped my arm before I could enter my room. It was then the accusing words tumbled out.

"Are you really giving up on them?" My tone sounded as devastated as I felt.

Cate shot a sideways glance at the guards down the hall and pulled me closer to the window. In a hushed tone, she said, "Of course not, but I know when it's time to back-off and regroup. All going well, they'll go to the reservation and not stay in the Compounds." She ran a hand through her hair. "Honestly, at this point, I don't see a way around the reservation. As long as the public stays content, at least they'll be out of the Compounds. Consider it a transition point before we find a way to set them free. And until we can convince the majority of the public to support us, scientific facts don't matter if they're too afraid."

"That's why you offered to educate the public? It's not actually to facilitate a smooth transition to the reservation, but to ultimately sway the public to our side by eradicating that fear?"

"Yes. Public education *will* help a smooth transition happen, but my end game is the bigger picture. To ultimately free them, we need votes. And to get votes, the public needs to trust what we're saying. Ultimately, until those votes are in our favor, we're fighting a losing battle."

Relief that she *hadn't* caved was followed by admiration as a grin spread across my face. "We'll need to organize a national campaign. The public needs to know and understand that the vaccine is safe."

Dr. Hutchinson pushed her dark rimmed glasses up her nose. "Yes, we'll also need to rally as many state representatives as we can. I personally know a few of them. We'll start there."

I twisted the handle on my door. "I'll get packed."

Cate nodded. "We'll go straight to the airport. From there, we'll fly to Seattle."

"Seattle?"

"I need you by my side, Meghan. It's no secret that I want you to be the Director of Compounds 10 and 11 one day. This is the perfect opportunity for you to work at my side, see how I manage Compounds, while we fight this new law."

I balked. "But we have a vaccine now. Won't the Compounds cease to exist?" I'd heard rumors of Dr. Hutchinson grooming me for her position, and my lab group loved to tease me about it, but I never dreamed anything would come of it. Even if the Kazzies were returned to the Compounds, for political reasons, it wouldn't be the same as before.

Cate shook her head. "Our labs are state-of-the-art. The Inner Sanctums may close, but our labs won't. You're not out of a job quite yet."

Her humorous jab caught me by surprise. She merely winked and pushed her door open and sailed inside. I was left standing in the hallway with her words swirling through my mind.

Grooming me to be the Director at Compounds 10 and 11? Had she really said that?

I pictured Davin. In South Dakota. I knew he'd never leave our state even if he did gain his freedom.

My hand shook when I opened my door.

OUR FLIGHT TO Seattle was long. It took six hours by the time we left D.C. I was glad to be airborne. The protestors had been at the airport again, throwing their tomato sauce/vinegar bombs and yelling rude and hateful comments. The police tried to control them, but at times, I feared they'd storm the runway.

I still hadn't talked to Sara, only because I wanted to be alone to have time to discuss it with her when we connected. I also hadn't heard from Davin. I checked my phone frequently, hoping to see a missed call from him. Nothing.

Biting my lip, I tried to not let the worry consume me, yet I kept seeing it from his perspective. I'd be incredibly hurt too if I thought he slept with someone else. While we weren't an official couple, we both had feelings for each other and we'd made that clear. And everything that we'd been through during the past year together . . .

I just need to talk to him and explain.

Puffy looking clouds skimmed the jet's wings as we descended into Seattle. Once below the clouds, the sky became a vast gray ceiling. Rain splattered the windows, and turbulence jostled me in my seat.

Dr. Hutchinson's eyes lit up when the Space Needle appeared. Even though broken windows were evident in the spire, it was still impressive looking. "Have you ever been to Seattle, Meghan?"

"No, other than Washington D.C., I've never been out of the Midwest."

I clasped my hands as the wheels touched the ground, the engines screamed, and the spoilers on the wings kicked into action.

"Have you always lived here?"

"No." She grabbed her purse from under the seat in front of her. "I grew up in Spokane. That's in eastern Washington."

We slowed to a crawl as the pilots taxied us to our ride.

Thankfully, I didn't spot any protestors lining this runway, but I was still cautious when I stepped out of the plane. Clinging to the railing tightly, I clutched my laptop bag as I surveyed our surroundings.

Nothing. Nobody was around. Just the breeze, rain, and waiting vehicle.

The driver rushed out of his seat when we disembarked. He reached my side and took my bag.

"Let me help." Before I could protest, he'd also taken Cate's bag and ushered us to the car.

We slipped into the backseat as the driver and pilot loaded our bags in the back. I felt a bit spoiled with their catering. I was perfectly capable of carrying my belongings, yet I also knew Dr. Hutchinson was a well-known figure in Washington. She had celebrity status.

Warm, humid air swirled into the vehicle when the driver slid into his seat. "How was your flight, ma'am?"

"Uneventful but fine." Cate clicked her seatbelt on. "I'm sure you've heard of my colleague, Dr. Forester. She lives in South Dakota and works at Compound 26."

The driver's eyes widened. "It's a pleasure to meet you. My wife's in awe of how much you've contributed to the vaccine at such a young age. She said you're a genius."

My cheeks turned pink. "I don't know if I'm a genius." I fiddled with my shirt. "I just have a good memory."

"Meghan's an extremely intelligent and talented scientist." Dr. Hutchinson pulled her sunglasses out. The evening sun, hanging low in the western sky, blazed through the cab. "Don't let her fool you."

The driver mumbled something about how he assumed the same before turning around in his seat and peeling us out of the airport.

I expected us to venture to another hotel. I assumed that's where they'd drop me off, so when the driver pulled into the driveway of a large house an hour later, I was a bit shocked.

"I hope you don't mind staying in my guest room?" Cate asked before opening her door.

"Oh . . . um . . . no, of course not."

I stared in awe at Dr. Hutchinson's home. It was built on a hill. Seattle's stunning skyline of neglected skyscrapers was visible in the distance. The house was two stories with large windows, a peaked roofline, and a freshly painted dark blue exterior. Any freshly painted house caught my attention, since paint was not something readily found in stores.

The neighborhood appeared only half abandoned. Many of the homes were large. It was obvious which ones were still occupied—lights shone from the windows and the lawns were cared for. On the flipside, the abandoned ones had boarded-up windows and overgrown yards. It was an all too common sight in today's world.

We said goodbye to the driver and stepped into the entryway in Cate's home. Heavenly scents and soft music greeted us.

"Is that you, Mom?" a voice called from a distant room.

Cate motioned for me to drop my bags. "That's my daughter, Harper." She kicked off her shoes and said in a raised voice, "Yes, sweetheart, just me."

A second later a young woman, probably in her late teens, came bounding into the foyer. She rushed to Cate and flung her arms around her. "You weren't gone long!"

Cate hugged her back. "Thankfully, no."

When the girl saw me, she let go of her mother. "Oh, hi. Sorry, I didn't know anyone else was here."

"That's all right." I waved. "I'm Meghan."

Recognition filled the girl's face. "Meghan Forester! From South Dakota!" She nudged her mom. "How does it feel to be around someone more famous than you?"

Cate laughed. "Meghan will be staying here until we get a few things straightened out. And from the smell of it, you're cooking dinner?"

Harper nodded. "Mushroom lasagna." She shrugged sheepishly in my direction. "I'm vegetarian. Hope that's okay with you."

"Absolutely fine. Trust me, anything's better than my cooking."

Harper and Cate shared a look before they both laughed.

A blush heated my cheeks at how flippant I'd been. I was obviously tired from the flight. I was usually more guarded around people, but perhaps it was the endless energy that seemed to emit from Harper and the familiar way Cate so easily invited me into her home that loosened my inhibitions.

Harper picked up one of my bags. "Come with me. I'll show you the guest room."

AFTER A VERY delicious dinner of mushroom lasagna and a fresh salad, I retired to my room for the night. I could tell that Harper and Cate wanted to catch up. Their close bond was obvious. I knew enough about Cate's past to know that she'd lost her husband in the First Wave. Luckily, she and Harper had managed to avoid infection. I felt so grateful that Cate still had her daughter. I could only imagine how devastating it was for those who'd lost their entire family.

Once I'd showered and changed into pajamas, I sat down on the bed. The guest room consisted of a double bed and single chair in the corner. It was simple yet comfortable. Much more along the lines of what I was used to. The luxurious and spacious accommodation at the White House had been as alien to me as the deep sea creatures pulled from the bottom of the ocean. I definitely felt like I could breathe here.

Lying back on the bed, I debated how I would broach the subject of my failure with the Kazzies. Sara had tried a few times to get in touch with me today, but I'd ignored her since I knew what she was going to ask.

I mulled over what to do. After checking my phone, my spirits sank that Davin still hadn't returned my calls. *I should call him now. Even though he's ignoring me, he deserves to know what happened.* And if he ignored me again . . . *Then I guess Sara will have to tell him.*

My heart rate picked up. With shaking fingers, I pulled out my cell phone. Since his number was top of my call list all I had to do was tap two buttons.

"Hello?"

I breathed a sigh of relief that he'd answered. "Hi, Davin."

"Oh . . . Meghan." His voice sounded strained.

"How are you?"

He cleared his throat. "Fine. How are you?"

I debated what to tell him first: that I hadn't slept with Mitch or that they were still moving to the reservation. I decided to get the harder one over with first.

"Well . . ." My breath caught. "Not good. We failed. *I* failed. You're all moving to the reservation."

I waited for his response.

It never came.

"But I'm not giving up," I rushed on. "Cate and I are in Seattle. We're going to begin an education campaign and rally the public's support. You'll have to go to the reservation for a short while, but—"

"Meghan, it's okay. I expected this to happen." His tone

was quiet. "I told you. It was too hopeful to think they'd scrap that new law. They had a hard enough time deciding to let us out of the Compounds at all. It would be a miracle if they let us be completely free."

"But complete freedom is what you deserve."

"Maybe, but I know that will probably never happen."

"Of course it will! I'm not giving up! I'll—"

"Stop, please. I need you to listen to me."

My fingers shook as I held my phone to my ear.

He took a deep breath and then began talking in what sounded like a rehearsed speech. "Meghan you need to accept that my fate will probably never change. I'll most likely die in here or on the reservation. You have no idea how much I—" His voice cut off as he cleared his throat. "You have no idea how much you mean to me or how in awe I am that you've tried so hard to free me and everyone else. But you need to realize that I'll probably always be in here. I'm always going to be infected. That's a stigma I'll carry with me for the rest of my life."

"But your infection doesn't define you or any of the other Kazzies."

"It may not to you, but it does to a lot of other people. And I . . ." He again seemed to struggle to get the words out. His voice turned hoarse. "And I want you to accept that what you're fighting for will probably never happen. I need you to understand that and not kill yourself with what you're trying to do. It kills me, Meghan, to see what kind of toll this takes on you.

I squeezed my eyes tightly shut as the tears flowed. "But I *want* to fight for you!"

He cleared his throat again. Emotion made his voice thick. "And I want you to lead your own life."

Tears cascaded down my cheeks. Here it was. He was saying it again. It was just like those two weeks he ignored me before I was exposed. He was gently yet firmly telling me that he wanted me to let him go. He truly believed he'd always be imprisoned.

I somehow managed to ask through my tears, "Is that really what you want?"

"What I want . . ." His voice caught. He took a deep breath before continuing. "What I want is for you to be happy. And happiness isn't going to come for someone who's fighting a war that can't be won."

"You don't know that! Things could change!"

He snorted quietly. "I suppose anything's possible, but I'm also a realist, Meg. I've lived in this Compound for seven years. For seven *years*, I've been at the whim of the men and women who run this place. I have *Makanza*. I'm infected. I'll always be feared by the public. Maybe the reservation is the compromise and is as good as it will ever be for me. I'll have to be okay with that. If that's to be how my life plays out then fine, I'll deal with it, but what I *can't* deal with," his voice shook, "is knowing that you lose sleep over me and everyone else. That you don't eat at times because you get so worried about what will happen to us. That you're putting your life on hold to help us. *That's* what I can't live with, and I won't. I want you to enjoy your life and forget about trying to save us."

I was speechless. I couldn't believe what I was hearing.

It was happening all over again.

Davin was once again pushing me away and making it clear he wouldn't consider a life with me. Now now. Not ever if he was never free.

"Davin . . ." Tears blinded me. I glanced out the window at the dark night. My tear streaked face stared back at me in the reflection. "I can't. I *can't* stop fighting. If I stop fighting, I'll stop breathing. *Please* don't take that away from me."

He sighed heavily. "I'm so sorry. You should have never had to take on our problems." He sounded so tired and defeated.

"You have nothing to be sorry about! It's the damn virus. As soon as it took Jer's life—" My throat tightened. I did my best to compose myself so my next words were clear. "As soon as it claimed the one human who I loved more than myself, I dedicated my life to stopping it. It's the only thing that's kept me going."

"And you *have* stopped it. You discovered a vaccine that works. You've inoculated the public. Your dedication has forged a new path for our country. You did what you set out to do. I'm in awe of all that you've done."

"But all of that doesn't mean a thing if . . ." I stopped myself. I almost told him that none of it mattered if *he* couldn't be free. It was a stupid, selfish thing to say. Of course, it mattered. Davin was one of twelve hundred Kazzies. To say that none of their lives mattered simply because I couldn't be with Davin was weak and childish.

I cleared my throat. "I can't give up. Please understand that."

He took a deep breath. "I know I can't make you forget about this and create a life for yourself without our needs following you everywhere you go, but please promise me one thing?"

"What?"

"Find someone," his voice turned gruff, "to . . . love . . . on the outside. Find someone to pour all of your passion and energy into that's not going to burden you or drag you down for the rest of your life." His tone grew quieter. "I wish . . ." I heard him shake his head. "No, wishing won't do anything, not in here. Not in my world. But promise me, Meg that you won't spend too much longer on this. I know that Mitch . . ." He took a breath. "I know that Mitch cares for you and that you care for him too. You should give him a shot. You could be . . ." He cleared his throat. "You could be happy with him."

"Mitch? No, Davin, I never—"

"Meghan, stop. I want you to move on with him, but I can't hear about it. I want you to be happy, but if I hear about him with you." He groaned. "I just can't, okay?"

"But I didn't—"

"I have to go. Another call's coming through, and it's probably my mom. I need to tell her that I'm moving to the reservation and that it's going to be my new home. Bye, Meghan."

"Wait!" The desperate word bubbled out of me just as he hung up. I stared at the phone, at the blank empty screen.

I sat there, unmoving, unable to believe what he'd said. *He wants me to be with Mitch. But he doesn't really, he just wants me to find someone who's not imprisoned in hopes that I'll be happy.*

The memory of Davin's lips on mine rose to the front of my mind. I closed my eyes as tears poured down my cheeks. It was possible that kiss had been our first and last.

Sobs shook my shoulders as I fell to my side on the bed. I drew my knees up. My world felt quiet and broken. It was exactly how I felt inside.

19 – PUBLIC EDUCATION

The next six weeks became a haze of traveling, speaking, campaigning, and fighting for a cause that most times felt impossible. Fortunately, Dr. Sadowsky understood the importance of what Cate, our political team, and I were trying to achieve. He extended my leave of absence from the Compound so I didn't have to stress about missing work.

Even though Davin had requested that I stop, I couldn't. Quite simply, I couldn't leave my friends to their fates.

The president also kept her word. She gave us special passes to cross state borders and offered her staff to help organize rallies, create fundraisers, and provide support for a political world that was as foreign to me as the country I was seeing. All of that resulted in a small army sweeping the nation, doing our best to increase education and awareness.

As each week passed, the dark circles under my eyes grew more prominent. I barely slept. At times, I didn't eat. My anxiety ran rampant from the close quarters we traveled in, the public speaking, the hands I had to shake, and the bodies that constantly pressed against me, but I didn't let it stop me. Even though I was living Davin's worst fears, I persevered. It was the only way to convince the public and stop the protests.

I barely noticed when my birthday came and went in August. I was officially twenty-four, but I kept that to myself. Since I'd never told the Kazzies my birthday, none of them knew. I didn't mind that a strained conversation with my parents was the only happy birthday I received. I was too tired to care.

When the end of August finally neared, the anniversary of the First Wave loomed. September 3. Once that date hit, the Kazzies would be moved to the reservation. Our time was running out.

And while on some days, I saw hope in our endeavors, on other days it felt impossible. Still, we carried on. Until the president agreed to a public vote to free the Kazzies, they would remain prisoners on Reservation 1.

By the time September 1 dawned, Cate and I had managed to visit over half of the United States. The other teams had covered the rest of it. Our six-week long tour had come to an end.

We all agreed to reconvene and pursue our cause again in October, but right now there was something else we needed to do.

Cate and I needed to return to our home states. In two days, our Kazzies would be moved to Reservation 1.

WHEN THE TIME finally came for Cate and me to part ways, we stood facing each other on the tarmac at Sioux Falls airport. She grasped my hands firmly. "Take care of yourself, Meghan. You look exhausted."

"I will. And you better too." Neither of us had slept much during the past six weeks.

She squeezed my hands again before letting go. "At least the Director won't be Dr. Roberts. Even though the Kazzies have to move to the reservation, they'll be happier there. They won't be locked up anymore."

I nodded acceptingly. The president had called Cate last week about the reservation's new Director. He worked for the CDC in upper management and had a military background. I hadn't heard much about him, but anyone was better than Dr. Roberts.

"See you in a few weeks." Cate re-boarded the plane.

I waited on the tarmac until they lifted into the sky. Once the jet disappeared into the clouds, I breathed in a breath of fresh air that smelled sweeter than anything I'd ever imagined.

I was home.

My cell phone buzzed in my purse. Fishing it out, I began walking to my car and sighed when I saw the text. Another one from Mitch.

Hey pretty lady. Are you back in town yet? :)

With a sigh, I dropped my phone back in my bag. I'd heard from Mitch every few days during my time away. Half the time, they were texts with no real purpose other than to flirt or say hi.

Most weeks I'd heard from Mitch more than I had from Davin. Biting my lip, I clutched my bag tighter to my side. *I'll deal with him later.* It was becoming increasingly apparent that my co-worker was actively pursuing me, but in the time I'd spent away, clearing things up with Mitch had been the furthest thing from my mind.

Fighting the anxiety that coming conversation provoked, I forced myself to walk to my car. Bone-deep wariness seeped through me. I checked my cell phone again, hoping for a message from someone else while I checked the time. Nothing. It had been four days since Davin and I spoke.

And six weeks since we've had a decent conversation longer than five minutes.

Since it was mid-afternoon, there was still enough time to visit the Compound and see how the progress was coming along. As I drove from the airport, I rolled down the window. Warm air flowed in.

It was hard to believe that almost a year ago, I'd begun my job at the Compound. So much had changed in that time. We'd developed a vaccine. The public was now immune. The Kazzies were being released from the Compound.

My love for Davin hadn't diminished.

I'd hoped time and time again over the previous months that my affection, admiration, and soul-searing love for a man I could never be with would fade. Unfortunately, the opposite had happened. I loved him even more now than I had six months ago.

He would most likely fill a vacant spot in my heart until the day I died. I'd never loved before like I loved him, and I didn't think I would ever love like this again.

With a deep sigh, I turned onto the Compound's frontage road. The outer perimeter guards assessed me with a new light in their eyes and respectful nods. I was vaguely aware that ANN had run constant coverage on what Dr. Hutchinson, our political teams, and I were doing. I'd been too busy to watch any of it. I had no idea if they portrayed us in a positive light. Anything less would be one more battle we'd have to fight.

"Dr. Forester. It's been a while since we've seen you." Private Williams presented his hand-held computer at my admittance door.

I placed my palm against it. It flashed green. "I've been a bit busy."

He pocketed the small computer. "I know. It's been all over the news what you and your group are doing."

"Good. We're trying to not only educate the public about the vaccine but to also raise awareness."

"Well, I can confidently say I think you're accomplishing both."

His words were exactly what I needed to hear. I had no idea if he said them out of kindness or truth. Regardless, it was nice to know that maybe, just maybe, we'd made a difference. Even if it was a small one.

Carol greeted me when I strode across the lobby. The guards at all of the access doors on my way to the Sanctum did the same. I knew Sara would be waiting for me when I stepped into the Sanctum. I'd told her during my flight back that I'd return to the Compound if I had time.

Instead of trying to speak to me telepathically, she waited in Garrett's cell. The large-eyed Kazzie, along with Sophie, Dorothy, Sage, and Victor were there. Everyone waited for me.

Everyone except Davin.

"Where is he?" I asked when I stepped into the watch room.

Sara approached the glass. "He's coming. Don't worry."

The guard pressed a button, and the back panel door slid open. A second later, Davin strode in.

When he stepped into the cell, he stopped. His eyes glued to mine.

Despite talking to one another in brief, awkward conversations during my time away, it hadn't been the same as seeing him in person. I'd missed his intense eyes, dark hair, broad shoulders, and steely chest that made me want to melt right into him.

I had no idea how long we stared at each other. It was only when the guard cleared his throat and Sophie giggled that I snapped out of my trance.

I took a deep breath. "I'm going in." I walked to the containment door. "No need to help me suit up, as I'm sure you know."

The guard opened the containment room door, and I stepped inside. I waited for the door to hiss closed behind me, seal, and the room to depressurize to match the pressures within the cells. When the dials completed their never-ending turns, the door hissed open.

All seven of my friends waited.

"Meghan!" Sara rushed forward and threw her arms around me.

The rest crowded around. Several patted me on the back. Sage ruffled the top of my head. Only Davin hung back, his hands stuffed in his jean pockets. His dark hair stood out on all ends, as if he'd been running his hands through it all afternoon. He kept his gaze averted.

Tears clouded my eyes as I regarded all of my friends. "I'm sorry that you have to move to the reservation."

Victor shook his head, his large red face as blazing as the setting sun. "We know you and your friends tried, Meg. You can't win 'em all."

Garrett nodded. His large, egg-like eyes blinked slowly. "We'll be okay. At least we'll get out of here."

Sophie tensed at Sara's side at the mention of the reservation.

I stepped back to get a better look at Sophie as Sara's gaze fell to assess me. "You look exhausted!" she said hotly.

I ducked my head and tried to see myself the way they

were. I hadn't look in a mirror . . . well . . . at all today.

"And skinny." Sage's eyes appraised me disapprovingly. "Didn't they feed you when you were touring the country?"

Dorothy shook her head with an envious smile. "Wish I could lose weight like that." She appeared as plump as ever.

I shuffled my feet against the concrete floor. I'd had breakfast, but I'd been too nervous to eat lunch. It was the thought of seeing all of them again and having to explain that our attempts had been futile that had caused a pit in my stomach. A pit that wouldn't let me eat.

My gaze sought Davin's.

A heavy frown marred his features. His sapphire eyes were as bright as ever. He put his hands on his hips. "When did you last eat?"

His deep words rolled over me. It took a second before my head was clear enough to reply. "This morning."

He stepped forward and took my hand. The feel of his calloused, thick fingers closing around my palm made my head spin.

"Come on. We're getting you dinner." He tugged me away and called to Garrett's guard, "Can you order large meals for both of us and have them sent to my cell?"

"Sure," the guard replied. "I'll do it now."

I expected everyone else to follow us. Their energy strummed nervously through the room, but they all hung back. I wasn't sure if it was Davin's stony expression or the way he stiffly walked past all of them. Whatever the case, none of them followed us out of the back door panel.

When it was just the two of us in the back hallway, all of my attention zeroed in on Davin's hand around mine. He still hadn't removed it.

He was warm. His palm was dry yet smooth. Only the

calloused pads were rough. I felt his strength in his firm grip. A shiver ran through me at the power he could evoke.

Yet as frightening as that power was, I only felt safe with him. I knew he'd never hurt me. I knew he'd give his life to protect me, just as I'd give my life to protect him.

But then his words came back to haunt me. *It can never be.*

"Where are we going?" I asked.

"I'm sure you can guess." He pulled me into the elevator and hit the top button. "A quick stop before we get you food." We glided up to the fourth floor and stepped out into the forgotten corridor

With every step he took, his arm brushed mine. Strong muscles in his forearms flexed when he tightened his hand on my palm. His heat seared my skin in the most delicious way.

"Do you want to sit down?" he asked when we reached the end of the hall. "There's something we need to talk about."

Oh oh. I wasn't sure I wanted to hear whatever he had to say. During our short conversations over the past six weeks, Davin had tried again and again to stop me from what I was doing. But those conversations had been brief. We'd both known that I wasn't letting go. We'd both known that I was ignoring his request to carry on with my life. Yet he still didn't know about Mitch.

He still didn't know that nothing had ever happened between me and my co-worker, and now that so much time had passed—I didn't know how to bring it up.

I pulled my hand away and crossed my arms just as Davin lowered himself to the floor. "I know what you're going to say."

"You do?"

I stepped back and took a deep breath. "And don't even bother. You're wasting your breath. I understand that you want me to move on with my life, forget all of you, let you face your uncertain future on your own, but I can't do that and I won't do that. So stop asking me to go away. I'm not going to."

A sad smile covered his face. "I know. I see that now, so I won't ask again."

"You won't?"

He shook his head. "Will you please sit now?"

With stiff movements, I lowered onto my knees. His expression turned grim again.

"You've lost at least fifteen pounds." Pain crossed his features as a flash of some other emotion I couldn't identify flickered in his gaze. "This is why I wanted to speak with you. Meghan, if you're going to spend all of your time fighting for us, you at least have to eat. You need to take better care of yourself."

I sighed. "I know. It's just . . . out there . . ." *How do I explain how hectic it was? How so many people were around me all day every day? How at times, it felt like I was underwater, unable to breathe while the weight of the ocean pressed down on me?*

His expression softened. "Let me guess. It was too much? All of the people? The demands?"

"Yeah," I breathed.

"And that's why I don't want you doing it," he grumbled.

He pulled his knees up and clasped his arms around them. Thick veins wound up his forearms, while his rounded shoulders bulged. More than anything I wanted to feel those arms around me. To hold me. Comfort me. Tell me that everything would be okay.

But he couldn't do that. We didn't know if everything would be okay. In two days, he and every other Kazzie in the country would be arriving at the reservation. None of us knew what would happen from there.

"How much have you been sleeping?" I felt his gaze on the dark circles under my eyes. Even though I hadn't looked in a mirror today, I knew they were as dark as ever.

"About four hours a night."

"Four hours?" He jumped to standing and paced the width of the hall. "Meghan, that's crazy! You're going to kill yourself with that kind of schedule!"

His shouts only pressed down on me further. Tears filled my eyes. I looked down so he wouldn't see them. I didn't have the energy to say anything to his anger. He was right. I was running myself ragged, but I'd rather do that and die early than do nothing and live to a ripe old age.

He paced a few more times. His movements grew faster and faster until the last few became a blur.

Throughout it all, I sat quietly. I didn't have the energy to fight him. Not today. Not when it was one of my last chances to see him, really see him, before he disappeared to the reservation.

It was only when a tear slipped out, against my will that Davin's hurried movements stopped. One second, he was a blur in front of me, the next he stood ramrod straight, his magnificent figure towering above.

"Jesus, Meg. I'm sorry." He fell to the ground and pulled me into his arms.

I sobbed against his chest. The last six weeks of fighting, trying, and rallying poured out of me. I'd tried so damned hard, and it hadn't done anything positive that I could see. Not yet anyway. And deep down, I feared it never would. If we were never able to sway the public, if we were never able to get the majority of representatives on our sides, then Davin would be forever locked away.

And that was a thought I couldn't bear.

The tears slid down my cheeks in messy rivers. I burrowed into his chest as he rocked me on the ground, crooning nonsensical things in my ear. His soap and aftershave scent was everywhere. I wanted to sink into him, become one with him in the way only a man and woman could.

But he'd never allow that.

It can never be.

I had no idea how long he held me like that. It wasn't until my tears ran dry and I hiccuped a few times that he loosened his grip.

"Come on," he said gently. He lifted me and carried me down the hall as if I weighed nothing at all.

From there, we descended back to the main floor. Sergeant Rose let us into Davin's cell. The guard's eyes widened when he saw me in Davin's arms.

"Is she okay?"

"No, she's barely eaten or slept in six weeks. Is the food here?"

"Yes. It should be in your tray system." Sergeant Rose clicked the panel open.

Davin set me on his bed and watched me with eyes so bright they seemed to see right into my soul. "I'm going to make sure you eat a proper meal tonight and then I want you to go home, take a shower, and go to bed. And tomorrow, you're to stay home, sleep, and eat more. That's it. That's all you're to do tomorrow."

I pushed up straighter. "But tomorrow is the last day you're in the Compound—"

He put a finger to my lips. "Meghan, I'm not budging on this one. Since you refuse to take care of yourself, I'm going to tell you exactly how you spend the next twenty-four hours, and if you don't . . ."

His threat fell flat. We both knew he would never actually threaten me. In fact, we both knew his demands could easily be ignored on my part, but the devastated look on his face and the way his eyes pleaded with me to do as he asked—I couldn't say no.

"Okay, fine. I'll stay home tomorrow and sleep and eat."

"And that's all you do?"

I sighed. "Yes."

20 - SECRET TUNNEL

I thought it would be hard to stay away. I thought for sure as soon as morning came I'd be bounding out of bed, more nervous energy kicking in as the Kazzies last full day at the Compound was finally here.

Only, that didn't happen at all.

Davin was right. I was exhausted.

Completely exhausted.

After a huge dinner with him at the Compound the night before, I'd stopped at the lab to say a quick hello to my co-workers before driving home. Mitch had tried to corner me, but I managed to hightail it out of there before *that* conversation. And true to my word, I'd showered, pulled on my pajamas, and climbed into bed.

The feel of my own bed, the softness of the sheets, and the way the moon shined through my window made the world disappear. I fell into a deep sleep that I didn't emerge from until late morning the next day. I couldn't believe that I'd slept so long.

As I groggily woke, my thoughts slowly sped up. I pictured

Davin last night as he sat across from me while we ate dinner. His unique blue eyes. The curl of his hair. His large hands, broad shoulders, and steely demeanor.

His image appeared so readily thanks to my eidetic memory.

More than anything, I wanted to return to the Compound and be at his side. I knew the Kazzies would be packing the few items they had. The van was due to arrive tomorrow morning to transport them to the reservation. I'd be riding with them. As the only researcher in Compound 26 who'd been exposed to the virus, I was the only one who could travel with them into the rez.

Because of everything that was happening, I thought it would be hard to spend the day at home. Instead, it went surprisingly fast. I made a quick trip to the South Dakota Food Distribution Center. More than a few people stopped and stared when they saw me. I liked to think that was because they recognized me from the news, not because I looked like a train wreck. I still had circles under my eyes, and Davin was right, I'd lost at least fifteen pounds.

It quickly became apparent, however, that it *was* from people recognizing me, not from my poor personal care. One woman actually stopped and thanked me for what I was doing. Her kind words and warm touch made my throat tighten. It was so different from the angry mobs, hateful jeers, and homemade food bombs that we'd encountered in random cities throughout the country.

"Thank you," I said to her before she turned. "I needed to hear that."

It was strange, to connect with a complete stranger and feel a bond that I rarely felt with those I knew. Perhaps exhaustion had also hindered my usual anxiety-provoked response. Regardless, when I returned home I felt a bit more energetic, but I still kept my promise.

I didn't go to the Compound.

I made simple food, so I couldn't burn it or render it inedible. One of my neighbors, Ameena, stopped by to say hello and told me she admired what I was doing. Amy also stopped by in the evening.

When her knock sounded on my door, I opened it to her barreling inside.

"It's so good to have you back!" She kicked her shoes off and hung her purse on a kitchen chair.

Since my apartment was so small, the front entryway practically opened up to the kitchen.

"Charlie and Mitch have been driving me crazy. It'll be good to have you back at my side in the lab."

I smiled genuinely. "I've missed you guys too."

Amy pulled out a kitchen chair. "So? How has the last month been? I've seen the crazy protests that have followed you and your group around the country, but it hasn't seemed all bad. There seems to be just as many people supporting the Kazzies. So that's good news right? A decent majority want them freed."

I nodded. "That's what we're hoping, and with time, we're hoping to grow that group of supporters. There's so much fear out there. People are convinced that they'll still die from *Makanza*, even though they've been vaccinated."

Amy snorted. "You can thank the MRI for that. We've done such a great job at keeping the public in the dark about the virus. I'm not surprised they're afraid. They don't know any better."

I sighed. "I know."

"So how are you feeling? You look like crap by the way."

Amy winked.

I smiled at her crass comment. I knew she didn't mean any ill will by it, and she was right. I looked terrible. "I slept thirteen hours last night, and I've eaten enough today to blow through half of my food allowance for the week."

"Good. You need to sleep and eat more. Ever since I've met you, you haven't had enough of either."

I pushed to standing from my chair and moved to the stove to boil the tea kettle. The simple task brought back memories of Sharon, Davin's mother. Every time I visited her in South Dakota, she always headed straight for the stove before pulling out her china tea set. It had become such a routine that I no longer waited for her to ask if I wanted tea. She knew I would.

"Tea?" I asked Amy.

She shrugged. "Sure."

A few minutes later, I settled again in the chair across from her. Tea steamed from our mugs. Even though it was still warm outside, there was something comforting about a hot cup of tea in the evening. During my weeks on the road, I didn't think I'd enjoyed that once.

I took a sip and set my cup down. "How did preparations go today?"

Amy ran a hand through her red curls. "Okay. There's not much to pack, so they're all ready to go. We spent most of our time reviewing the rules on the reservation."

My hand stilled. I set my teacup back down. "Rules?"

"Apparently, the Director of the reservation has strict rules he's enforcing."

"Do you know much about him?"

She shook her head. "Nope, other than he's a former CDC big wig and was in the military at one point."

Tea sloshed over the sides of my cup when I picked it up. "I don't understand why they need rules on the reservation. Aren't the Kazzies supposed to live there the way we all live normally?"

"Yes and no from what I've heard." Amy finished her drink and leaned back. "They announced this morning that they'll have strict rules about keeping a certain distance from the perimeter, and visitors are allowed only under certain conditions. And as you know, anybody who does visit has to go through the three week quarantine process afterward, unless they have the money to spend on the blood test to confirm *Makanza* is no longer active inside them."

I set my cup down. "That seems like a good way to keep people from visiting. How many people can afford that test? And not many can afford to take an entire three weeks off from work, so that will keep people from visiting too."

"I know." Amy tapped her chin. "I thought the same thing."

A warm breeze from the open living room window fluttered papers on my counter. That warm air did little to warm me inside. "Did you know we heard in D.C. that Dr. Roberts may be the reservation's director?"

"What?" Amy's eyebrows rose to her forehead.

"I know. Luckily, that didn't happen."

"No kidding." Amy shook her head.

We both sat in silence for a moment. I attempted to drink my tea again. Thankfully, I managed not to spill.

"Do you know what's going on about the border crossing rules?" Amy set her empty cup down. "There's really not a need for them anymore, and how are the Kazzies' friends and family members supposed to visit them on the reservation if they can't leave their state?"

"Last I heard from Cate's political contacts, there's talk of the borders reopening, along with banning curfew, but right now, it's all talk. Nothing's been decided."

Amy rolled her eyes. "Figures." She checked her cell phone. "Sheesh. Speaking of curfew, it's getting late. I better get going."

I glanced at the clock. It was already eight at night.

I walked with Amy to the door. She threw her shoes on and picked up her purse. "See you bright and early tomorrow morning?"

I nodded tightly. Tomorrow we were moving the Kazzies.

Tomorrow we'd see the reservation.

WHEN I ENTERED the Sanctum the next morning, excitement hung in the air. The guards were frantically moving about, organizing the Kazzies' removal from their cells. The van had arrived. It waited outside. The meager belongings the Kazzies owned had been packed, decontaminated, and stored in the vehicle. All seemed ready to go.

Now, it was just a matter of moving my seven friends.

Dr. Sadowsky stood in the Sanctum, issuing orders. All of the Kazzies would need to be suited up. From there, they'd go through the decontamination process before being marched out.

Energy buzzed within the Kazzies' cells. I could only imagine what they felt. Sara, Sophie, Sage, Victor, and Dorothy had come to live in Compound 26 nine years ago. They hadn't been outdoors since. For Davin and Garrett, it had been seven years.

I studied Davin as he followed Sergeant Rose's instructions for donning his suit. His movements were stiff. At one point, he dropped his boot. His hands shook when he picked it up. I'd never seen him so nervous. So unsure.

"Are you ready?" I asked when he was fully suited.

His only reply was a curt nod.

All of the Kazzies entered their containment rooms and went through the purifying process. I waited for Davin to emerge into the watch room. It would be the first time he'd left the Sanctum since he arrived.

When the door hissed open, my breath caught in my chest. He stepped into the room beside us. Neither Sergeant Rose, Mitch, Charlie, Amy, nor I said a word.

It was finally happening.

Davin and my friends were finally leaving the Compound.

Davin's gaze stayed on me. I couldn't be sure, but his lips seemed to tremble. I stepped forward and clasped his hand. He held mine tightly in return.

One by one, researchers emerged with their Kazzies from the watch rooms. We all began the slow march down the hall.

When we reached the outer perimeter of the Sanctum, the guards leading us turned down a separate corridor. It was a place I'd never ventured before. It had always been off limits.

"This way please." The guard opened a door using a keycard, fingerprint, and retinal scan.

I knew it must lead to something ultra secure if it required a retinal scan. That was only used for access *into* the Compound. Never had I needed a retinal scan once inside.

The door opened to a wide stairwell.

"Where are we going?" Gerry asked. The tall, olive skinned researcher stood by the Sisters.

Sara and Sophie held hands.

"This leads to a tunnel. It's one way to exit the interior," the guard replied.

No wonder they need retinal scans.

One by one, the Kazzies and their researchers stepped through the door. I stayed at Davin's side. The wide stairwell gave us plenty of room.

"This isn't creepy at all." Charlie ran his hand along the concrete walls. "Nope, definitely not. Secret door that opens to a subterranean tunnel with dimly lit walkways. Nothing at all strange in the slightest."

Mitch chuckled.

He walked just behind me. His large hand suddenly settled on my shoulder and squeezed. "You sure you don't want me to go first, Little Megs?"

Davin stiffened beside me.

I shrugged Mitch's hand off. "I can manage."

"Yeah, she's a big girl, Mitchy." Amy's smart tone cut through the damp air as we descended. "Last I checked, she didn't need any man paving the way for her."

If I didn't know better, Davin's lips twitched up.

Everyone carried on, following the guards down. It seemed to take forever until we reached the bottom of the stairs. Once we did, a long straight tunnel stretched out in front of us. It was so long, I couldn't see the end.

Charlie began whistling the tune for the X-files.

I peeked up at Davin. His gaze stayed at the end of the tunnel. All of the Kazzies seemed more and more tense the longer we walked.

I glanced over my shoulder after we'd been traveling through the tunnel for at least five minutes. The twins weren't far behind. Even from the distance, sweat was visible on Sophie's forehead through her viewing shield. Sara clutched her hand tightly. Together, in their pure white biohazard suits, they looked like astronauts walking on the moon, except Sophie didn't seem steady. She seemed to be relying heavily on

Sara to support her.

I slowed my steps. "Sophie? Are you okay?"

She stumbled when I said her name. Sara caught her, but barely.

When Sophie took her next step, her knees gave out. I lunged to catch her head before it cracked on the floor. An alarm sounded on her wrist.

Red light flashed.

The airtight seal had broken. *Makanza* particles seeped out of her suit.

Amy's eyes widened. Gerry gasped. The other researchers that were close enough to realize what happened jumped back.

"Stay calm!" I eyed them all firmly. "You've all been vaccinated. You'll be fine!"

Victor's researchers' eyes widened fearfully. Victor's red brow furrowed in disgust when they took large steps backward, away from Sophie.

My chest swelled with anger. "If you're afraid to be here, wait at the door! You'll all have to go into quarantine anyway!" The weeks and weeks of frustration poured out of me in those two sentences. Gone was the anxious Meghan, the one afraid to speak up in front of crowds. If Victor's researchers didn't know to act better than they were, they *didn't* deserve to be here.

Davin kneeled at my side. He must have done it sometime between Sophie falling and me yelling at my co-workers.

"Sophie?" His voice was gentle. "I'm going to lift you."

She didn't reply. A faraway look glazed her eyes.

Davin stood. Sophie dangled limply in his arms. "Sophie?" His voice grew quiet.

She blinked and then looked around. "What's going on?"

"You fainted and fell," I replied. "Do you want Davin to

carry you?"

A blush stained her cheeks. It was like she suddenly understood that he held her. "Um, no. I'm fine now. I'll walk."

Davin gently set her down as I fixed her suit, sealing it again. Her wrist light flashed green. Sophie wobbled initially when I finished fiddling but then regained her footing before returning to Sara's side.

When I turned to assess who still remained in our group, I was appalled to see that at least half of the researchers had retreated to the stairwell and waited like scared, herded sheep.

Disappointment so strong it threatened to choke the life right out of me coursed through my veins. *How are we supposed to convince the public the Kazzies are nothing to fear if their own researchers, who understand the science behind the vaccine, won't stay by their sides?*

And in that moment, it all felt so impossible. So inexplicable.

Davin's right. I'm fighting a war I cannot win.

A large palm closed over my hand, fingers entwining through mine. I looked at my hand blankly, as if it belonged to someone else, and then I followed the white suited-up arm attached to the person holding my hand.

Davin gazed down at me.

The emotion flooding his eyes spoke volumes. He squeezed my fingers, almost painfully, but it was what I needed. It grounded me. Anchored me.

This was why I was fighting. *This* was why I cared so much.

"Let's go, Meg." His words were so quiet through his hood that I knew the others standing only yards away hadn't heard him.

I nodded. It was all I could manage.

The guards ahead had frozen into statues. Without a superior to tell them what to do, they were like deer caught in headlights.

I addressed them firmly. "You've been vaccinated. You'll be fine, but you'll be required to either be quarantined for three weeks or have your blood tested after you've gone through the initial symptoms."

The guards blinked.

"Do you understand?" I said more forcefully.

Both nodded.

Mitch cleared his throat and appeared on my other side. "We're still with you, Megs. We won't leave your side."

My heart filled, even more, when Amy and Charlie stepped closer.

"We know the vaccine works." Amy squeezed my other hand. "Let's go."

We continued the long march down the tunnel. When we finally reached the end, a single door stopped us from going farther.

The guard fingered a switch on his communication device. "We're here, but there was an incident."

He quickly rattled off how everyone had been exposed and then turned and searched for me. "The van's in place. When this door opens, they all . . ." He nodded at the Kazzies behind me. "They'll need to climb in the back and have a seat."

"We're ready." My voice didn't waver.

Both guards were required to use their keycards, codes, and retinal scans before the door opened. When it did, blinding sunshine poured into the tunnel.

Davin brought a hand up, shielding his eyes. The others did the same.

With the door fully open, the van appeared on the other

side. It waited but so much more did as well. Fresh air swirled into the tunnel. The sounds of birds flying overhead sang through the breeze. And the sun . . .

The sun was so amazingly bright on the eastern horizon.

I turned to see how the Kazzies were doing.

They all stood motionless. Staring at the outside.

Staring at freedom.

Tears poured down the twins' faces. Davin's hand squeezed mine harder. Dorothy audibly wept before falling to her knees, while Victor, Sage, and Garrett all stood ramrod straight, their tight expressions speaking volumes.

"This is where we say goodbye, Meghan." Amy's voice broke the quiet. "We can't go any farther. We'll need to go into quarantine."

I nodded and did something I never did. I pulled her into a hug.

Her hair tickled my face, and her apple blossom shampoo flooded my nose. "Thank you."

"You can always count on me." She squeezed tighter.

I knew that Mitch, Charlie, Amy, Gerry, and the other researchers would all have to move into quarantine now. I could only hope none of them experienced second stage symptoms like I had. But I knew they'd all be fine. The vaccine worked.

"I'll see you when I get back." I squeezed Amy one last time.

Mitch, Charlie, and Gerry all said their goodbyes. I thanked the other researchers who had stayed and not run. With emotions charging through the air, the seven Kazzies and I climbed into the van while the blazing sun shone through the windows.

21 – THE RESERVATION

The ride to the reservation was long. An MRRA soldier drove. He'd said hello when we entered the van and hadn't said one word since.

All of the MRRA soldiers and guards that would work inside the reservation had been vaccinated and exposed to *Makanza*. They were like me. We were all safe and immune from the virus.

Other than the driver, it was just me and the Kazzies. Everyone was quiet, not just the soldier. My friends stared out the windows as if mesmerized by the changing landscape. Rolling hills, prairie grass, and ghost towns flew by as we drove mile after mile.

I sat beside Davin. His body was still, his movements absent. Tension poured from him, yet he made no move to turn from the window. I could only imagine how uncomfortable he felt in his suit. The Kazzies were required to wear them until they entered the reservation. It was an awfully long time to stay suited up. The material didn't breathe and felt suffocating at times.

Yet, Davin didn't seem to mind. His gaze stayed on the landscape, his bright blue eyes filled with emotion. After seven years of being locked away, everything out here must look so new.

A few hours later, we entered the abandoned town of Mobridge. The van slowed. It was hard to see ahead, but snippets of the reservation and the land across the Missouri river appeared.

A tall fence.

Large gates.

Watch towers dotting the horizon.

The government had spared no expense at keeping the reservation secure. I swallowed audibly.

Two other vans were in front of us. From the license plates, I knew who they brought. Minnesota and Iowa had also driven their Kazzies to the reservation.

As we inched across the bridge, everyone perked up.

"This is it?" Dorothy tried to peer ahead, but it was hard to see with the angle the van waited at. The only thing apparent was the giant fence enclosing the reservation.

"Looks like there are more Kazzies ahead." Victor nodded at the Minnesota and Iowa vans. "How many Kazzies are in their Compounds?"

"Nine in Minnesota and eight in Iowa," I replied. "Their Kazzies have strains none of you have."

"The giant freak show." Sage's deep voice rolled out of his hood. "No wonder they want to keep us locked up."

A mewling sound came from Sophie. Sara gripped her hand tightly.

The van inched forward. When it was our turn to enter the large gates, we all peered out the windows. Like we'd been told, the fence had barbed wire at the top while guards stood at their stations with guns in hand.

It really is like a prison.

My stomach sank. "I have to get you out of here!" The fevered whisper escaped my lips.

Davin's sad gaze met mine. "It's better than the Compound. Just remember that. You can't save all of us."

My heart broke at how Davin had so easily and readily accepted his fate. He thought I was wasting my time. He'd told me he understood better than I did how the MRI and Compounds worked.

What if he's right?

When we'd fully entered the reservation, the guards waved us to a parking area. At this section of the rez, there wasn't anything around. No buildings. No houses. The town wasn't in sight. Only vast rolling plains with grassland swaying in the breeze.

The van's back doors opened. Makanza Research and Response Agency soldiers flanked the door's sides. None of them wore suits.

At least the MRRA has enough sense to know the vaccine works.

"All right, Compound 26." One guard waved us forward. "Step down. You'll be checked in and shuttled to the town. Homes have been established for you. You're to wait in your houses until our first gathering tomorrow morning. No Kazzies are allowed out of their residences until all have attended the meeting where the rules on the reservation will be explained."

I cocked my head. *I thought they'd already learned the rules back at Compound 26.*

The guard's eyes alighted on me. Surprise shone in his irises. "Dr. Forester."

I hopped out of the van. Bright sunlight beat down, and

scents of wildflowers drifted in the breeze.

I put my hands on my hips. "What other rules do they have to learn? Our researchers already reviewed the rules this morning with them."

He shook his head. "I'm not sure, ma'am. I'm following orders."

With a wave of his hand, he ushered my seven friends to an area to remove their suits. One by one, they filed past me.

I tucked my hair behind my shoulders as the breeze picked up. "I've been vaccinated and exposed as you know. I'll wait so I can accompany them to their homes."

He cleared his throat. "Ma'am, most researchers leave their Kazzies at this point. There's no need for you to stay."

I felt Sara studying me from the distance as she removed her suit. I opened up readily when she knocked on our mental link. *What's going on?* she asked.

They're telling me I can leave now, that other researchers haven't continued to the town, but don't worry. I'm not going anywhere.

The guard eyed his companion. "Can she go to the town, Summers?"

He shrugged, holding his assault rifle casually. "I guess. I don't know. No one else has asked to do that."

"I'll be accompanying them." My usual response around new people faded. I didn't just ride in a van for five hours to not see them to their new home.

The second guard shrugged. "I think it's fine." He turned to my friends. "Finish removing your suits!"

Clicks and hisses sounded from Dorothy and Garrett as two soldiers helped them. The twins, Davin, Sage, and Victor all kicked off their pants and boots. Each stretched before smiling.

It was the first time any of them had felt a breeze against

their skin in years.

In parking spots only ten yards over, other Kazzies from different Compounds were doing the same. My eyes widened when wings appeared under the bottom of a tall female's arms. Strain 15. With that infection, a Kazzie's arms became attached to the latissimus dorsi muscle. The skin thinned and when a Kazzie stretched their arms, the skin stretched with it, like wings. Their bones also became hollow. Essentially, they could fly. Of all the strains, they looked the least human.

The guard eyed the tall woman warily. Another snickered and made a comment under his breath. One of the Kazzies in the group yelled something at the guards. I gasped when the guard muscled the Kazzie back with his gun, telling him to watch what he said.

"Hey!" I stepped forward. "Is that necessary?"

The guard ignored me.

Throughout it all, the tall woman kept her head down, her gaze averted.

It was a look too many Kazzies carried.

With a hammering heart, I turned back to my friends. All seven of the Kazzies from Compound 26 were no longer inhibited by their suits. And each of them stared in wonder at the surroundings, taking in deep, gulping breaths of fresh air.

"It smells . . ." Sara grinned and then laughed. "I don't know. Fresh? Good?" She grabbed Sophie's hand. "Do you remember what it smelled like outside back home?"

A tentative smile spread across Sophie's face. "Not like this."

"That's because you girls grew up in the city." Dorothy tilted her face to the sun. "Cities smell nothing like the true outdoors."

I swirled around as Garrett, Victor, and Sage all joined in

the rising spirit. Only Davin had disappeared.

"Where did he go?"

One of the soldiers nodded to the side of the van. "There."

I rounded the corner to see Davin squatting by the van. His hands were in the dirt. He rubbed them back and forth along the earth. I approached him and hunkered down at his side. "Davin?"

He stayed quiet as his hands moved on the ground. His strong fingers dug into the soil, coming away dark and dirty.

When he finally looked up, tears filled his eyes. "Do you know how long I've wanted to feel the earth? To touch the land my ancestors cultivated?" He lifted a cupful of dirt and let it fall onto his other palm. "I may not be free, but I have this."

My throat tightened as tears clouded my vision. I grabbed his arm and squeezed.

Davin was finally outside again, smelling the breeze, feeling the earth, connecting to the natural world in a way he never could in the Compound.

His eyes met mine. "Thank you." Cupping my palm, he sifted dirt onto it. "Thank you for this."

Cool, moist dirt covered my hand. Never before had I understood how precious feeling something like that was.

"All right. Let's get moving!" the first guard called as the sound of approaching vehicles reached my ears.

In the distance, two MRRA trucks drove toward us, coming from deeper within the reservation.

Davin stood and pulled me with him. The driver that drove us from the Compound pulled the van to an area near the gates. Workers there wore biohazard suits and carried large canisters of decontamination spray. Every surface within the van was thoroughly covered.

Even though any remnants of *Makanza* that had escaped from Sophie's suit in the tunnel had long disintegrated, I wasn't surprised by the unnecessary process. Since *Makanza* only survived on surfaces for ten minutes I knew it was nowhere in that van, yet that didn't change procedure. *Not taking any chances.*

"Dr. Forester?" the guard shuffled to my side as the MRRA soldiers lined my friends up. "You may leave now if you'd like."

I watched the MRI employees from Minnesota and Iowa hop back into their vans before they restarted and began driving away. I was the only MRI researcher now in the reservation.

My arms crossed as I met his gaze. "I'm staying."

Davin and the others had joined the Kazzies from Iowa and Minnesota. All of them eyed each other warily. It was the first time any of them had met Kazzies with different strains.

The soldiers began asking each Kazzie for their identifying information as they were catalogued into the reservation's roster. After each answered the questions, a device was held to their wrists before something blasted into their skin.

"What's that?" My tone grew hard.

The guard glanced over his shoulder. "It's a tracking device. We need to know where each Kazzie is at all times. In case any try to escape."

"You're *tracking* them?" My voice rose.

The trucks that had been approaching from the distance reached us. Dust swirled around the wheel's rims as they ground to a halt. I turned accusingly to the guard as slamming doors sounded behind me.

The guard cocked his head. "Of course we are. How else can we guarantee they stay behind the fence?"

A commotion drew my attention. Davin faced one of the guards, refusing to give them his arm. "You're not putting that in me." His voice grew deadly quiet.

Sage stood just behind Davin. His expression was hard. Sparks flew from his fingers. "You're not putting that in me either."

I tensed as my arms fell to my sides. Energy flew around Davin and Sage as they squared off against the soldiers.

My gaze flew to the twins. They stood to the side. Sara held Sophie as her sister cried. Sophie clutched her wrist as a single drop of blood dripped down her blue arm.

They've already tagged her!

I jumped forward, trying to diffuse the situation.

"Stop! This is crazy! You can't put tracking devices in them! There's a fence around the entire perimeter. How can they possibly escape? There's no need for this!" I pushed hair from my eyes as the breeze picked up. "Who's your superior? I'd like to speak with him or her. This was *never* mentioned in the law when it was decided the Kazzies would come to the reservation."

Heavy, stomping steps sounded behind me, coming from where the trucks had parked before a voice reached my ears.

"Dr. Forester, still causing problems I see."

I stiffened as my breath caught in my throat. *No!*

No, no, no! He can't be here!

I turned as if an invisible hand manipulated me. The world slowly spun in front of my vision as if I were a top moving in slow motion. But I didn't want to see. I didn't want to believe that he stood behind me.

A growl erupted from my side. Davin's hands fisted into tight balls, his knuckles grinding against one another.

And when the slow spin stopped and I stood facing him, I

stared up into eyes that I remembered too well. Gray eyes that emitted coldness and revenge.

"What are you doing here?" My words came out in a whisper.

Dr. Roberts smiled. "My job. I'm the Director here."

"No!" Davin roared, and before I could do anything, he lunged at my former boss.

22 – DEVASTATED

It all happened so quickly. One second Davin was at my side, the next he was on top of Dr. Roberts, pinning him to the ground.

A vicious snarl emitted from Davin's lips. He wrapped his hands around Dr. Roberts' neck, his grip choking the life out of Compound 26's former lab director.

"Davin, no!" I flew at him.

But the soldiers kicked into action before I could reach him. They grabbed hold of Davin's arms and tried to pull him back.

They couldn't.

They didn't stand a chance against Davin's strength.

Dr. Roberts' face turned blue. His eyes bulged.

The rest of the Kazzies stood around, wide-eyed, not interfering. More sparks flew from Sage's hand as if he couldn't control himself amidst the heightened emotions.

The rest looked as shocked as me as to what was unfolding.

Wind whipped across the prairie as I screamed at Davin to

stop and tried to pull him back, but it was like he didn't hear me. He was out of control.

Out of nowhere, another soldier appeared. He jumped onto Davin's back and jammed a syringe into Davin's neck. With a forceful plunge, the syringe's contents flooded into Davin's system.

He fell unconscious in seconds.

I kneeled at his side as he slumped onto the ground. Wind blew across his face, rustling locks from his forehead.

"Davin?" He didn't respond when I tapped his cheek. "Davin!"

I whirled around, looking accusingly at the solider who'd drugged Davin. "What did you give him?"

The guard spoke in a calm voice. "A drug to keep him under until we can transfer him somewhere safer." It was only then I saw the rows of syringes in the guard's belt.

My eyes widened. *They knew something like this might happen! They came prepared to sedate them if needed!*

I eyed his belt again while I cradled Davin's head. Rage burned my insides, like a fire in an inferno. "Is that really necessary?" The words choked out of me.

With the help of two guards, Dr. Roberts sat up, coughing violently. "He's as unpredictable as a rabid dog!" Dr. Roberts coughed again and rubbed his throat.

The guards helped him to stand. Dr. Roberts smoothed back his hair and straightened his uniform. Bruises were already forming around his neck. "Of course it's necessary!"

Heat rushed to my cheeks. "You tortured him for years! You cut him mercilessly without anesthetic! You cut him off from his only family member on this planet and *intentionally* hurt him time and time again! How would you react if you encountered someone like that?"

Dr. Roberts sneered. "Still the Kazzie lover. You're no better than them."

Anger burned in me so brightly, I could barely breathe. *How is he the Director? He's not supposed to be here!* Laying Davin's head down, I stood. The wind picked up again, whipping around us.

In a cold voice, I said, "Why are you here? You weren't the appointed Director."

"It so happens that the appointed Director, as you call him, was in a car crash two days ago. He suffered several horrific injuries and is no longer able to do this job. I was runner-up, so here I am."

He seemed delighted at his renewed power.

My hands clenched into fists. "But you hate them! If you hate them so much, *why* are you here?"

He stepped closer until our shirts touched. His cold gray eyes met mine. "To make sure they *stay* here."

BEFORE I KNEW what was happening, Dr. Roberts called for an MRRA vehicle and gave the soldier driving it strict instructions to take me back to Sioux Falls. Under no circumstances was he to turn around or deviate from that course.

"You can't do this!" I stood in the prairie, my friends behind me. All of them huddled together with the Kazzies from Minnesota and Iowa. "I won't get in that car!"

I made a move to go to Davin, who was still unconscious on the ground, but Dr. Roberts blocked me. He was surprisingly fast given his age.

"Let me go to him!" I tried again. Dr. Roberts blocked me a second time.

"Get in the car, Dr. Forester!"

I glanced over my shoulder at my friends. Sara gave me a desperate look while Sophie mewled quietly, staring at the ground. Sparks still flew from Sage's fingers. *At least he hasn't electrocuted anyone.* But other than Sage's obvious anger, none of them reacted. They'd all resorted to their usual behaviors—the way they'd reacted when they were at Dr. Robert's mercy within Compound 26.

Blatant fear and submission.

"For the last time, *get* in the car, Dr. Forester!" My former boss pointed at the vehicle. A vein bulged in his neck.

"No. I'm not leaving them." I leveled his icy stare with my own.

Surprise was evident in his irises.

We stared at one another as prairie wind blew the tall grass around us, making it look like waves rolling in the ocean. In the distance, thunderclouds grew. Lightning crackled on the horizon.

"What makes you think you have any power here?" Dr. Roberts put his hands on his hips. "Do you really think because you're Dr. Hutchinson's new pet that you can do as you please? That you're above the law?" He stepped closer. "The MRRA will *always* be the first line of defense against another outbreak. The president understands that. The government understands that. *I* have the power here, and you better get used to that."

"I'm not leaving, and I won't let you do this to them, not again."

He leaned closer until I could see the tiny pores on his face. "I'd like to see you try to stop me."

Tears threatened to spill onto my cheeks as the anger within me grew. All of my friends watched as thunder boomed in the distance. The twins' eyes pleaded with me, but deep down, I knew there was nothing I could do.

Dr. Roberts was right. I had no power here.

A scream threatened to erupt from my throat. I clamped my lips closed. Never had rage and frustration rallied in me so deeply that I couldn't control myself, but that was how I felt right now.

Out of control.

If this was even an ounce of what Davin felt, I could understand why he acted like he did. He'd endured *years* of torture under Dr. Roberts' commands. I'd merely worked at Dr. Roberts' side, having to stomach his sadistic practices until we discovered the vaccine which effectively stopped him.

My eyes sought Davin. He still lay on the ground. The only movement was his chest rising and falling with deep, slow breaths. *At least he's still alive.*

"Summers!" Dr. Roberts barked. "Help me get her in the car!"

The MRRA soldier approached in halting steps, his eyes wide. "Sir?"

"You heard me. Help me get her in the car!"

"No." I clenched my teeth tightly and took a step back. "I'll go, but I'll return. I'm going to stop you."

Dr. Roberts opened the car door as more thunder cracked. The wind picked up as the atmosphere became as charged as the situation unfolding. "I'd like to see you try."

THE DRIVE BACK to Sioux Falls passed in a blur. Sara and I spoke almost the entire way.

We're in a van right now. They're driving us to the town.

How's Davin?

I don't know. They took him in a separate vehicle.

Rain splattered the windshield for most of the drive. A few

times, the soldier driving tried to initiate small talk, but small talk had never been my forte. Besides, I was too consumed with listening to Sara.

There are hundreds of small houses. I guess this is where we'll live. They're saying it's the Kazzie neighborhood.

How's everyone else doing?

Okay. I guess. Nobody's saying much. Oh wait . . . We're stopping now. They're starting to have people get out.

My breath sucked in, which got a funny look from the soldier. *What's happening?*

They're splitting us into groups of two. It seems it will be two Kazzies to each house. They just had Garrett and Victor enter a home. It looks like they're locking them inside.

I could feel her fear as the minutes ticked by.

Now, it's our turn. They're telling Sophie and me to enter a house. She breathed a sigh of relief. *It seems we'll be living together.*

Good, and remember, do what they say. It seems safest.

She nodded numbly and proceeded to enter the house before she and her sister were locked inside. Sara gave me the rundown of the home, explaining what it looked like. After another hour passed, in which nothing further happened, we agreed to shut down our conversation so she could talk to the other Kazzies.

Keep me updated if anything changes.

I felt her nod. *I will.*

My nails were in shreds by the time we reached the Compound. I'd bitten them to the qwik. I numbly stepped out of the vehicle, and the soldier promptly sped off.

The sun was close to setting. It was already nine at night. Curfew had arrived, but I didn't care. I raced into the Compound to my lab. I needed to find my co-workers and tell them what happened. Barreling through the doors, my eyes grew wide when our dark, vacant lab stared back at me. I smacked my hand to my forehead.

Amy, Mitch, and Charlie are in quarantine!

I took a deep unsteady breath before I hurried down the hall to my office. I'd left my laptop and bag in there. It had never occurred to me to take my things to the reservation.

With shaky fingers, I pulled out my cell phone. It slipped from my grip and clattered to the floor. Cursing, I picked it up and held it firmly before tapping in the familiar number.

Dr. Hutchinson answered on the first ring.

"Cate!" My voice came out panicked. I tried to calm down, but my heart beat so wildly. All I could think about was the horrible pain Dr. Roberts was undoubtedly inflicting on Davin at this very second. It ate at my soul.

Rustling sounded on the other end. "Meghan? Is that you? What's wrong?"

A sob shook my chest. *I'm losing it. Calm down!* I took another deep breath. "Dr. Roberts is the Director on the reservation! He's running the place! It's not the man from the CDC!"

Her sharp intake of breath followed. "Please tell me this is a joke."

"It's not! He said the original appointee had a car accident two days ago and is no longer fit for the job. So now Dr. Roberts is in charge. Does that mean you didn't know they'd appointed him either?"

"No." She paused. I could picture her biting her lip and running a hand through her hair. I'd spent enough time with her to know what she did when she was worried. "They never announced that. Oh, Meghan . . . This is awful! I never dreamed they'd actually let *him* be in charge."

The way she sneered his name indicated her feelings for

my former boss matched my own. Her voice strengthened. "How are the ones from my Compound doing? Were they there?"

I shook my head. "I don't know. I tried to get into the town where they'll be living, but they wouldn't let me. They . . ." I choked on another sob.

Her voice grew wary. "What? What happened?"

"They drugged Davin, and they're implanting tracking devices in all of them. When I spoke up, Dr. Roberts forced me to leave." I explained the awful situation in which Davin had turned on Dr. Roberts. "They wouldn't let me go to the town. I have no idea how they're treating them. Everything is locked up so tight up there. It's a world of its own."

She made a disgruntled sound. "We need to stop this."

"I know, but I don't have the sway you do. Can you call the president and arrange another meeting as soon as possible?"

Rustling again sounded on the other end. "Yes. I'll call right now. Pack your bag. We're flying to D.C. tomorrow."

23 - MEETING

We traveled to D.C. the next day. The entire flight my heart beat erratically. I had no idea what was happening on the reservation. I had no idea if Davin was being treated fairly or if he was being tortured again. Since Sara didn't know, my only inside connection, I was completely in the dark.

Sara and Sophie were still locked in their new home. Nobody had come for them. The initiation meeting, that explained the rules on the reservation, had been canceled. They hadn't been given an explanation as to why.

My stomach rolled at the thought of what could be happening. Images of the way Dr. Roberts' brutalized Davin kept flashing through my mind. The Chair. Bloody puncture wounds. Being locked in the Experimental Room.

I gripped the armrests of my seat tightly. Stratus clouds hung above us as we descended into Dulles International Airport. Cate had managed to pull a few strings. We had a meeting with the president scheduled for late morning. It was currently 10 a.m. on the east coast.

We'd need to hurry.

Cate's foot tapped on the floor as the jet's wheels hit the runway. The familiar scream of the engines and squeaking breaks followed.

"We'll have to be succinct." She unclicked her seatbelt and stood as the plane taxied along the runway. "The aide said we'll only have twenty minutes of the president's time."

I swallowed uneasily. *How can we change the course of the future in only twenty minutes?*

"Having Dr. Sadowsky's testimonial will help, I hope." I cleared my throat after I said the words. My anxiety had returned in full-force and with it came the feeling that I was being swallowed whole by an invisible force, eager to suck me into its dark embrace.

Just breathe. Remember what Davin said. When you feel a panic attack coming, close your eyes and breathe.

As Cate grabbed her bags while the pilot opened the cabin door, I reached to the back of my mind and mentally knocked on my connection with Sara.

At least ten seconds passed before she opened. *Meghan?*

I breathed a sigh of relief. *Hi. How's it going? Are you okay?*

Yes, for the time being. Oh, Meghan . . . it's so . . . It's weird here.

I swallowed tightly. *And Davin? How is he?*

I felt her shake her head helplessly. *I'm sorry. I still don't know.*

Her response was like a kick in the gut. Each time we'd spoken, she'd said the same thing. She was fine. Sophie was fine. The other Kazzies were fine, but she had no idea about Davin. When they'd hauled him away, unconscious from the drug they'd administered to him, he'd been taken somewhere.

And she still had no idea where.

Worst of all, she couldn't reach him. That either meant he was still unconscious or too drugged to communicate.

Neither option made me feel better.

Do you know anyone who's seen him?

No. They're still keeping us restricted in our new homes. We're not allowed to leave until we've gone through the initiation meetings. They say we still have two more weeks before all of our meetings and training are over, but those meetings haven't started. I guess all of the Kazzies haven't arrived yet.

Oh, Sara. I'm so sorry. Cate and I are working right now to get you out of there. How's everyone else doing?

I felt her shrug. *Okay, but . . .* She seemed to struggle to find the words. *You know this is the first time any of us have seen other Kazzies. I didn't even know what some of the strains could do. Did you see that woman with wings? And there was a guy I saw on the street, walking with two guards, he had super long arms and cupped hands.*

Guilt filled me when she said that. It only then dawned on me that we should have educated them more about what they'd see. I smacked my hand to my forehead as cool air swirled into the jet's cabin. The pilot had opened the door and lowered the stairs.

"Meghan? Are you coming?"

My head snapped up when Cate's voice registered.

"Um, yeah." It was strange to be talking to two people at once. I felt fairly certain from the peculiar expression Cate wore that I hadn't done a good job at hiding my facial expressions while I'd been conversing with Sara. And I had just smacked myself in the forehead for no apparent reason. *Nice one, Meg.*

I explained to Sara where I was. We once again shut down our connection as Cate and I stepped out of the jet. Stiffening, I waited for the jeers, food bombs, and insults to come.

Nothing happened.

The runway was empty.

"Looks like the protestors have left."

Cate nodded. "From what I've heard, since the Kazzies were moved to the reservation, the protests here have died down. Senator Douglas probably told them to go home."

She tucked a strand of hair behind her ear as our ride pulled up.

We slipped into the backseat of the car and sped away. The jet would stay put. This wouldn't take long. By lunchtime, we'd know if Dr. Roberts would still be the Director of the reservation.

THIRTY MINUTES LATER, we pulled through the White House gates. The familiar lawn, guards, and fence passed by. I balled my hands into fists when we stopped at the same door we'd entered last time.

A staff member greeted us. "This way please." He waved us to the door.

Cate and I stepped out. Birds chirped from the trees overhead while a breeze caressed our cheeks. We were ushered inside. With hurried movements, two aides beckoned us down the halls. "You'll need to be quick. She has a conference call with the prime minister in Australia in thirty minutes."

A few steps later, I was once again entering the Oval Office. The president sat at her desk. This time, she wasn't on the phone.

"Dr. Hutchinson and Dr. Forester, good morning." She pushed to standing. A loose fitting blouse adorned her top. Plain brown dress pants covered her lower half.

"Thank you for seeing us on such short notice." Cate shook her hand.

"Of course." The president waved the aides away. "We'll be fine."

I shook the president's hand after Cate. Thankfully, my palm didn't feel sweaty, only cool.

After we sat on the couches, the president angled her body toward us. Despite her focused demeanor, I still noticed the dark circles under her eyes and worry lines around her mouth. The new direction our country had taken seemed to be taking a toll on everyone.

"What can I do for you today?" She folded her hands in her lap.

Cate took charge. "We came to discuss the state of the reservation. It's only recently come to our attention that Dr. Roberts, the former lab director of Compound 26, is now in charge. We have concerns about that."

The president's eyebrows rose. "Is that so? He came very highly recommended. As you probably know by now, the decision to put him in charge was only made a few days ago as the original appointee suffered a car crash. Since Dr. Roberts was runner-up, he was the next logical choice."

"Can I ask who recommended him?" I sat further forward.

"Several top officials in the MRRA. Dr. Roberts has an extensive military background, and given his specialty in medicine as well as working with the Kazzies previously, it seemed like the best fit."

Cate and I exchanged a look. It didn't go unnoticed.

"If you have something to say, just say it." The president's tone was firm.

"Have you been informed of his past behavior at Compound 26?" I reached into my bag to pull out Dr. Sadowsky's testimonial. "He abused the Kazzies horribly at my facility. It went on for years before it was stopped."

The president's brow furrowed. "What do you mean?"

I handed her the letter from Dr. Sadowsky. "Dr. Roberts

had special mechanics installed within Compound 26. One of those items was called the Chair. It was a mechanical apparatus that restrained a Kazzie from any movement so barbaric medical practices could be done on them." I pulled out the pictures and handed them to her.

The president's eyes widened as she studied the photos.

She next read Dr. Sadowsky's brief letter. It stated that Dr. Roberts had indeed been treating the Kazzies unjustly. Following that, she studied the photos again.

I leaned forward. "He also subjected the Kazzies to experimental treatments, and almost all of those treatments were against the Kazzies' will. Dr. Roberts treated them like lab rats, cutting into them with no anesthetic, locking them in isolation for weeks at a time, and it's my belief that he wanted to sabotage the work Compounds 10 and 11 were doing with mind-body genomics."

The president studied everything I gave her while the clock ticked menacingly on the wall. Our time was almost up.

"This is incredibly disturbing." She shuffled the papers together and set them down. "Do you feel he would subject the Kazzies to inhumane treatments on the reservation?"

"Most certainly. Just yesterday, when we transported our Kazzies to the reservation, he treated them horribly." I explained how Davin had been drugged and hauled away like a common criminal.

The president continued to frown, her look contemplative. "It was well known that the Kazzies may need to be sedated once they arrived. That action was approved."

My eyes widened. "It would have been nice if we'd been told that. Not only did we walk into that situation blind, but our Kazzies did too. They had no idea what to expect."

The president took a deep breath. "I hear your

frustrations, but you need to understand that a lot has been orchestrated in a short time. I apologize that it wasn't executed as well as it could have been."

Cate leaned forward. "What about Dr. Roberts? Are you going to remove him?"

The president's frown deepened, a penchant look crossing her features. "I am indeed disturbed by the things you've shown me, and I take them very seriously. I also understand your concerns, and I will look into it."

She paused as if debating a few things. Eventually, she shook her head. "At the moment, I'm going to keep Dr. Roberts in charge. We've had too many upheavals as it is. The protestors are still running rampant. They may not be active within D.C. anymore, but I'm still receiving reports of groups trying to stop the small progress you all made during your educational tours this summer. If I remove Dr. Roberts now, it could signify that we don't have control of the reservation or that we jumped into it unprepared. I can't send that kind of message right now."

My mouth dropped.

She held her hand up. "But, I believe what you've brought to me needs to be addressed. I'll arrange for a few officials to closely monitor the activities on the reservation. I can assure you that the Kazzies won't be subjected to abuse."

My heart rate sped up. "But how can you guarantee that? This is crazy!" The challenging question bubbled out of me. I couldn't believe what I was hearing. We'd just presented the president with solid proof of the past behaviors of Dr. Roberts, yet she wasn't going to remove him. Instead, she was going to keep him in charge and arrange for a few people to "monitor" activities within the reservation. And her decision was all based off public perception.

Her tone dropped to glacial levels. "It's hardly crazy. It's how you keep a country running that's barely functioning as it is. And I *did* say I would monitor the going-ons inside. Hopefully, you can understand that there are a number of objectives we're trying to achieve right now. Showing chaos or disorganization to the American people will not work to our advantage."

"But you *will* look into this," Cate interjected. "And soon?"

"Of course." The president smoothed her blouse.

The door opened to her office. The same aides stepped back in. "They're ready for you."

The president nodded briskly and stood. She held out her hand. "Thank you both for stopping by and informing me about your concerns."

I forced a smile and took her hand. "Thank you. Please do consider what we've said."

Cate also said her thanks, but the blood whooshing through my ears became so loud I couldn't hear her. The sudden realization that I'd come again to D.C. in hopes of helping the Kazzies to only fail a second time kept pummeling my thoughts. With it came the deep, mind-numbing fear that nothing would be done to stop Dr. Roberts.

Nothing anytime soon.

24 – INSIDE

Clouds drifted by my window as we flew across the country. We'd be landing in South Dakota in two hours. I couldn't get there fast enough.

Since it was obvious we'd get little to no help from D.C., it really came down to two choices. One, we waited to see if things improved on their own, hoping that top officials within the government stopped abuse on the reservation. Or two, we did something about it ourselves.

Ultimately, my choice was made the second I left the president's office.

I closed my eyes and, for a brief moment, let myself remember the kiss Davin and I had shared. It felt like another lifetime in which that had happened. The hardness of his chest. The soft feel of his lips. The way he pulled me so tightly to him. So much time had passed since those few minutes in the forgotten corridor.

I wanted to hold onto the memory and never let it go. Fear at the thought of never seeing him again wrapped around me, like icy tentacles from the deep. Davin had believed that once he was in the reservation we'd become a thing of the past. Until now, I'd never thought he could be right.

His words came back to haunt me as they had again and again over the past weeks.

It can never be.

My hands dug into my knees as I turned toward Cate. "I'm not going to leave them there, Cate. I can't."

Worry lines creased her forehead. "It may take time, but the president is our best bet. One call from her and everything could change. Dr. Roberts could be ousted in an afternoon."

"And if she doesn't make that call?"

Cate frowned and adjusted her glasses. "Then . . ."

"Exactly. Then what? We're stuck. I can't let that happen. I'm going back to the reservation."

"Meghan. Think clearly. There's nothing we can do right now."

Yes, there is. There's always something that can be done.

But I didn't tell her that. I knew she'd try to talk me out of it, so I numbly nodded and played along, while inside, I began to plan.

AFTER WE LANDED in Sioux Falls, my first stop was at the Compound. Since it was only day two, my co-workers would still be in quarantine.

When I strode into the Sanctum, my co-workers were all hanging out in cell four. All twenty cells had been opened for the exposed researchers.

Amy, Mitch, and Charlie were playing cards, but all of them stood and approached the watch room when I stepped up to the control panel.

Mitch grinned, a knowing twinkle in his eyes. I pushed aside the anxiety that provoked. He still didn't know any future between us was already foreclosed.

I'll deal with that later.

"What's up, stranger?" Amy's smile faded when she got a better look at me. "What's wrong?"

I nodded to the guard. "You can take a break. I'll be in here for a bit."

"Of course, ma'am."

Once he left, I took his seat and told them what had transpired over the past twenty-four hours.

"Dr. Roberts is running the reservation?" Mitch shook his head. "You've got to be kidding me."

"And the president is *still* keeping him in charge after you showed her what he's done?" Amy asked incredulously.

I nodded. "They're not going to make Dr. Roberts step down. He's going to stay in charge of the reservation, and worst of all, I still have no idea how Davin's doing."

Charlie frowned heavily. "Unbelievable."

I ran an agitated hand through my hair. "The president said things are too volatile right now. That she needs to give the impression to the public that we're controlling the virus. She fears if she removes Dr. Roberts that it will cause more upheaval."

Amy snorted. "What a crock of shit."

Charlie seconded her opinion. "Sounds like typical political BS."

Mitch put his hands on his hips. "So there's nothing we can do."

I shook my head. "That's not an option for me. I'm driving back up there."

"Now?" Charlie's eyebrows rose.

Amy rolled her eyes. "No, genius . . . next week."

Their usual banter helped calm my racing heart.

"What are you going to do?" Amy asked.

My brow furrowed. "I'm going to try to get into the reservation. I need to know how our Kazzies are doing. And I need to speak with Dr. Roberts. I know he probably won't listen to me, but I need to try."

"But how are you going to get in?" Mitch crossed his arms.

"I have no idea. That's partly why I'm here. I wanted to see how you were all doing, but I also wondered if you had any ideas that would make them admit me."

"We're fine." Amy swirled her hair up into a ponytail. Red curls still escaped to frame her face. "None of us have shown any symptoms yet. Only one of the researchers has run a fever. He's probably going to go through the same thing you did."

Poor guy.

"That's a fairly high rate of zero symptoms or only mild symptoms." I tapped my fingers on the panel. "That's great odds."

"Exactly." Mitch shook his head. "Now, if only the damned government would pay attention to that."

I checked my watch. Time was ticking. "So . . . any ideas to get me into the rez?"

"First off, curfew's coming up." Charlie glanced at the clock too. "Are you still sure leaving this afternoon is a good idea?"

Mitch clapped Charlie on the back. His eyes shone with excitement. "Actually, my friend. That's exactly why she should go."

I cocked my head at Mitch's excited expression. "Care to explain?"

Mitch rubbed his hands together. "I was just going to do that."

THE DRIVE TO Mobridge was long and excruciating. My co-workers plan to get me into the reservation seemed feasible. It could work, or it could completely backfire. However, it was all I had to go on.

The miles sped by as darkness loomed. Since it was technically summer, we were still on summer curfew hours. Come a few weeks, that would change.

Unless they decide to do away with curfew all together. We could only hope.

I had twenty minutes to spare when I drove into Mobridge. Hopefully, that would work to my advantage. Mitch's idea had been for me to approach the gates as darkness fell and to ask to be admitted for the night.

Given the MRRA secured each state's borders and enforced curfew, they'd have two options. One, they could admit me for the night. Or two, they could call the State Patrol and have them send an officer to collect me. Given it would probably take the Patrol at least an hour or two to reach Mobridge, it wasn't a very practical option.

I could only hope they chose option one.

The barbed wire fence was the first thing I noticed about the perimeter when I pulled up to the main gate. I wasn't the only one here, though. Several cars lay scattered in the surrounding prairie. Their occupants were nowhere to be seen.

A light shone on my vehicle when I parked. A loud voice blaring through a speaker followed. "State your name and intention for approaching Reservation 1."

Under my breath, I muttered to myself, "A megaphone and spotlight? Is that necessary?"

I opened my door and stepped out. The light was so bright I shielded my eyes. "It's Dr. Meghan Forester."

I fished my credentials out of my pocket and held them

up. "I'm with Compound 26, and I wish to enter."

The speaker clicked on again, a high pitched sound followed, but then it turned off. At least a minute passed. I guessed whoever was on the other end was trying to figure out how to answer me.

Another click sounded and a different voice bellowed, "State your intentions, Dr. Forester. You know having MRI credentials does not give you ungoverned access here."

"I'm aware of that." I ducked my head. "Can you turn the light off please? It's blinding."

The light clicked off. Only the setting sun illuminated the sky. Already stars were peeking through.

"State your intentions." The authoritative voice sounded again.

"I would like to enter. I wish to speak with Dr. Roberts."

"Dr. Roberts has retired to his quarters for the night."

Inside, I breathed a sigh of relief. *That's what I hoped.* A cool prairie breeze washed over my cheeks. I pushed my hair behind my ears. "That's fine. I can speak with him tomorrow, but I still need to enter. With no hotels in sight, I have nowhere to stay."

"That is not our concern, Dr. Forester. The State Patrol can be here in two hours. You're not the first they've had to collect."

So that explains the empty vehicles.

I swallowed uneasily and tried a different tactic. "You do realize that I'm not a normal bystander trying to get a look at the Kazzies . . . Private?" I let the word hang.

"It's *Sergeant* Beckenworth. I'm in charge of the night guard."

"I apologize, Sergeant Beckenworth, but like I was saying, I'm employed by the Makanza Research Institute. I am not a common criminal, nor am I a thrill seeker trying to break into Reservation 1. I am a former colleague of Dr. Roberts, and I wish to speak to him. However, I can wait until tomorrow. Perhaps you can give me the respect I deserve and open these gates. I need a place to stay for the night."

"I . . ." The Sergeant seemed at loss for words.

"You do realize if it weren't for what I discovered that you wouldn't have a job?" I cringed inwardly at the arrogance of that statement, but I also knew it may help. "The only reason this reservation is here is because of what *I* discovered. And the only reason you'll never catch *Makanza* is because of what *I* discovered."

I had to force the words out. What I was saying was ridiculous. Granted I had paved the way for the vaccine, but the original theory had been born in Dr. Hutchinson's Compounds, and it was the massive undertaking by thousands of MRI scientists that had resulted in the vaccine.

Hopefully, Sergeant Beckenworth wouldn't know that.

"Well . . . I suppose . . ." He cleared his throat. "I suppose we could let you in for one night. You'll be contained within a guest house, however."

I quickly smothered my grin. "That's absolutely fine. Thank you."

When the gates opened, they creaked and groaned. The mechanical superiority of the Compound was absent here. These gates probably rarely opened, unlike the Compound which admitted hundreds of workers each day.

I slid back into my vehicle and pulled forward. My car's headlights cut through the night, illuminating the pavement ahead that snaked through the hills.

An MRRA soldier waved to the paved parking area. "Park your car here. You'll be escorted to a house for the night."

I did as he instructed before cutting the motor. "May I stay with the infected people from my Compound tonight?"

He frowned. "No, ma'am. You're to stay in the house we place you in."

My shoulders sank. "Of course."

As I waited for a vehicle to escort me to the town, I knocked on the mental door that linked me to Sara. She answered readily.

Hi, Meghan. How's everything going?

I smiled inwardly. *I'm here, Sara. I'm at the reservation, and I'm in.*

THE DRIVE INTO town seemed to take forever. I spent the entire time staring out the window, trying to catch a glimpse of my friends or other Kazzies, but the reservation was mostly empty prairie. Only nature stared back at me.

When the first homes appeared at the edge of town, two things quickly became apparent.

One, everything was new. Two, the reservation as it used to be no longer existed.

"Did they destroy the original buildings?" I asked my driver.

Even though it was dark, I had still seen large pits filled with burned debris before we'd entered the town.

"Yes, ma'am," the soldier replied. "Everything was bulldozed and burned years ago. The MRRA did that after the Second Wave."

"So the entire town is newly constructed?"

"Yes, ma'am. A grocery store, school, small clinic, general store, entertainment facility, and houses were built this summer for the Kazzies. They have everything they need to begin a new life."

His tone echoed pride. *He actually believes containing the Kazzies to a reservation is fair and just. He truly believes they're doing the right thing.*

"How is the town setup?"

"It's two Kazzies per house, and since there's around twelve hundred Kazzies, we had to build six hundred homes. They're small, so it wasn't too much work."

"So the Kazzies all live in this area?"

"Yes, ma'am. The town is setup in a grid system. Ten houses per block, five streets, and twelve interconnecting streets. They're all in one area so it's easier to maintain their whereabouts. We also track them with devices imbedded in their wrists."

I bristled at that reminder. Through clenched teeth, I asked, "So where am I staying?"

"In one of the unoccupied Kazzie houses. We built a few extra just in case."

"And the MRRA soldiers stationed here? Where do you all live?"

"Our barracks are in several locations throughout the reservation, ma'am."

I angled my body toward his. "And how long will you be stationed here?"

"Two years, although I can leave for four two-week periods over that timeframe."

"And what about the Kazzies' families? Where will they stay when they visit?"

"Uh . . ." His gripped tightened on the steering wheel as we turned onto a street. "We don't have accommodations for them, ma'am."

"So where do they stay?"

He shrugged. "I suppose I don't know."

We pulled up to a small, newly built house. It was simple on the outside. Real wood clapboard siding, a small chimney, a few windows, and a newly shingled roof.

"This is where you'll be staying tonight, ma'am. We'll tell Dr. Roberts first thing in the morning that you'd like to see him."

Since I only had my purse and small bag that I'd packed for D.C., on the off chance I'd had to spend the night there, I didn't have much to carry. Once the soldier let me into the house, he gave me a quick tour before telling me goodnight.

The second he left, I raced to the front door. I had no intention of staying in this house tonight.

Only, when I went to let myself out, the door wouldn't budge. I tried again.

They've locked it from the outside!

I rattled the door handle, but as much as I tried, it wouldn't give. I slapped my palms against it in anger. *They call these homes, but they're truly just fancy prison cells.*

Pacing the small living room, I tapped into my connection with Sara. *I'm in a house, but I'm locked inside. I can't get out.*

She sighed sadly. *I know. We're all still locked in our homes. That hasn't changed. They only let us leave for our first initiation meeting this afternoon, but they picked us up and escorted us to it.*

So when will they stop locking the doors? When will you be allowed to come and go as you please?

I'm not sure. They haven't told us any details like that yet, but it sounds like locking us in at night will be the norm. I'm not sure about the daytime.

Which house are you in?

Sophie and I live in house eight on the third street, block ten.

I groaned. They were so close yet so far away.

Gripping my head in frustration, I spun away from the

door. It was only when I stopped, wanting to punch a pillow on the couch, that I really looked at my surroundings for the first time.

The living room was small and sparsely furnished. There was a couch, coffee table, and chair. A cold fireplace took up a third of one wall. Next to the living area was a kitchen. It held the basics: a stove, sink, oven, and a kitchen table with two chairs. I opened one of the cupboards. Canned foods and shelf stable items stared back at me.

So you do all of your own cooking?

I felt Sara nod. *Yes, we're supposed to, but Sophie and I don't know how to cook, so the soldiers brought us a cookbook and told us to figure it out.*

I grimaced. Since I was the world's worst cook, I'd be no help to them. *Is it going okay?*

We haven't starved yet if that's what you mean.

I tried to laugh at her joke but couldn't. Things were worse here than I thought.

And everyone else? How are they fairing?

Victor and Garrett share a home. Dorothy's rooming with another woman she just met. And Sage is supposed to share a house with Davin.

My heart stopped as I waited for the news. I'd been too scared to ask her earlier. As of this morning, she still didn't know how he was doing. *Do you know anything yet?*

He's alive. I know that much. About two hours ago, I felt him try to connect with me, but . . .

My heart thumped painfully. *But what?*

We got cut off again. I think they keep giving him something to keep him subdued. It makes his brain too fuzzy, so we can't talk.

I stopped rifling through the kitchen cupboards and sank against the counter. *Do you really think they keep drugging him?*

It's the only thing that explains why I can't speak with him.

Tears moistened my eyes. Now, more than ever, I knew I needed to see Dr. Roberts. I couldn't allow him to keep abusing Davin. I had no idea how I'd stop it, but I knew I had to try.

25 - AGREEMENT

I barely slept that night. It didn't help that guards regularly patrolled the streets, shining bright spotlights up and down the street as they went. They'd already passed twice. Each time, the bright light shone through my curtains.

The new bed in the small bedroom was comfortable enough, but my mind wouldn't allow me to rest. All night long, dreams plagued me of what they were doing to Davin.

To keep him continually subdued meant he was receiving sedatives around the clock. Images of deranged psychiatric hospitals, in which patients sat in wheelchairs, drool escaping a corner of their mouths while glassy eyes gazed off into the distance, unseeing, kept bombarding my mind.

I knew it was what they were doing to Davin. It was the only way to keep him from lashing out. It was what Dr. Roberts had done to him for years. Only now, nobody was watching. Giving Dr. Roberts absolute control in the reservation meant he could do as he pleased.

Fears of him killing Davin or creating an "accident" in which Davin fell victim to some horrendous tragedy also plagued me. Who was to say Dr. Roberts wouldn't grow tired of having to control Davin and would decide that an untimely death was easier to deal with.

For all I knew, nobody would question Davin's disappearance. If Sharon wasn't allowed into the reservation, nobody would know that he was gone. I could only hope whoever the president appointed to monitor activities here would do their job.

If she appoints anyone at all.

She seemed so busy even though I knew she meant to control what happened here. I still wasn't convinced she would.

When a knock on the small home's front door came after sunrise, I was already awake and dressed. I'd been too nervous to eat and only had a cup of coffee for breakfast. The caffeine swam through my system. I couldn't sit still.

"Dr. Forester? I'm Private Foden." The soldier that opened my door looked like all the rest. Military garb, a young face, and shoulders that stood straight and proud. He pushed the door open wider. "Please, come with me."

I grabbed my belongings and followed him out the door. The rising sun and surrounding prairie grass and flowers did little to distract me. "Where's Dr. Roberts?"

"He's waiting for you at the main office."

"And what about the infected people from Compound 26? Where are they?"

"In their homes, ma'am. Probably still sleeping." He smiled after he said it and such innocence flashed in his eyes that I knew he truly believed nothing nefarious had been done to them.

"And Davin Kinder? Where's he?"

He opened my car door. "Davin who?"

"Davin Kinder. He's a Kazzie from my Compound. How is he doing?"

He cocked his head. "I'm sorry, ma'am. I'm afraid I don't know. I'm not familiar with that name."

My throat threatened to close and choke the life out of me. I told myself to calm down and keep breathing. Sara had felt Davin try to connect yesterday. *That means he's still alive. He's not dead. He's still alive.*

THE DRIVE TO the main office felt like a long, lumbering hike up a mountain. Even though Private Foden drove at highway speeds, it still felt too slow. When we finally pulled up to the military camp, we stopped in front of barracks that looked plain and big. A dozen buildings with long domed roofs filled the land here.

Once inside, I kept my eyes open for my former boss. I didn't see him anywhere.

"This way, ma'am." The guard waved down a hallway and led me forward.

He ushered me into a simple room. Bright fluorescent lights glowed overhead. The room was simple. No windows. A table and two chairs.

It felt like an interrogation room.

Since I heard the door lock behind Private Foden after he left, I didn't bother trying it. It didn't matter since not a minute passed before a door in the corner opened and Dr. Roberts marched in. He looked as he always did. Military apparel, a short haircut, gray eyes that seemed colder than the frozen arctic.

Gripping a chair back tightly, I tried to hide my fear. I knew that I had to be very careful with what I revealed. If I gave any indication to having insider information about the reservation, Dr. Roberts would grow suspicious. He was a smart man. He wouldn't be fooled. I needed to keep the information Sara gave me a secret.

"Dr. Forester." His tone was as glacial as his eyes. "I wasn't surprised when I awoke this morning to the message that you'd returned to the reservation. I can't say that I'm happy about it."

I met his stare despite fear quaking inside me. "I'd like to know how the Kazzies from Compound 26 are doing."

"I'm sure you would." He crossed his arms, a smug look on his face.

"Where's Davin?"

"He's contained."

I gripped the chair tighter. "Contained where?"

Dr. Roberts cocked an eyebrow. "Is this why you came here? Twenty questions?"

"I came here to ensure that he's safe."

Amusement entered his eyes. "He's just fine."

I made myself breathe deeper and used the chair to steady me. Since Dr. Roberts seemed hell-bent on not revealing anything, I tried a different tactic. "The president is aware of what's going on here."

"I've heard." His gaze turned hard.

He has? I knew if I dwelled on that, I'd lose my train of thought. Shaking myself, I said, "If she hears of how you're treating Davin, you'll be removed from your position."

He smirked. "Why do I find that hard to believe? The president knew certain measures would need to be taken. She approved a number of the practices here. I'm calling your bluff, Dr. Forester. You don't fool me."

I swallowed tightly as an angry expression grew on my former boss' face.

"And just so you know," he said coldly, "I've heard you've been busy. Just yesterday you were in Washington D.C. From what I hear, you were once again trying to sabotage my career. This time you were asking the president herself that I be removed from my position." Fury emanated from him.

For a moment, I just stared. If he knew about my meeting with the president then he had insider contacts in the nation's capital. It seemed that Dr. Roberts' reach stretched wide and far.

He has even more power than I'd realized.

"I . . ." I cleared my throat as I felt myself losing this battle. "You have to understand my concerns. At Compound 26, you hardly treated the Kazzies fairly."

He sneered and stepped closer. I resisted the urge to step back even though the tips of his shoes nearly brushed mine. "So that warrants you trying to fire me? That warrants you again interfering with my career? And for what? Your damned love for those Kazzies?" Rage glowed in his eyes.

"I just want them safe. That's all."

Dr. Roberts' gaze stayed on me. Silence filled the room before he reached into his pocket and pulled out his phone. He smirked again. "I have something to show you."

"What?" I eyed the phone warily.

He hit a button and a video opened. My breath sucked in. It showed Davin and my friends by the entrance gates to the reservation. There was no sound, only our silent images. A flash of me appeared in the background. *It's a video of the day they were admitted to the reservation.*

"What is this?"

Dr. Roberts smiled as the video continued. The recording jostled and swung to the side. Dr. Roberts appeared in the frame. He stood behind me.

In the video, I spun slowly toward him, my long hair whipping around my shoulders. You couldn't hear what we said, but it didn't matter, only a few words emitted from our mouths before Davin lunged at my former boss.

I gasped as the struggle ensued. I'd seen it firsthand, but somehow, seeing it on video made it seem a hundred times worse. It looked like Davin was an out-of-control, dangerous man. Dr. Roberts looked like an innocent bystander.

That's not at all the reality!

The video cut out after Davin was drugged and the guards helped Dr. Roberts to a stand. My hands shook. I could barely get my next words out. "Why did you show me that?"

"Because I'm going to show this to the world. They'll all see what your Kazzies are like and why they need to stay contained."

My entire body began to shake. Frustration constricted my throat, making it hard to speak. "You *know* that Davin's not normally like that! You *know* that you tortured and abused him for years! You treated him appallingly and never paid the price for it!"

"Well, Dr. Forester," my former boss pocketed his phone, "that's simply your opinion. You have no proof of that."

It felt like the room was spinning, like I was on a horrible never-ending roller coaster ride. Taking deep gulping breaths, I said, "What do you want? What do I need to do so you don't show anyone that?"

He raised an eyebrow. "What makes you think I'll negotiate with you?"

"Because you're not the only one who can blackmail. I have access to the Compound's archived video feed. I can pull up the videos of you torturing the Kazzies, of the barbaric practices you've done to them. I can show *that* to the world."

His smile disappeared. Never mind that I could never do that without incurring the president's wrath. She was aware of Dr. Roberts' previous actions yet still decided to keep him in charge. She wanted to maintain the façade of order and control. I could only hope *he* never learned that, otherwise, he could call my bluff.

Crossing his arms, my former boss leveled me with an icy stare. "You don't have the guts to do that."

I squared my shoulders. "Go ahead and show the world that video. You'll see what happens if you do."

With a furious growl, he turned and stormed to the opposite side of the small room. He paced the room as his hands clenched into fists. "I still have control of them! I can still drug Davin for as long as I want!"

Hearing that he was indeed drugging Davin made my stomach sink. "You *can't* keep doing that! You could kill him!"

Dr. Roberts stopped pacing. His eyes brightened in manic glee, and in that moment I saw it. *He's crazy. He's completely insane!*

"You have no control here, Dr. Forester. *I'm* still the Director. *I* make the decisions on how dangerous Kazzies are contained."

He's not going to stop. No matter what I say, he's going to keep abusing Davin. I knew my only chance at keeping Davin safe may fall on the officials that the president promised to send to the reservation. *But what if she doesn't? Or what if they never find out what's really going on?*

With a deep shuddering breath, I wracked my brain for what I could do. I didn't have much time, but I needed to do something. With my mind racing, it suddenly dawned on me what Dr. Roberts may agree to. It was exactly the kind of thing that would please him. It felt like my heart ripped from my chest when I said the words. "I have a proposal for you."

"A proposal?"

I licked my dry lips and nodded tightly. "I know you blame me for what happened at Compound 26, that you feel it's my fault you left your job there. So what if I promise to never come back here? You know how much that would hurt me. It would be an eye for an eye. If you promise to release Davin from where he's being kept, and if you promise to not drug him, I promise to never speak with or contact the Kazzies again."

Dr. Roberts crossed his arms. An aching ten seconds passed. "You'll never set foot on the reservation again in exchange for Davin being released and not being drugged?"

I nodded shakily. "Yes."

He laughed. "An eye for an eye. It does seem quite fitting. You've tried twice now to ruin me. And since I can't ruin your career since you're the golden girl of the MRI, it does seem fair to take the next best thing from you. Your Kazzies."

The world around me grew smaller and smaller. *He's going to do it. He'll agree to this.* It felt like the ceiling was caving in on me. I gripped the chair back more. *Breathe, Meghan. Just breathe.*

When I finally felt like I could speak, I said, "If I never come back here, and if I never speak to them again, you'll give me your word that you won't harm them?"

"Yes."

I felt like I was making a deal with the devil. I swayed against the chair. *Keep it together, Meghan!*

"I'll need more than just your word. I'll need proof that they're not being drugged."

His gaze hardened. "Fine. What kind of proof do you need?"

I thought quickly. "Weekly blood tests from not only

Davin, but Sage, the twins, Victor, Dorothy, and Garrett too. I'll process those samples myself to ensure that they're truly from them. If the DNA doesn't match up, and if I find any hint of drugs or barbiturates in *any* of their systems, the deal's off."

His nostrils flared. "Fine. Weekly blood tests, but that's it. That's all you're getting."

I swallowed audibly. A part of me screamed to not do it. My heart bled inside at the thought of giving up Davin. Of giving up ever seeing or speaking to him again.

The other part cried at how he would react. He'd think I'd left him. He'd think I'd done as he'd said and given up on him. I wasn't sure what hurt more.

But it will keep him safe. For the time being, he'll stay safe, and Dr. Hutchinson and I will continue our work and hopefully have Dr. Roberts removed from power. If he's removed, I'll get to see Davin again.

My soul burned brighter as a new purpose flashed to life inside me. To bulldoze the fence around Reservation 1 and integrate the Kazzies back into society. To forever eradicate the barriers the Kazzies faced in our culture.

It was the only thought that kept me going. Knowing that the possibility still lived of this all going away, of this nightmare fading and morning once again coming, the sun once again brightening my life—a life that had plunged into darkness.

Taking a deep breath, I stood straighter and said in as firm of a voice as I could manage, "All right, Dr. Roberts. You have a deal."

26 – SAYING GOODBYE

I left the reservation shortly after that. It was only when I'd been escorted to my car by Dr. Roberts himself that it truly sank in what I'd done.

I'd given up Davin.

I'd given up my friends.

But I'd done it all to keep them safe.

When I started my car, I tapped on the mental door that linked me to Sara. I knew what I needed to do, but it didn't make it any easier.

She answered readily. *Meghan? Where are you? How's it going? Did you see Dr. Roberts? Are they going to let us out?*

I inhaled deeply. My fingers shook as I shifted my car into drive. *Yes, I saw him. He's going to let Davin out of wherever he's being kept, and he's going to stop drugging him.*

Sara squealed in glee. *Oh, Meghan! That's wonderful! How did you do it?*

I . . . I knew the time had come. I'd known as soon as I made the deal with Dr. Roberts that I'd have to do this too, but I didn't want to accept it. I didn't want to face it. Not yet.

I need you to know something, Sara. I need you to know that I love you like a sister.

I know. Of course, I know that. Her tone turned wary. *What's wrong? You're sounding weird.*

And please know, no matter what happens, that will never change.

Okay, Meghan, you're scaring me now. What the heck's going on?

I've decided to do what Davin keeps telling me to do. I swallowed tightly. *I've decided to move on and put all of this behind me. Davin's right. I need to find someone on the outside. I can't keep fighting for all of you.*

What?

The pain in her voice almost undid me. Forcing the tears back, I continued. *Tell Davin he's right. I need to give Mitch a shot. It's time to try to make my own life out here. So now, I have to say goodbye.*

Goodbye? What do you mean, goodbye? Meghan?

She waited for me to explain, but I couldn't. If I told her about the deal Dr. Roberts and I had made, it would inevitably get back to Davin what I'd done.

Sara would do her best to keep it a secret, but it was only a matter of time before she slipped or said something she didn't mean to. She had so many people in her head. It wouldn't be the first time she'd accidentally let something through.

And I couldn't let that happen. If Davin knew what I'd done, if he knew that Dr. Roberts had threatened me, he'd fly into a rage. He wouldn't care that it would get him locked up. His safety wouldn't occur to him. He'd again go after my former boss, and I knew then our deal would be off. Dr. Roberts would be forced to drug Davin and keep him contained.

And if keeping him contained led to an accidental drug overdose . . .

My heartbeat increased wildly.

I couldn't let that happen.

I forced myself to take a deep breath. The only way to ensure that Davin believed I'd stopped seeing him was if I'd done it on my own free will. If Davin thought I'd finally followed his advice and decided to forge a life for myself without him and the Kazzies holding me back, he'd accept that I was gone.

He wouldn't fly into a rage. He wouldn't hurt my former boss or any of the MRRA soldiers. He'd quietly accept that I was gone and always would be.

It was the only way. It was the only way I could keep him safe.

Meghan? Meghan, talk to me! What's going on?

I ignored Sara's anxious cries. In the back of my mind, I felt the connection that tied me to Sara. It was like an invisible thread that connected our psyches. It was there. Always there. Only now, I needed to make it go away.

I'm sorry, Sara, but it's time for me to start my life anew. Tell Davin that he's right. I need to begin my own life. Tell him that . . . I swallowed tightly. Getting out the next words was harder than I thought they'd be. *Tell him that Mitch and I have decided to start dating. Davin's been encouraging me for weeks to be with Mitch, so that's what I'm going to do.*

She started to argue and frantically asked me what I was talking about, so I said the one word that I dreaded saying more than anything.

Goodbye.

And with that, I cut the string.

I felt our connection disappear, the way a breeze snuffs out a candle. One second it was there, the next it wasn't. I wanted to cry at how easily it was broken.

Tears poured down my face as my car sped along the highway. The morning sun shined overhead. Birds flew across the horizon. The world kept turning.

Yet to me, the world had stopped. Everything that I loved and cherished fell behind me as the miles passed by.

I kept telling myself it was for the best. Davin and my friends would be drug-free. Cate and I would continue working to free them, but it could be months, even years, before that happened. But for the time being, they'd be safe.

It was now possible they'd be allowed to live normal lives until I found a way to get them out, yet all I could think about was how I'd just said goodbye to the only sister I'd ever had, and I'd just turned my back on the only man I'd ever loved.

CONTINUE THE STORY

Section 12, book three in The Makanza Series

To free them, she'll risk everything.

THANK YOU FOR READING!

If you enjoyed *Reservation 1*, please consider posting a review on Amazon. Authors rely heavily on readers reviewing their work. Even one sentence helps a lot. Thank you so much if you do!

♥ ♥ ♥

If you enjoy Krista Street's writing, make sure you visit her website and join her newsletter to stay up-to-date on new releases. Links to her social media are also available at the bottom of every page.

www.kristastreet.com

THE LOST CHILDREN TRILOGY

Krista Street's bestselling series on Amazon.com

Four months ago, Lena woke up in a dark alleyway with no recollection of who she is. The only clues to her past are a mysterious tattooed symbol and a supernatural power: the ability to see evil in people.

While struggling to regain her memory, she follows a strange guiding instinct to a small Colorado town. There she finds other young men and women with similar stories, similar tattoos, and a multitude of superhuman powers. Among them a man she's intensely attracted to, yet with no memories of him, she has no idea why.

As Lena and the others explore their powers and try to figure out who and what they are, they make a frightening discovery. Those who know the answers to their questions are hunting them. And if they find them, these superhumans may not survive.

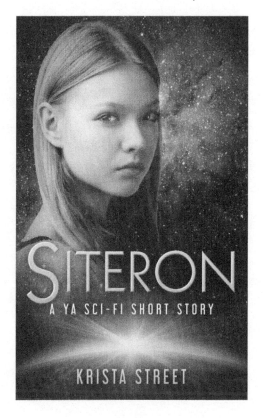